For Jane

PENGUIN BOOKS

THE STORY OF LUCY GAULT

Books of the Year Choice

'A novelist working at full power in a tale of intense and intensifying sadness' Julian Barnes, *The Times Literary Supplement*

'Trevor at his best' John Mortimer, *Observer*

'Trevor writes with extraordinary sensitivity and insight. A sad book, full of longing for a way of life and people forgotten' Terry Wogan, *Oldie*

'Humane warmth and rich detail make every page of this work by a superlative novelist at the height of his powers pulse with vitality' Peter Kemp, *Sunday Times*

'Lovely, elegiac' Jane Shilling, *Sunday Telegraph*

'Deserves a high place among novels' Eric Christiansen, *Spectator*

'Elegant, elegiac, ambitious' John Bowen, *Oldie*

'The real Booker winner' Susan Hill, *Daily Telegraph*

William Trevor was born in 1928 at Mitchelstown, County Cork, and spent his childhood in provincial Ireland. He attended a number of Irish schools and later Trinity College, Dublin, and is a member of the Irish Academy of Letters. He now lives in Devon.

He has written many novels, including *The Old Boys*, winner of the Hawthornden Prize; *The Children of Dynmouth* and *Fools of Fortune*, both winners of the Whitbread Fiction Award; *The Silence in the Garden*, winner of the *Yorkshire Post* Book of the Year Award; *Two Lives*, which was shortlisted for the *Sunday Express* Book of the Year Award and includes the Booker-shortlisted novella *Reading Turgenev*; *Felicia's Journey*, which won both the Whitbread Book of the Year and *Sunday Express* Book of the Year Awards; *Death in Summer*, and most recently *The Story of Lucy Gault*, shortlisted for the Man Booker Prize. He is a celebrated short-story writer, and his recent collection, *The Hill Bachelors*, won both the Macmillan Silver Pen Award and the *Irish Times* Literature Prize.

In 1977, William Trevor was awarded an honorary CBE in recognition of his valuable services to literature, and in 1999 he received the prestigious David Cohen British Literature Prize in recognition of a lifetime's literary achievement. In 2002, he was awarded an honorary knighthood in recognition of his valuable services to literature.

The Story of Lucy Gault

WILLIAM TREVOR

PENGUIN BOOKS

PENGUIN BOOKS

Published by the Penguin Group
Penguin Books Ltd, 80 Strand, London WC2R ORL, England
Penguin Putnam Inc., 375 Hudson Street, New York, New York 10014, USA
Penguin Books Australia Ltd, 250 Camberwell Road,
Camberwell, Victoria 3124, Australia
Penguin Books Canada Ltd, 10 Alcorn Avenue, Toronto, Ontario, Canada M4V 3B2
Penguin Books India (P) Ltd, 11 Community Centre,
Panchsheel Park, New Delhi – 110 017, India
Penguin Books (NZ) Ltd, Cnr Rosedale and Airborne Roads,
Albany, Auckland, New Zealand
Penguin Books (South Africa) (Pty) Ltd, 24 Sturdee Avenue,
Rosebank 2196, South Africa

Penguin Books Ltd, Registered Offices: 80 Strand, London WC2R ORL, England

www.penguin.com

First published by Viking 2002
Published in Penguin Books 2003

I

Set in Monotype Dante
Printed in England by Clays Ltd, St Ives plc

ISBN-13: 978-0-141-04989-2

www.greenpenguin.co.uk

Penguin Books is committed to a sustainable future
for our business, our readers and our planet.
The book in your hands is made from paper
certified by the Forest Stewardship Council.

ONE

I

Captain Everard Gault wounded the boy in the right shoulder on the night of June the twenty-first, nineteen twenty-one. Aiming above the trespassers' heads in the darkness, he fired the single shot from an upstairs window and then watched the three figures scuttling off, the wounded one assisted by his companions.

They had come to fire the house, their visit expected because they had been before. On that occasion they had come later, in the early morning, just after one. The sheepdogs had seen them off, but within a week the dogs lay poisoned in the yard and Captain Gault knew that the intruders would be back. 'We're stretched at the barracks, sir,' Sergeant Talty had said when he came out from Enniseala. 'Oh, stretched shocking, Captain.' Lahardane wasn't the only house under threat; every week somewhere went up, no matter how the constabulary were spread. 'Please God, there'll be an end to it,' Sergeant Talty said, and went away. Martial law prevailed, since the country was in a state of unrest, one that amounted to war. No action was taken about the poisoning of the dogs.

When daylight came on the morning after the shooting, blood could be seen on the sea pebbles of the turn-around in front of the house. Two petrol tins were found behind a tree. The pebbles were raked, a couple of bucketfuls that had been discoloured in the accident taken away.

Captain Gault thought it would be all right then: a lesson had been learnt. He wrote to Father Morrissey in Enniseala, asking him to pass on his sympathy and his regret if the priest happened to hear who it was who'd been wounded. He had not sought to inflict an injury, only to make it known that a watch was being kept. Father Morrissey wrote back. *He was always the wild one in that*

3

family, he concluded his comments on the event, but there was an awkwardness about his letter, about the choice of phrases and of words, as if he found it difficult to comment on what had occurred, as if he didn't understand that neither death nor injury had been intended. He had passed the message on, he wrote, but no acknowledgement had come back from the family he referred to.

Captain Gault had been wounded himself. For six years, since he had come back an invalid from the trenches, he had carried fragments of shrapnel in his body, and they would always be there now. His injury at that time had brought his military career to an end: he would remain for ever a captain, which was intensely a disappointment, since he had always imagined achieving much higher rank. But he was not, in other ways, a disappointed man. There was the great solace of his happy marriage, of the child his wife, Heloise, had borne him, of his house. There was no other place he might more happily have lived than beneath the slated roof of its three grey storeys, the stone softened by the white woodwork of the windows and the delicate fanlight above a white hall door. Flanking it on its right was the wide high archway of a cobbled yard, with cobbled passageways leading to an apple orchard and a garden. One half of the circle on to which the front rooms looked out was the gravel sweep; the other was a raised lawn that was separated from steeply rising woods by a curve of blue hydrangeas. The upstairs rooms at the back had a view of the sea as far as the sea's horizon.

The origins of the Gaults in Ireland had centuries ago misted over. Previously of Norfolk – so it was believed within the family, although without much certainty – they had settled first of all in the far western reaches of County Cork. A soldier of fortune had established their modest dynasty, lying low there for reasons that were not known. Some time in the early eighteenth century the family had moved east, respectable and well-to-do by then, one son or another of each generation continuing the family's army connection. The land at Lahardane was purchased; the building of the house began. The long, straight avenue was made, lines of chestnut trees planted along it on either side, the woodlands of the glen laid out. Later generations planted the orchard, with stock from County Armagh; the garden, kept small, was created bit by bit. In 1769 Lord Townshend, the Lord Lieutenant, stayed at Lahardane; in 1809 Daniel O'Connell did when there wasn't a bedroom unoccupied at the Stuarts' Dromana. History touched the place in that way; but as well-remembered, as often talked about, were births and marriages and deaths, domestic incidents, changes and additions to this room or that, occasions of anger or reconciliation. Suffering a stroke, a Gault in 1847 lay afflicted for three years yet not insensible. There was a disastrous six months of card-playing in 1872 during which field after field was lost to the neighbouring O'Reillys. There was the diphtheria outbreak that spread so rapidly and so tragically in 1901, sparing only the present Everard Gault and his brother in a family of five. Above the writing-desk in the drawing-room there was a portrait of a distant ancestor whose identity had been unknown for as long as anyone of the present could remember: a spare, solemn countenance where it was not whiskered, blue unemphatic eyes. It was the only portrait in the house, although since photography had begun there were albums that included the images of relatives and friends as well as those of the Gaults of Lahardane.

All this – the house and the remnants of the pasture land, the seashore below the pale clay cliffs, the walk along it to the fishing village of Kilauran, the avenue over which the high branches of the chestnut trees now met – was as much part of Everard Gault as the features of his face were, the family traits that quite resembled a few of those in the drawing-room portrait, the smooth dark hair. Tall and straight-backed, a man who hid nothing of himself, slight in his ambitions now, he had long ago accepted that his destiny was to keep in good heart what had been his inheritance, to attract bees to his hives, to root up his failing apple trees and replace them. He swept the chimneys of his house himself, could repoint its mortar and replace its window glass. Creeping about on its roof, he repaired in the lead the small perforations that occurred from

5

time to time, the Seccotine he squeezed into them effective for a while.

In many of these tasks he was assisted by Henry, a slow-moving, heavily made man who rarely, in daytime, removed the hat from his head. Years ago Henry had married into the gate-lodge, of which he and Bridget were now the sole occupants, since no children had been born to them and Bridget's parents were no longer alive. Her father, with two men under him, had looked after the horses and seen to all that Henry on his own now saw to in the yard and the fields. Her mother had worked in the house, her grandmother before that. Bridget was as thickset as her husband, with strong wide shoulders and a capable manner: the kitchen was wholly in her charge. The bedroom maid, Kitty Teresa, assisted Heloise Gault in what had once been the duties of several indoor servants; old Hannah walked over from Kilauran once a week to wash the clothes and sheets and tablecloths, and to scrub the tiles of the hall and the stone floors at the back. The style of the past was no longer possible at Lahardane. The long avenue passed through the land that had become the O'Reillys' at the card table, when the Gaults of that time had been left with pasture enough only to support a modest herd of Friesians.

Three days after the shooting in the night Heloise Gault read the letter that had come from Father Morrissey, then turned it over and read it again. She was a slender, slightly built woman in her late thirties, her long fair hair arranged in a style that complemented her features, imbuing a demure beauty with a hint of severity that was constantly contradicted by her smile. But her smile had not been much in evidence since the night she had been woken by a shot.

Even though in the ordinary run of things she was not pusillanimous, Heloise Gault felt frightened. She, too, came of an army family and had taken it in her stride when, a few years before her marriage, she was left almost alone in the world on the death of her mother, who had been widowed during the war with the Boers. Courage came naturally to her in times of upheaval or grief, but was not as generously there as she imagined it would be when she reflected upon the attempt to burn down the house she and her child and her maid had been asleep in. There'd been, as well, the poisoning of the dogs and the unanswered message to the young man's family, the blood on the pebbles. 'I'm frightened, Everard,' she confessed at last, no longer keeping her feelings private.

They knew each other well, the Captain and his wife. They had in common a certain way of life, an order of priorities and concerns. Their shared experience of death when they were young had drawn them close and in their marriage had made precious for them the sense of family that the birth of a child allowed. Heloise had once assumed that other children would be born to her, and still had not abandoned hope that one more at least might be. But in the meanwhile she was so convincingly persuaded by her husband that the lack of a son to inherit Lahardane was not a failure on her part that she experienced – and more and more as her only child grew up – gratitude for the solitary birth and for a trinity sustained by affection.

'It's not like you to be frightened, Heloise.'

'All this has happened because I'm here. Because I am an English wife at Lahardane.'

She it was, Heloise insisted, who drew attention to the house, but her husband doubted it. He reminded her that what had been attempted at Lahardane was part of a pattern that was repeated all over Ireland. The nature of the house, the possession of land even though it had dwindled, the family's army connection, would have been enough to bring that trouble in the night. And he had to admit that the urge to cause destruction, whatever its origin, could not be assumed to have been stifled by the stand he'd taken. For some time afterwards Everard Gault slept in the afternoon and watched by night; and although no one disturbed his vigil, this concern with protection, and his wife's apprehension, created in the household further depths of disquiet, a nerviness that affected everyone, including in the end the household's child.

*

Still eight but almost nine, Lucy had made friends that summer with the O'Reillys' dog. A big, frolicsome animal – half setter, half retriever – it had crept into the O'Reillys' yard a month or so ago, having wandered from a deserted house – so Henry's guess was – and been accepted after some hostility by the O'Reillys' working dogs. Henry said it was a useless creature, Lucy's papa that it was a nuisance, particularly the way it scrambled down the cliffs to offer its company to whoever might be on the strand. The O'Reillys had given the dog no name and would hardly have noticed – so Henry said – if it had wandered off again. When Lucy and her papa had their early-morning swim, her papa always sent it back when he saw it bounding over the shingle. Lucy thought that hard, but did not say so; nor did she reveal that when she bathed by herself – which was forbidden – the nameless dog blustered excitedly about at the edge of the sea, which it did not ever enter, and sometimes ran about with one of her sandals in its mouth. It was an old dog, Henry said, but in Lucy's company on the strand it became almost a puppy again, eventually lying down exhausted, its long pink tongue lolling from its jaws. Once she couldn't find the sandal it had been playing with, although she spent all morning searching. She had to root out an old pair from the bottom of her clothes-press and hope no one would notice, which no one did.

When the Lahardane sheepdogs were poisoned Lucy suggested that this dog should be a replacement for one of them, since it had never really become the O'Reillys'; but the suggestion met with no enthusiasm and within a week Henry began to train two sheepdog pups that a farmer near Kilauran had let him have at a bargain price. Although devoted to both her parents – to her father for his usually easygoing ways, to her mother for her gentleness and her beauty – Lucy was cross with them that summer because they didn't share her affection for the O'Reillys' dog, and cross with Henry because he didn't either: all that, in retrospect, was what that summer should have left behind, and would have if there hadn't been the trouble in the night.

Lucy wasn't told about it. Failing to rouse her from sleep, her

8

father's single shot became, in a dream, the crack of a branch giving way to the wind; and Henry had said that the sheepdogs must have gone on to poisoned land. But as the weeks went on, the summer began to feel different, and eavesdropping became the source of her information.

'It'll quieten,' her papa said. 'There's talk of a truce even now.'

'The trouble will go on, truce or not. You can tell it will. You can feel it. We can't be protected, Everard.'

Listening in the hall, Lucy heard her mama suggest that maybe they should go, that maybe they had no choice. She didn't understand what was meant by that, or what it was that would quieten. She moved closer to the slightly open door because the voices were lower than they had been.

'We have to think of her, Everard.'

'I know.'

And in the kitchen Bridget said:

'The Morells have gone from Clashmore.'

'I heard.' Henry's slow enunciation reached Lucy in the dog passage, which was what the passage that led from the kitchen to the back door was called. 'I heard that all right.'

'Past seventy they are now.'

Henry said nothing for a moment, then remarked that at times like these the worst was always assumed, the benefit of any doubt going the wrong way in any misfortune there'd be. The Gouvernets had gone from Aglish, he said, the Priors from Ringville, the Swifts, the Boyces. Everywhere, what you heard about was the going.

Lucy understood then. She understood the 'deserted house' the nameless dog had wandered from. She imagined furniture and belongings left behind, for that had been spoken of too. Understanding, she ran from the passage, not minding that her footsteps were heard, not minding that the door to the yard banged loudly, that hearing it they would know she'd been listening. She ran into the woods, down to the stream, where only a few days ago she had helped her papa to put in place a line of crossing stones. They were going to leave Lahardane – the glen and the woods and the seashore, the flat rocks where the shrimp pools were, the room she woke up in, the chatter of the hens in the yard, the gobbling of the turkeys, her footsteps the first marks on the sand when she walked to Kilauran to school, the seaweed hung up to tell the weather. She would have to find a box for the shells laid out on the window table in her bedroom, for her fir-cones and her stick shaped like a dagger, her flint pebbles. Nothing could be left behind.

She wondered where they would go, and could not bear the thought of somewhere that was impossible to imagine. She cried to herself among the ferns that grew in clumps a few yards from the stream. 'It'll be the end of us,' Henry had said when she had listened, and Bridget had said it would be. The past was the enemy in Ireland, her papa said another time.

All that day Lucy remained in her secret places in the woods of the glen. She drank from the spring her papa had found when he was a child himself. She lay down on the grass in the place where the sun came into the woods. She looked for Paddy Lindon's tumbled-down cottage, which she had never managed to find. Paddy Lindon used to come out of the woods like a wild man, his eyes bloodshot, hair that had never known a comb. It was Paddy Lindon who'd found her the stick shaped like a dagger, who'd shown her how to get a spark out of a flint pebble. Some of the roof of the cottage had fallen in, he'd told her, but some of it was all right. 'Amn't I destroyed by the rain?' he used to say. 'The way it would drip through the old sods of the roof, wouldn't it have me in the grave before I'm fit for it?' The rain taunted and tormented him, like a devil sent up, he said. And one day her papa said, 'Poor Paddy died,' and she cried then, too.

She gave up looking for where he'd lived, as so often she had before. Becoming hungry, she made her way down through the woods again, to the stream and then out on to the track that led back to Lahardane. On the track the only sound was her footsteps or when she kicked a fir-cone. She liked it on the track almost better than anywhere, even though it was all uphill, going back to the house.

'Will you look at the cut of you!' Bridget shrilly reprimanded her in the kitchen. 'Child, child, haven't we trouble enough!'

'I'm not going away from Lahardane.'

'Oh now, now.'

'I'm never going.'

'You go upstairs this minute and wash your knees, Lucy. You wash yourself before they'll see you. There's nothing arranged yet.'

Upstairs, Kitty Teresa said it would surely be all right: she had a way of looking on the bright side. She found it in the romances Lucy's mother bought for her for a few pence in Enniseala and she often passed on to Lucy tales of disaster or thwarted love that turned out happily in the end. Cinderellas arrived at the ball, sword fights were won by the more handsome contender, modesty was rewarded with riches. But on this occasion the bright side let Kitty Teresa down. As make-believe fell apart, she could only repeat that it would surely be all right.

*

'I belong nowhere else,' Everard Gault said, and Heloise said that by now she belonged nowhere else either. She had been happier at Lahardane than anywhere, but there would be revenge for the shooting, how could there not be?

'Even if they wait until the fighting's over, that night won't be forgotten.'

'I'll write to the boy's family. Father Morrissey said to try that.'

'We can live on what I have, you know.'

'Let me write to the family.'

She did not protest. Nor later, when the weeks that went by drew no response to the letter; nor later still when her husband took the pony and trap into Enniseala and found the family he had offended. They offered him tea, which he accepted, thinking this to be a sign of reconciliation: he was ready to pay whatever was asked of him in settlement of the affair. They listened to this suggestion, barefoot children coming and going in the kitchen, one of them occasionally turning the wheel of the bellows, sparks rising from the turf. But no response came, apart from the immediate civilities. The son who had been wounded sat at the table, disdainful of the visit, not speaking either, his arm in a sling. In the end, Captain Gault said – and was embarrassed and felt awkward saying it – that Daniel O'Connell in his day had stayed at Lahardane. The name was legendary, the man the beloved champion of the oppressed; but time, in this small dwelling at least, had robbed the past of magic. Those three lads had been out snaring rabbits and had lost their way. They shouldn't have been trespassing; no doubt about that, it was admitted. Captain Gault didn't mention the petrol tins. He returned to Lahardane, to another night-time vigil.

'You're right,' he admitted to his wife a few days later. 'You have always had a way of being right, Heloise.'

'This time I hate being right.'

Everard Gault had been missing in 1915; and waiting, not knowing, had been the loneliest time of Heloise's life, her two-year-old baby her greatest comfort. Then a telegram had come, and soon afterwards she had closed her eyes in selfish relief when there was the news that her husband had been invalided out of the army. As long as they lived, she vowed to herself, she would never again be parted from him, her resolve an expression of her gratitude for this kind misfortune.

'All the time I was there I could feel them thinking I had intended to kill their son. Not a word I said was believed.'

'Everard, we have one another and we have Lucy. We can begin again, somewhere else. Anywhere we choose.'

His wife had always brought Everard Gault strength, her comforting a balm that took away the weary pain of small defeats. Now, in this greater plight, they would manage. They would live, as she had said, on what she had herself inherited; they were not poor, though they would never be as well-to-do as the Gaults had been before the land was lost. Somewhere other than Lahardane, their circumstances would not be much different from their circumstances now. The truce that had come at last in the war was hardly noticed, so little was it trusted.

In the drawing-room and in the kitchen the conversations continued, the same subject touched upon from two different points of interest. Rendered disconsolate by all she heard, the upstairs maid asked questions and was told. Lahardane was Kitty Teresa's home too, had been for more than twenty years.

'Oh, ma'am!' she whispered, red in the face, her fingers twisting the hem of her apron. 'Oh, ma'am!'

But if it was the end of things for Kitty Teresa, it was not, as they had imagined it would be, entirely so for Henry and Bridget. When plans were made, it was put to them that they might continue their occupancy of the gate-lodge as caretakers of the larger house, that for the time being at least the herd would be made over to them to give them a continuing livelihood.

'You'll do better with the creamery cheque,' Heloise estimated, 'than with what wages we could afford. We think that fair.' Only passing time, the Captain added, could settle all this confusion.

They would be going to England, Heloise said at last to her child, after she'd promised Kitty Teresa to look out for another position for her and had given old Hannah notice.

'For long, is it?' Lucy asked, knowing the answer.

'Yes, for a long time.'

'For ever?'

'We don't want it to be.'

But Lucy knew it would be. It was for ever for the Morells and the Gouvernets. The Boyces had gone up to the North, Henry said, the house was under auction. She guessed what that meant from his voice, but he told her anyway.

'I'm sorry,' her papa said. 'I'm sorry, Lucy.'

It was her mother's fault, but it was his fault too. They shared the blame for old Hannah's miserable silence and Kitty Teresa's eyes gone red and her apron soaking with the tears that streamed on her cheeks and her neck, causing Bridget twenty times a day to tell her to give over. Henry slouched glumly about the yard.

'Oh, who's a fashion plate!' her papa exclaimed, pretending in the dining-room when one morning she wore her red dress.

At the sideboard her mama poured out tea and carried the cups and saucers to the table. 'Cheer up, darling,' her mama said, her head on one side. 'Cheer up,' she begged again.

Henry passed by the windows with the milk churns on the cart and, not cheering up in the least, Lucy listened to the clomp of the horse's hooves fading on the avenue. Two minutes that took: once at breakfast her papa had timed it with his pocket watch.

'Think of a poor little tinker child,' her mama said. 'Never a roof over her head.'

'You'll always have a roof, Lucy,' her papa promised. 'We all have to get used to something new. We have to, lady.'

She loved it when he called her lady, but this morning she didn't. She didn't see why you had to get used to something new. She said she wasn't hungry when they asked her, even though she was.

Afterwards on the strand the tide was coming in, washing over the sand the seagulls had marked, over the little piles the sand-worms made. She threw stems of seaweed for the O'Reillys' dog, wondering how many days were left. No one had said; she hadn't asked.

'You go on home now,' she ordered the dog, pointing at the cliffs, putting on her papa's voice when she wasn't obeyed.

She walked on alone, past the spit of rocks that stuck out like a finger into the sea, crossing the stream where the stepping stones were. When she had climbed a little way up through the woods of the glen she could no longer hear the sea or the sudden, curt shriek of the gulls. Slivers of bright light slipped through the dark of the trees. 'I've never seen the half of the old glen,' Paddy Lindon used to say. Every year, he'd once told her, he cultivated potatoes on the clearing he'd made beside his cottage, but this morning she didn't have the heart to go looking for it again.

'Who's coming to Enniseala with me?' her papa invited that afternoon, and of course she said yes. Her papa leaned back in the trap, hugged into its curve, the reins loose in his fingers. The first time he was in Enniseala, he said, was when he was five, brought in to have the fraenulum of his tongue cut.

'What's fraenulum?'

'A little snag underneath your tongue. If it's too tight you're tongue-tied.'

'What's tongue-tied?'

'It's when you can't speak clearly.'

'And couldn't you?'

'They said I couldn't. It didn't hurt much. They gave me a set of marbles afterwards.'

'I think it would hurt.'

'You don't need anything like that.'

The marbles were in a flat wooden box with a lid that slid on and off. It was still there, beside the bagatelle in the drawing-room. She had to stand on a footstool when they played bagatelle, but she knew these were the marbles he'd been given then because once he'd told her. He'd forgotten that. Sometimes he forgot things.

'There's a fisherman in Kilauran can't speak at all,' she said.

'I know.'

'He does it on his fingers.'

'Yes, he does.'

'You see him doing it. The other fishermen understand him.'

'Well, there's a thing! Would you like to hold the reins now?'

In Enniseala her papa bought new suitcases in Domville's because they didn't have enough. One of the shopmen came out from the office and said he was sorry. He wouldn't have believed it, he said. He'd never have thought he'd live to see the day. 'Please God, you'll be back, Captain.'

Her papa kept nodding, not saying anything until he held his hand out and called the shopman Mr Bothwell. The new suitcases hardly fitted into the trap, but they did in the end. 'Now,' her papa said, not getting into the trap himself but taking her hand in a way that made her guess where they were going.

He could move the door of Allen's without the bell ringing. He opened it a little and reached up for the catch at the top, then pushed the door so that they could walk in. He reached over the counter and lifted the glass jar down from the shelf and tipped the sweets into the scoop of the scales. He slipped them into a white paper bag and put the bag back on the scales again and put the glass stopper back on the jar. Liquorice toffee and nougat were what he liked and so did she. *Lemon's Pure Sweets* it said on the silver-coloured wrappers of the liquorice toffees.

While he was weighing them she wanted to giggle, as she always did, but she didn't because it would have spoilt everything. He pulled the door in and the bell rang. 'Four pence ha'penny,' he said when the girl with the plaits came out from the back. 'You're a holy terror!' the girl said.

He always held the reins himself when they were on a street. He held them tight, sitting straight up, jerking one and then the other, now and again releasing one of his hands in order to wave at someone. 'What's it mean "and County"?' she asked when they had passed all the shops.

'And County?'

'Driscoll and County, Broderick and County.'

'The Co. is not for County, it's for Company. "And Company Limited." The Ltd means Limited.'

'It's for County at school. County Cork, County Waterford.'

'It's just the same abbreviation. Shortening a word so there won't be too much written on a map or above a shop.'

'Funny they're the same.'

'You like to have the reins now?'

There was a smell of leather in the trap, but it was stronger when the new suitcases were opened in the house. The trunks were half full already, their lids held upright by straps that folded away when they were closed. Henry measured the windows for boarding.

'Who's never been on a train before?' her papa said, the way he did, as if she were still only three or four. He used to go away by train himself, away to school three times a year. He still had his trunk and his box, his initials painted on them in black. She asked him to tell her about the school and he said he would later, on the train. Everyone was busy now, he said.

'I don't want to go,' she said, finding her mama in their bedroom.

'Papa and I don't want to go either.'

'Why are we then?'

'Sometimes we have to do things we don't want to.'

'Papa wasn't trying to kill those men.'

'Did Henry tell you that?'

'Henry didn't. And Bridget didn't.'

'You're not nice when you're cross, Lucy.'

'I don't want to be nice. I don't want to go with you.'

'Lucy –'

'I won't go.'

She ran from the room and ran down to her crossing stones. They came to find her, calling out in the woods, but everything she said to them on the way back they didn't hear. They didn't want to hear, they didn't want to listen.

'Will you come to the creamery with me?' Henry said the next day, and she shook her head dolefully. 'Shall we have tea outside?' her mama said, smiling at her. And her papa said the cat had her tongue when the tablecloth was spread on the grass and there was lemon cake, her favourite. She wished she hadn't gone to Enniseala with him, she wished she hadn't asked him about his fraenulum and what was written over the shops. All the time they were pretending.

'Look,' her papa said. 'The hawk.'

And she looked up although she hadn't meant to. The hawk wasn't more than a dot against the sky, circling round and round. She watched it and her papa said don't cry.

*

The weeping of Kitty Teresa was no longer heard in the bedrooms because Kitty Teresa had gone already, gone home to Dungarvan when another position couldn't be found for her. She would come back the day they came back themselves, she promised before she left. No matter where she was she'd come back.

'They've rented a place,' Bridget said in the kitchen, and Henry took from the shelf above the range the piece of paper with the address on it. He didn't say anything at first and then he said so that's that. 'Only till they're fixed permanent,' Bridget said. 'They'll buy a place, I'd say.'

In the yard Henry sawed the wood for boarding the windows. Lucy watched him, sitting on the ledge beneath the pear tree that was spread out against the yard's long east wall. It was on her way back from school that she'd begun to bathe on her own, weighing her clothes down with her satchel and running quickly into the sea and out again, drying herself any old how. Henry knew; she didn't know how but he did. When she slouched off now he probably guessed where she was going. She didn't care. She didn't care if he went away to tell on her. It wasn't like him to do that, but the way things were he might.

In the field above the cliffs she heard the chiming of the Angelus bell in Kilauran. Sometimes you heard it, sometimes you didn't. The sound still carried to her while she was pulling off her clothes on the strand. It was lost when she ran into the sea and waded out. This was always the best part – walking slowly through the waves, the coldness rising, invigorating on her skin, the pull of the under-tow at her feet. She spread out her arms to swim beyond her depth, then floated with the tide.

The strand had been empty in both directions when she'd left it. Without being able to see clearly as she swam back to it, she knew that what seemed to be moving there now was the O'Reillys' dog chasing its own shadow on the sand. It often did that; while she watched, it stood still for a moment, gazing out to where she was, before beginning its play again.

She turned on her back to float. If she ran away she'd take the short cut Paddy Lindon used to talk about. 'Take to the high woods the steep side,' he used to say. 'Go long enough on and there's the road for you.'

She swam towards the shore again and when the water became shallow she walked through the last of the waves. The dog was nosing about on the shingle and she knew that her clothes had been pilfered, that whatever had been taken would already be buried in the shingle or the seaweed. When she began to dress she found that her summer vest had gone but when she looked in the ragged line of seaweed and in the shingle she couldn't find it.

Helpless in its disgrace, scolded all the way up the cliff, the nameless dog cringed piteously, until there had been punishment enough. The matted, untidy head was pressed against Lucy's legs then, to be stroked and patted and embraced. 'Home now,' she ordered and, fierce again, watched while disobedience was considered and thought better of.

In her room, she replaced from among the clothes that had been packed already the vest that had been lost. He never went any other way, Paddy Lindon used to say, when he'd be heading for the processions in Dungarvan or for the Sunday hurling. When his luck was in, a cart would go by on the road and he'd hail it.

*

'This is specially yours,' her papa said.

He had gone back to Domville's to get it. It was blue, not like the other suitcases, and smaller because she was small herself. Leather, even though it was blue, he said, and showed her the keys that fitted its lock. 'We mustn't lose the keys,' he said. 'Shall I keep one?'

She couldn't smile, she didn't want to cry. All her things, he said, all her precious things would fit in it, the flintstones, the dagger stick.

'One day we'll have *L.G.* put on the lid.'

'Thank you, Papa,' she said.

'You go and put your things in it.'

But in her room the blue suitcase remained empty on the window seat, its lid closed, one of the keys that opened its lock still tied to its handle.

*

'I understand,' Bridget said when it was explained to her that it might be a little time before some at least of the possessions left

19

behind were sent for. The instruction was given that Henry and she should walk through the rooms occasionally, since things sometimes went wrong in an empty house. Lucy heard all that.

The sheets for draping the furniture were ready in the hall. Upstairs on the first landing there was a pile for the jumble sale, the clothes they didn't want to take with them. Some of Lucy's were there too, as if everything now was being taken for granted.

'Oh now, you mustn't, darling.' Her mama was in the doorway of her bedroom but Lucy didn't look up, her face pressed hard into her pillow. Then her mama came in and put her arms around her. She wiped away the tears and there was the same scent on her handkerchief, always the same it was. It would be all right, her mama said. She promised it would be.

'We have to say good-bye to Mr Aylward,' her papa said later, finding her in the apple orchard.

She shook her head, but then he took her hand and they walked through the fields and along the strand to Kilauran. The O'Reillys' dog watched them from the top of the cliffs, knowing better than to follow them, because her papa was there.

'Couldn't I stay with Henry and Bridget?' she asked.

'Ah no, no,' her papa said.

The fishermen were spreading out their nets. They saluted, and her papa saluted them back. He said something about the weather and one of them said it was grand altogether these days. Lucy looked about for the fisherman who talked with his fingers, but he wasn't there. She asked her papa and he said that man was maybe still out with his boat.

'I'd be all right with Henry and Bridget,' she said.

'Ah no, darling, no.'

She reached up for his hand, turning her head away so that he wouldn't know she was trying not to cry. When they came to the schoolroom he lifted her up to see in at the window. Everything was tidy because it was the holidays, everything left as Mr Aylward said it must be, the four empty tables, the benches pulled in to them, the charts hanging up. *Bayonets were first made in Bayonne.*

Cider is the juice of apples. The blackboard was clear, the duster folded by the chalk box. The shiny maps – rivers and mountains, the counties of England and Ireland – were rolled up on the shelf.

'We need a bit of time,' her papa said in Mr Aylward's house, his head inclined in her direction, and she knew he didn't mean all three of them when he said we.

'Ah, well, of course,' Mr Aylward said. 'Of course.'

'It breaks my heart,' her papa said. 'To tell you the truth.'

Yet what else could he have done, he asked Mr Aylward, when he'd looked down at the shadows standing there, knowing there would be petrol somewhere as well, knowing that whoever was there had poisoned the dogs? He'd been nervous, firing in the dark, he said. No wonder he'd never made a soldier.

'There isn't any man in a family wouldn't have done the same,' Mr Aylward said.

A sheepdog from Lahardane had gone on to poisoned land before, Henry had said; not that that dog had died, but even so. Henry wanted everything to be all right, pretending too.

'You keep the poetry up, girl,' Mr Aylward said. 'She's right good at learning her poetry, Captain.'

'She's a good little girl.'

Mr Aylward kissed her, saying good-bye. Her papa finished what was in the glass he'd been given. He shook hands with Mr Aylward, and Mr Aylward said that it should come to this. Then they went away.

'Why'd they bring petrol with them?' she asked.

'One day I'll tell you about all that.'

They passed the fishermen, who were now repairing the nets they'd laid out. It was the place where the women had stood, gazing out at the sea when the *Mary Nell* had not returned. The women had been there when she passed on her way to school, and again on her way back, their black shawls pulled tight, nearly hiding their faces. The storm that had wrecked the *Mary Nell* was over then, the sun was even shining. '*Bestow thy blessing*,' they had prayed with Mr Aylward, '*that they may be kept safe in every peril of the deep*.' But

21

that same day there was the sound of the women's keening. No fisherman came back, none was rescued, because the Ballycotton lifeboat had been beaten back by the gales. No drowned body was washed up with the smashed planks and ragged strips of canvas, with the splinters of mast and boom. 'A man's not given back from that sea,' Henry said. 'In living memory and before.' From miles out, the sharks hurried in when there were wrecks.

As she passed by the fishermen with her father, the sound of the keening, the mournful wail that carried over the half doors of the cottages, seemed to Lucy to be there again, a forlorn echo of a terrible time returning in a time that was terrible also. The cheerfulness that came now and again to Lahardane wasn't real and only lasted for as long as they remembered to pretend.

'I don't want to leave Lahardane,' she said on the strand.

'None of us wants to, lady.'

He bent down and lifted her up, the way he used to when she was little. He held her in his arms and made her look out over the calm sea, looking for the man who spoke with his fingers, but she couldn't see a fishing boat, nor could he. He put her down again and wrote with a pebble on the sand. *Lucy Gault*, he wrote. 'Now, that's a lovely name.'

They climbed the cliff at the place where it was easy, up to the field next to the O'Reillys' turnip field, where there'd been barley last year. When Mr O'Reilly was weeding whatever crop was there he'd wave to her.

'Why must we go?' she cried.

'Because they don't want us here,' her papa said.

*

Heloise wrote to her bank, in England, to explain what was about to happen and to seek advice about her holdings, all of which were in different areas of enterprise within the Rio Verde Railway Company. For generations there had been a family connection with the renowned railway, but in the present circumstances – since for a time at least her inheritance would play a greater part in her life and that of her husband and their child – her tentative query did not seem out of place and the bank's response confirmed its wisdom. Steadfast and prosperous for almost eighty years, the Rio Verde Railway was at last beginning to display signs of what might possibly be the onset of commercial fatigue: Heloise was recommended to consider disposing of all, or the greater part, of an investment that for so long had served her family well.

In Enniseala the Captain sought confirmation or otherwise of this advice from his solicitor and friend of many years, Aloysius Sullivan, who was as knowledgeable about financial matters as he was about the law. He shared the bank's opinion: with plenty of trading acumen left, and its accumulated funds to draw on, the Rio Verde Railway would certainly not collapse overnight, but even so a more diversified portfolio was his suggestion also.

'No need to think about it before we leave,' Captain Gault reported when he returned to Lahardane. Echoing again the view of the bank, the solicitor had confirmed as well that this wasn't something to decide about in a hurry.

They talked about being in England then, of the many other practicalities they would have to see to when they were less distracted by emotion. How different their lives would be! each thought but neither said.

*

The straw fish-baskets hung in a row in the long scullery beside the cold room. They were flat and they didn't hold much so Lucy took two, one at a time, on different days. She took bread from the bin in the pantry, a heel of white the first time, then heels of brown or soda, whatever would not be noticed. She wrapped them in the shop paper that was kept in the drawers of the kitchen dresser. She filled one basket and then the other with the packages, with apples and scallions and food she took from her plate in the dining-room when no one was noticing. She kept the baskets in a shed in the yard which no one went into, hidden behind a wheelbarrow that had fallen apart.

She rooted among the jumble on the landing for a skirt and jumper. She made a bundle of them in an old black coat of her mother's: at night it would be cold. On the landing there was no sound except the rustling she made herself, and when she took the clothes to her hiding place she met no one on the back stairs, no one in the dog passage.

*

On the afternoon of the day before the day of the departure Captain Gault went through his papers, feeling that it was something he should do. But the occupation was tedious and, abandoning it, he dismantled instead the rifle he had fired in the night. He cleaned its parts purposefully, as if anticipating their use in the future, although he did not intend to take the rifle with him.

'Oh, all this will fall into place,' he murmured more than once, confident in his reassurance to himself. Leaving, arriving, the furniture one day settled around them again: time and circumstance would arrange their lives, as in exile so many other lives had been arranged.

He returned to leafing through his papers, conscientiously doing his best with them.

*

Heloise secured the leather straps on the trunks that were ready to go, then attached the labels she had written. Wondering if she would ever see again all that had to be left behind, she distributed camphor balls in drawers and wardrobes, in sleeves and pockets.

This was the empty time of day. No matter what excitements there might earlier have been, or in what way the day so far had been different from other days, the house was quiet now. No rattle of pans disturbed the hours before evening came, no music on the gramophone in the drawing-room, no chatter of voices. Betraying nothing of the chagrin the task induced, Henry carried downstairs the trunks and suitcases that had been packed. On the kitchen table Bridget spread out on her ironing blanket the shirt collars the Captain would require on his travels. In the depths of the range the heaters for her iron had just begun to glow.

*

When Lucy passed the open door of the kitchen, Bridget did not look up. Henry was not in the yard. Only the orchard was noisy, the rooks scattering from among the apple branches when her presence disturbed them.

She went the steep way, as Paddy Lindon had advised, avoiding the easier track through the glen in case Henry was out on it. She didn't know how long her journey to Dungarvan would take; Paddy Lindon had never been precise about that. She wouldn't know where to look for Kitty Teresa's house when she got there, but whoever gave her a lift would. Kitty Teresa would say she'd have to take her back, but it wouldn't matter because everything would be different by then: all the time she'd thought about running away Lucy had known it would be. As soon as they discovered she wasn't there, as soon as they realized what had happened, it would be different. 'It breaks my heart, too,' her mama had said. 'And papa's. Papa's most of all.' When Kitty Teresa brought her back they'd say they'd always known they couldn't leave.

She passed a moss-encrusted rock that she remembered from some other time when she was here, then a fallen tree that wasn't familiar at all, with spikes where it had cracked off that could catch you if it was dark. It wasn't dark now, no more than gloomy, like it always was in the high woods. But darkness would come in an hour or so and she'd have to get to the road before it did, although there wouldn't be any chance of a cart going by until the morning. She hurried and almost at once she stumbled, thrown forward, her foot caught in a hole. Pain spread from her ankle when she tried to move it. She couldn't stand up.

*

'Lucy!' Captain Gault called out in the yard. 'Lucy!'

There was no answer and in the milking parlour he shouted down the length of it to Henry.

'Tell Lucy if you see her I've gone to say good-bye to the fisherman we missed the last time.' By the avenue and the road, he said, back by the strand. 'Say I could do with a bit of company.'

He called her name again at the front of the house before he set off on his own.

*

'She was here earlier,' Bridget said. 'I saw her about.'

It wasn't unusual; Lucy often wasn't there. Meeting Bridget on the stairs, Heloise had made her enquiry without anxiety. It could be, Bridget supposed, that there was the dog over at the O'Reillys' to say good-bye to.

'You've been a strength to me, Bridget.' In that quiet, untroubled moment Heloise paused before returning to the suitcases in her bedroom. 'All these years you've been a strength to me.'

'I wish you wouldn't be going, ma'am. I wish it was different.'

'I know. I know.'

*

On the avenue Captain Gault wondered in what circumstances he would again move through its shadows, beneath the long arch of branches that stole most of the light. On either side of him the grass, deprived, was a modest summer growth, yellow here and there with dandelions, foxgloves withering where they had thrived in the shade. He paused for a moment when he came to the gate-lodge, where life would continue when the house was abandoned. Now that an end had come, he doubted this evening that he would ever bring his family back to live at Lahardane. The prediction came from nowhere, an unwelcome repetition of what, these last few days, he had privately denied.

On the pale clay road beyond the gates he turned to the left, the berried honeysuckle scentless now, September fuchsia in the hedges. They would not for long have to rely on Heloise's legacy. Vaguely, he saw himself in a shipping office, even though he hardly knew what the work undertaken in such places involved. It didn't much matter; any decent occupation would do. Now and again they would return, a visit to see how everything was, to keep a connection going. 'It isn't for ever,' Heloise had said last night, and had spoken of the windows opened again, the dust sheets lifted, fires lit, flowerbeds weeded. And he'd said no, of course not.

In Kilauran he conversed with the deaf and dumb fisherman, as he had learnt to in his childhood: gestures made, words mouthed. They said good-bye. 'Not for too long,' he left his silent promise behind, and felt a falsehood compounded here too. He stood for a while on the rocks where sea-pinks grew in clumps. The surface of the sea was a dappled sheen, streaked with the last faint afterglow of sunset. Its waves came softly, hardly touched with foam. There was no other movement on it anywhere.

Had he been right not to reveal to Heloise, or to his child, the finality he had begun to sense in this departure? Should he have gone back to that family in Enniseala to plead a little longer? Should he have offered more than he had, whatever was felt might settle the misdemeanour he had committed, accepting that the outrage of that night was his and not the trespassers' who had come? Climbing down the rocks on to the shingle, shuffling over it to the sand, he didn't know. He didn't know when he walked on, lingering now and again to gaze out at the empty sea. He might have said to himself on this last night that he had too carelessly betrayed the past and then betrayed, with easy comforting, a daughter and a wife. He was the one who was closest to place and people, whose love of leftover land, of house and orchard and garden, of sea and seashore, fostered instinct and premonition. Yet when he searched his feelings there was nothing there to guide him, only confusion and contradiction.

He turned towards the cliffs, crunching over the shingle again. Lost for a while in the trees, his house re-appeared, a light coming on in an upstairs window. His foot caught on something among the stones and he bent to pick it up.

*

'Lucy!' Heloise called and Henry said she might have gone after her father. He hadn't seen her to pass on the Captain's message but, contrary as she was these times, she'd maybe been hiding about in the yard somewhere and had heard it for herself. She hadn't spoken a word to him for three days, nor to Bridget either. The way things were, it wasn't surprising she hadn't come in for her tea.

Heloise heard him shouting Lucy's name in the yard sheds. 'Lucy!' she shouted herself in the apple orchard and in the field where the cattle were, which was the way back from the O'Reillys'. She passed through the gate in the white railing that separated the fields from the turn-around in front of the house. She crossed the gravel to the hydrangea lawn.

It was she who had first called it that, just as it was she who had discovered that the Lahardane fields had once been known as Long Meadow and Cloverhill and John Joe's and the river field. She'd always wanted to hear those names used again, but nobody had bothered when she suggested it. The hydrangeas were heavily in bloom, their blue still distinctive in the darkening twilight, bunching out around the semi-circle they formed along a grey stone wall. They were the loveliest of all Lahardane's features, she had always thought.

'Lucy!' she called through the trees. She stood still, listening in the silence. She went further into the woods, coming out twenty minutes later on the track that ran down to the stream and the crossing stones. 'Lucy!' she shouted. 'Lucy!'

She called out her child's name in the house when she returned to it, opening the doors of rooms that weren't used, climbing up to attics. She went downstairs again. She stood by the open hall door, and in a moment heard her husband returning. She knew he was alone because there were no voices. She heard the gate she had passed through earlier creaking as he opened it and closed it, the latch falling into place.

'Is Lucy with you?' she raised her voice again to ask.

His footsteps on the gravel halted. He was hardly more than a shadow.

'Lucy?' she said.

'Isn't Lucy here?'

He still stood where he had stopped. There was something white in his hand, a shaft of lamplight from the open hall door spilling over it.

2

'Holy Mother of God!' Bridget whispered, her face gone pallid.

'I'm telling you.' Henry nodded slowly. They were down on the strand, he said. The Captain had come up through the fields and then they'd both gone back to the strand.

'He found her clothes. The tide was going out and he walking over from Kilauran. That's all was said.'

It couldn't be that, Bridget whispered. It couldn't be what he was saying. 'Holy Mother, it couldn't!'

'The tide would take anything with it. Except what was caught up in the stones. He had clothing in his hand.' Henry paused. 'A while back I wondered was she going bathing on her own. If I'd have seen her at it I'd have said.'

'Would she be over on the rocks? She was low in herself all this time. Would she be over where she'd get the shrimps?'

Henry didn't say anything, and then Bridget shook her head. Why would any child take off her clothes on a strand unless it was to bathe in the sea, the last bathe she'd have in it before they left?

'I wondered it too,' she said. 'Her hair a bit damp a few times.'

'I'll go down. I'll bring them a light.'

When Bridget was left alone she prayed. Her hands felt cold when she pressed them together. She prayed aloud, stifling her tears. A few minutes later she followed her husband, through the yard and the apple orchard, out into the grazing field and down to the strand.

*

They stared through the dark at the empty sea. They did not speak, but stood close to one another as if fearful of being alone. Softly,

30

the waves lapped, the sea advancing, each time a little more with the turn of the tide.

'Oh, ma'am, ma'am!' Bridget's exclamation was shrill, her footsteps noisy on the stones before she reached the sand. A while ago she'd thought it, she cried, the words tumbling over one another, her features scarcely seeming to be her own in the flickers of Henry's lamp.

At a loss, Captain Gault and his wife turned from the sea. Could there be hope, somehow, in this agitation, some grain of hope where there had been none before? In their bewilderment, for a moment, there was all that, the same for both of them.

'I'm not saying she ever said a word, ma'am. It's only Henry and myself thought it. We should have said it to you, sir.'

'Said what, Bridget?' There was a weary politeness in the Captain's tone, and patience while he waited for an irrelevancy: already expectation had shrunk away to nothing.

'All I'd notice was her hair was a bit wet when she'd come in.'

'From bathing?'

'If we'd known it for sure we'd have told.'

There was a silence, then Captain Gault said:

'You're not to blame, Bridget. No one will ever think that.'

'Her forget-me-not dress she was wearing, sir.'

'It wasn't her dress.'

Her summer vest, Heloise said, and in silence again they walked towards where it had been found.

'We told her lies,' the Captain said before they reached the place.

Heloise didn't understand. Then she remembered the reassurances and the half promises, and remembered knowing that the promises might not be kept. Disobedience had been a child's defiance, deception the coinage they had offered her themselves.

'She knew I'd always bathe with her,' the Captain said.

The splinter of driftwood that had snagged what the Captain had picked up was still there, its pale, smooth surface just visible in the dark. Henry moved the lamp, looking for something else, but there was nothing.

As if somehow it had acquired a potency of its own in feeding on circumstances and events, the falsity that beguiled the Captain, and his wife and their servants, was neither questioned nor denied. The house had been searched, the sheds in the yard, the garden, the orchard. Even though nothing had suggested that so late in the evening the missing child might have been in the woods, her name had been called out there; the O'Reillys' kitchen had been visited. The sea was what remained. It seemed no more than the mockery of wishful thinking that its claims, so insistently pressed by what facts there were, should not be accepted.

'Will you come over to Kilauran, Henry, and we'll take a boat out?'

'I will, sir.'

'Leave the lamp with them here.'

The two men went. Hours later, on the spit of rocks that broke the long expanse of sand and shingle, the women they left behind found a sandal among the shrimp pools.

*

The fishermen at Kilauran learnt of the loss when they rowed in at dawn from their fishing. They reported that all night they'd seen nothing from their boats, but the superstition that long ago had enriched their fishermen's talk was muttered again among them. Only the debris of wreckage, and not much of that, was left behind by the sharks who fed on tragedy: the fishermen, too, mourned the death of a living child.

*

As the surface of the seashore rocks was pitted by the waves and gathered limpets that further disguised what lay beneath, so time made truth of what appeared to be. The days that passed, in becoming weeks, still did not disturb the surface an assumption had created. The weather of a beautiful summer continued with neither sign nor hint that credence had been misplaced. The single sandal found among the rocks became a sodden image of death;

32

and as the keening on the pier at Kilauran traditionally marked distress brought by the sea, so silence did at Lahardane.

Captain Gault no longer spent his nights at an upstairs window but stood alone on the cliffs, staring out at the dark, calm sea, cursing himself, cursing the ancestors who in their prosperity had built a house in this place. Sometimes the O'Reillys' nameless dog plucked up courage and came to stand beside him, its head hunched down as if it sensed a melancholy and offered a sympathy of its own. The Captain did not turn it away.

Here and in the house, all memory was regret, all thought empty of consolation. There hadn't been time to have the initials inscribed on the blue suitcase, yet how could there not have been time since time so endlessly stretched now, since the days that came, with their long, slow nights, carried with them a century's weight?

'Oh, my darling!' Captain Gault murmured, watching yet another dawn. 'Oh, my darling, forgive me.'

*

For Heloise, the torment had a variation. Clawed out of the past, spread rawly through her suffering, the happy years of her marriage felt like selfishness. In all the rooms of the house she had come to as a bride there were memories of what had been so greedily hers – of gramophone music danced to with Everard's arms lightly about her, and the sluggish tick of the drawing-room clock while they read by the fire, the high-backed sofa drawn up, the crackle of logs in the grate. Disappointed but safe at least, he had come back from war. The child who had been born was growing up; Lahardane offered a living as well as a way of life. Yet if Everard had married differently, the unforgiving end of this chain of circumstances would not have come about; there was always that.

'No, no,' he protested now, attributing blame elsewhere. 'If ever they come back I'll shoot them dead.'

Again, for both of them, the sheepdogs lay poisoned in the yard, their bodies cold on the cobbles. Again Henry raked the sea-gravel where blood stained the pebbles.

'We could not explain more,' Heloise whispered, but her guilt did not lessen: to their child she had not explained enough.

*

'I wonder, though, will they go now?' Bridget speculated when the preparations for leaving did not begin again. 'I doubt they care what happens to them.'

'Isn't it fixed, all the same?'

'What was fixed is different now.'

'You'd say Kitty Teresa'll be fetched back? And Hannah with her?'

'I'm not saying what I don't know. Only that I wouldn't be surprised how things would be.'

Bridget's belief had always been that affection for the place would bring Captain Gault and his wife back when the country was quiet again and some settlement could be reached about the wounding. In hopeful speculation, she had found particular significance in the fact that the herd was not to be sold.

'I'd say they'd go,' Henry said. 'I'd say they'd want to go now.'

*

The relevant formalities were completed as fully as possible, all that the circumstances allowed. Captain Gault's declaration was starkly empty of sentiment, but the Registrar's clerk who came to Lahardane to transcribe it was moved and sympathetic.

'Why should we wait longer now?' Heloise asked when the man had gone. 'If the Kilauran fishermen are right in what they believe, there's nothing more. If they are wrong, there is, for me, a horror I do not want to know. If I am different from all the mothers in the world, if they would creep about the shingle and the pools for ever seeking a thread of ribbon they may remember, then I am different. If I am unnatural, and weak and full of a fear I do not understand, then I am unnatural. But I can only say that in my merciless regret I could not bear to look down and see my child's fleshless bones and know too much.'

Their sorrowing was their common ground, yet separated them.

One spoke, the other hardly heard. Each turned away from useless pity. No premonition helped them now, no voice in a dream, no sudden instinct. Heloise packed the last of their luggage.

During the bleak time that had passed she had requested, in a telegram to her bank, that the Rio Verde share certificates should be forwarded to her husband's bank in Enniseala. She revealed this to him as he was setting out to make what new last arrangements were necessary with Aloysius Sullivan.

'But why on earth should they be sent to us now?' He stared at her in bewilderment. 'All the way to us over here when we're about to leave?'

Heloise didn't answer. She wrote a note instead, empowering him to receive the certificates on her behalf.

'It's how I want it,' she said then.

This eccentricity lingered with Captain Gault while he did as his wife requested. Could it be that the shock of a summer's events, and being so distraught, had left behind an aftermath as terrible as any of the events themselves? Valuable documents had been unnecessarily entrusted to the post and were next to be exposed to the hazards of a journey back to the island they had come from. The disposal of the shares could have been arranged without the forwarding of any documents at all; only Heloise's instructions were necessary. In the letter that outlined the bank's reservations about the future of the railway company, this had been stated.

In Enniseala he was tempted to hand back the bulky envelope he collected, to ask that it be safely returned to where it had come from, to say there had been an error, perhaps understandable in the circumstances. But he did not do so, did not arrive back at Lahardane with some tacked-together excuse. Instead he handed over what he had been given, and passed on, too, the good wishes of Aloysius Sullivan. The envelope's contents were scrutinized, the solicitor's good wishes nodded away as if they were of no possible interest, although Heloise had always been particularly fond of Aloysius Sullivan.

That evening they might have walked together, in the house, in the orchard and the garden, through the fields. But Captain Gault did not suggest it and did not go on his own, as he had before. The apple trees, the bees of his hives, the cattle that had been his pride still drew him, but it was his wife who mattered more. It was a cruel last straw if what appeared to be was so.

Sombre and silent, drinking in solitude, he tried not to wonder if there was punishment in this. For had not, after all, the people risen up, and was not that the beginning of the hell which had so swiftly been completed in this small corner? He could not know that, as certainly as the truth had no place in an erroneous assumption, so it had none in such fearful conjectures of damnation. Chance, not wrath, had this summer ordered the fate of the Gaults.

*

On the train to Dublin, Heloise was silent. She hated, as much as she hated the seashore they had left behind, the fields and hills they passed among, the woods and copses, the quiet ruins. She asked no more than to be separated for ever from landscape that had once delighted her, from faces that had kindly smiled, and voices that had spoken gently. A rented villa in a Sussex suburb was not far enough away: for days she'd known that, but had not said it. She did so now.

The Captain listened. It was not beyond his understanding or his sympathy that the wife he had brought to Lahardane thirteen years ago should wish, in leaving it, to travel on and on, further and further, until some other train deposited them where strangers did not excite comment or curiosity. Their future in pleasant, easy England, once imagined, could not be imagined now.

'The Sussex address is the one we've left behind,' he said, needing to say something. But neither Sussex nor its suburbs nor its villas, nor England's tranquillity, concerned him. What did was his wife's face gone thin and white, her staring so at the landscape with deadened eyes, her voice without its timbre, her folded hands seeming like a statue's. But even so he felt relief as well. She had not acted in confusion when she'd sent a telegram to her bank, only with determination that she might more firmly close down the past. The documents he had collected for her went with them in their luggage, to become their livelihood wherever the end of their journey was to be.

'Anywhere,' she said. 'Anywhere will do.'

In Dublin, at King's Bridge Station, Captain Gault sent the telegram that cancelled their tenancy of the house in England. They stood, an island with their luggage, when he had done that. 'We are at one,' he said, for although Heloise's fragility still alarmed him, they shared the mood reflected in the nature of their departure, and the desire to lose themselves, to rid themselves of memory. Offering comfort, he said all that.

Heloise did not reply, but said as they travelled across the city to the docks:

'It's strange that going away doesn't sadden us in the slightest way. When once it seemed unbearable.'

'Yes, it's strange.'

In this manner, on Thursday the twenty-second of September 1921, Captain Gault and his wife abandoned their house and unknowingly their child. In England, unnoticed, the rush of town and country went by. Church spires and village houses, the last of the sweet-peas in small back gardens, the sprawl of runner beans on careful wires, geraniums in their final flush, might have been something else. France when it came was just another country, although nights were spent there. *We have travelled on*, Captain Gault wrote to the solicitor in Enniseala, one of three sentences on a sheet of hotel writing-paper.

3

Bridget polished the furniture before she covered it with old bed sheets that had never been thrown away. She cleaned the windows before the boards were nailed in place. She scrubbed the steps of the uncarpeted back stairs and the dog-passage flagstones. She packed away eiderdowns and blankets.

In the darkened house on the morning when there was nothing left to do except in the kitchen and the sculleries, where daylight still prevailed, Henry walked about the upstairs rooms with a lamp. The air there was already stale. That evening they would lock up.

The two were melancholy. On each of the few days that had passed since the Gaults' departure there had been the expectation that one of the fishermen would arrive with news that something had caught in their nets or on an oar. But no one had come. Would the Gaults want to know if anyone had? Bridget wondered, and Henry had shaken his head, unable to answer that.

In the hall he lifted the globe from the lamp and quenched the wick. In the dairy he washed out the churns he had earlier brought back from the creamery. 'I've a wall to see to,' he called out to Bridget when she appeared at the back door of the house, and he saw her nod across the distance that separated them. He wondered what it would feel like, sitting down for the last time at the kitchen table when he returned. A bit of bacon she was cooking.

The sheepdogs hurried in the yard when Henry whistled, and Bridget watched them pushing at one another behind him when he set off. 'It'll keep fine,' she raised her voice to comment.

'I'd say it would all right,' he said.

Bridget did not feel that her prayers had let her down. It was enough to have prayed, God's will that He had not heard her. They

38

would settle into the way things were to be; they would accept it, since that was how it had to be. Old Hannah would come to the gate-lodge the odd time and one day even Kitty Teresa might, although she was a fair enough distance away. More likely, though, Kitty Teresa wouldn't want to come visiting. After the carry-on there'd been with her when she had to leave, that would maybe be too much for her.

Most of all you'd miss this big old kitchen, Bridget thought when she entered it again. She would still come down to the yard to feed the hens for as long as hens were there; she'd find new tasks outside. When first she had come to the kitchen with her mother she used to play in the yard, and when it was raining she'd sit by the fire in the meal shed, blowing at the turf with the wheel-bellows, watching the sparks.

At the sink she scrubbed the surface of a pan, its enamel chipped in a way that had been familiar to her for years. She rinsed it and dried it, returning it to its place, wondering if the day would come when she'd use it again, and in a sudden wave of optimism believing that she would, that with time's healing they'd come back. She brought the piece of bacon to the boil on the range.

*

Henry didn't remember the black coat when he saw it. He had often seen it worn, years ago, but he didn't recognize it now. It hadn't been there before was what he thought. The last time he came up here after stones for a gap in O'Reilly's sheep wall there had only been high weeds in that corner. He stood looking at the coat, not moving further in to the ruins, telling the sheepdogs to stand back. Slowly he lit a cigarette.

The stones he was after were there, as they'd been before, fallen out of the walls, lying among the nettles. He remembered Paddy Lindon sitting at the table of which only the legs and a single board were left. The nettles around it were beaten down, a path made to the corner where the coat was. Two straw fish-baskets were lying there, and he could see flies on brown apple-cores.

He tried to make sense of it, and when a kind of sense came he didn't want to go closer. One of the sheepdogs whined and he told it to shut up. He didn't want to lift the coat to look, but in the end he did.

*

In the yard one of the dogs gave a single bark, and Bridget knew that Henry had returned. That dog always barked once when it came back to the yard, a habit Henry was trying to break it of. At the range she pushed the saucepan of potatoes on to the heat and poured boiling water over the cabbage she had cut up. She laid out knives and forks on the table and then heard Henry's footsteps in the passage. When she looked round from the range he was standing in the doorway. He had a bundle in his arms.

'What's that?' she said, and he didn't make any kind of reply, only came on into the kitchen.

*

All the way down through the woods he had hurried, anxious to relinquish the effort of understanding, on his own, what still didn't make sense enough. Surely the stillness in what he carried was the stillness of the dead? Again and again he laid it down to see, and even reached out to close the eyes that stared at him, for how in that dank place after so long could there still be life?

In the kitchen the smell of bacon boiling crept through his confusion, as reality settles the fragments of a dream. The clock ticked brightly on the dresser, steam rattled a saucepan lid.

'Mother of God!' Bridget cried. 'Oh, Mother of God!'

*

The child's lips were stained with blackberry juice. There was a sick look about her, her cheeks fallen in, dark hollows beneath her eyes, her hair as ragged as a tinker's. In Henry's arms she was covered with an old coat of her mother's. Filthy it was.

Henry spoke at last. He said he'd gone for the stones to Paddy

Lindon's cottage. As often it was, his face was empty of expression even while he spoke. 'More happens in a ham,' Bridget's father had once said about Henry's face.

'Sweet Mother!' Bridget whispered, crossing herself. 'Sweet Lady of Mercy!'

Henry slowly made his way to a chair. The child was starved, so weak you'd say she couldn't live: unspoken, these comments tumbled about in Bridget's thoughts, as earlier they had in Henry's, bringing with them the same confusion. How could she have come in from the sea? How could she be here at all? Bridget sat down, to steady the weakness in her knees. She tried to count the days, but they kept slipping about. Ages it felt like since the night on the strand, ages before the Gaults had gone.

'There's food she took from the house,' Henry said. 'Sugar sandwiches she maybe lived on. And thank God for it, there's water in that place.'

'She was never in the woods, Henry?'

Every morning Bridget carried her rosary from the gate-lodge to the kitchen and placed it on the shelf above the range. She pushed herself up from the table to find it now, gathering it between her fingers, not telling the beads but finding solace in their touch.

'She ran off,' Henry said.

'Oh, child, child . . .'

'She's frightened by what she done.'

'Why d'you do a thing like that, Lucy?'

Her own voice sounded foolish, Bridget thought, and hearing it she experienced the guilt of foolishness. Wasn't she to blame for not mentioning the bathing? Wasn't the child forever playing her games in the glen and above it in the woods – why wouldn't she have reminded them of that? Why wouldn't she have said it was all fancy, what the fishermen believed?

'What possessed you, Lucy?'

One of her ankles was in a bad way, Henry said. When they came into the yard she'd wanted to be on her feet but he hadn't let her down. You wouldn't know when it was the ankle got like it

41

was. It was maybe smashed up, you couldn't tell. He said he'd go over for Dr Carney.

'Will I carry her above first?'

He wouldn't say more, Bridget said to herself, until the bedraggled child was upstairs. Nothing would be passed on before that and then he'd say how he happened on her, what she'd said to him if she'd said anything at all. The child was so silent now she might never open her mouth again.

'Wait till I fill a couple of jars for the bed.'

Bridget returned her rosary to the mantel-shelf and pulled the kettle that had boiled back on to the heat of the range. The water steamed and spluttered almost at once. The Captain, the mistress, Henry going up and down the strand, poking at the shingle: the Devil's fools, as she'd been herself, making everything worse. In a glare of light, Bridget saw them now, absurdly there.

'Are you hungry, Lucy? Are you starved?'

Lucy shook her head. Henry had sat down too, his brown hat cocked forward a bit, as if it had been knocked on the way through the woods and he hadn't remembered to set it right when he put his burden down on the chair.

'The dear help her,' Bridget whispered, and felt tears warm on her cheeks before she knew she was crying, before she knew that foolishness was neither here nor there. 'Thanks be to God,' she whispered, her arms suddenly around Lucy's thin shoulders. 'Thanks be to God.'

'You're all right now, Lucy,' Henry said.

Bridget filled two hot-water jars. There was a kind of exhaustion in the child's eyes. An agony it seemed like, dully there.

'Are you sick, Lucy? Is there pain in your leg?'

The eyes registered for an instant what might have been a denial, but still there was no response, nothing said, no movement. Henry got to his feet, to take the unresisting body into his arms again. Upstairs, while Bridget held the two lamps she'd lit, he laid it down on the bed from which the sheets and blankets had been taken away a week ago.

'Wait there till you'll see Dr Carney himself,' Bridget instructed. 'Get him back here quickly. Take the trap, don't walk. I'll manage now.'

She rummaged through the bedclothes she had folded away in the landing hot-press and found a nightdress.

'What we'll have is a bath,' she said when she had made the bed as best she could without disturbing the limp form that lay there. But the bath would have to wait until the doctor had been, and she ran hot water into a basin in the bathroom and carried it back. She could hear a clattering outside and guessed that Henry had put a ladder up and was removing the window boards from Lucy's bedroom before he went for Dr Carney. You'd think he'd know better than to waste time over that. Her crossness came as a relief.

'Would I boil you an egg when we have you washed? Egg in a cup, Lucy?'

Again Lucy shook her head. The ankle could have a bone broken the way it looked, black more than blue, swollen up like a big ball. The whole leg had gone useless, trailing like something dead.

'Wait till I take your temperature,' Bridget said. There was a thermometer somewhere, but she couldn't think where and wondered if, anyway, it had gone from the house. They'd have to leave it to Dr Carney. 'We'll get you nice and clean for him.'

The child was dirty all over, her feet, her hands, her hair tangled, scratches on her arms and face. Her ribs stood out, the flesh of her stomach loose beneath them. A boiled egg mashed up with toast in a cup was what she always loved. 'Maybe the appetite'll come back when Dr Carney's been.'

The water in the basin went grey at once. Bridget poured it away in the bathroom and filled the basin again. What had he meant, sugar sandwiches? That cottage had fallen down. Had the child been in it ever since? Was it some childish thing, wanting to stay there for ever because she didn't want to go away? Was it only that that had caused this terrible commotion, and grief like you wouldn't witness in a lifetime? She should have told him to send a wire to the address they'd left. Then again he'd have to call in at the

43

gate-lodge for the bit of paper and she hoped he wouldn't think of it himself, because of the delay.

'Mama and Papa have gone away,' Bridget said. 'But they'll come back now.'

She put one jar halfway down to warm the cold sheets, the other at the bottom. She undid the window catch and pulled the top window down a little. Henry had wrenched off several of the boards, but some remained.

'Dr Carney won't be long,' she said, not knowing what else to say.

*

'Sure, it's all there.' In the hall Henry gestured with his head, vaguely indicating the bedroom he had taken the window boards from. 'There's nothing else only what she'll tell you.'

'Nothing else? And she after walking back from the dead!'

She couldn't have walked an inch, Henry said. She'd have walked too much as it was, getting to where he found her. He wouldn't have found her at all if he hadn't been thinking to fix the place where the sheep were getting in again.

'What's that about sugar sandwiches?'

There were pats of butter in a bit of newspaper, and grains of sugar left. There were apples she'd have taken off the trees, not ripe yet but she'd eaten them, because the cores were thrown down. She'd managed rightly, Henry said.

'Is the child away in the head, Henry?'

'Arrah, not at all.'

'Did she know what she was doing when she went off?'

'She did of course.'

'We need get word to Mr Sullivan. And word sent to England.'

'I was thinking that.'

The doctor diagnosed a broken bone that would have to be investigated further, and damage to the surrounding ligaments, internal bleeding, fever, a high temperature, lack of nourishment. He advocated beef-tea or hot milk, no more than a slice of thin toast to begin with. Henry returned with him to Kilauran, to send the necessary telegram. In the kitchen Bridget toasted a single slice of bread at the bars of the range.

They'd have to sleep in the house tonight. Henry reached that conclusion on the way back to Lahardane; it occurred to Bridget while she carried the tray upstairs. They couldn't leave the child on her own, not the way things were, never mind another attempt to set the place on fire. Until whatever arrangements could be made, until the Captain and Mrs Gault returned, they'd have to be there.

'What did you say in the wire?' Bridget enquired when Henry returned.

Lucy found alive in the woods, the message had gone to England.

4

They stayed in Basel, calculating there the kind of life Heloise's legacy would support. There was some anxiety at first in case she had been more optimistic than the facts allowed when she'd anticipated there would be money enough; in fact there was. The Captain's only assets, being the house and land they had left behind, would remain untouched unless some unforeseen circumstance dictated otherwise. Employment in a shipping office or something similar would not be easy to find abroad; fortunately it would not be necessary.

It was while discussing all this that the Captain realized they now saw the future differently, that although they shared so much in what had befallen them they were less at one than they'd seemed to be when he had called it that. In the brief time that had elapsed since their departure he had begun to sense that he'd been wrong to imagine he would not ever wish to return to the house they had abandoned. But he sensed as well that Heloise's contrary feelings had strengthened with every mile they had covered. Exile was what she longed for, where all her faith was, and her hope. He did not intend to cajole her out of that; looking after her was more his task. She was still a shadow of the woman she had not long ago been.

They moved on when the business they had chosen to do in Basel was complete. They went south, to Lugano, and stayed for a few days by its peaceful lake. On a cloudless autumn afternoon they crossed the border to Italy and then, again, went slowly on.

'A ruin?' Aloysius Sullivan said. 'A *ruin?*'

Bridget explained. She mentioned what was taken away in the fish-baskets, and the unripe apples. Mr Sullivan briefly closed his eyes.

'She was cross, the way things were. She had it in mind to run off so's they'd maybe take notice of her.' And Bridget told what she had further conjectured, and the few facts she had learnt – about the spiky branches that were a hindrance in the gloom of the woods, the added burden of the coat brought for warmth when night would come, the fallen branches stumbled over. 'She had blood oozing out from the scratches on her face. She could taste it and it frightened her. Poor scrap, she dragged herself on with everything she was carrying until by chance she came to Paddy Lindon's place for shelter. In the daylight again she tried to come back to the house here but the way the foot had swollen up she couldn't get more than a few steps. She was afraid for it when she went out after the berries. She was afraid again when the food ran down. Someone'd come was what she always thought. When no one did, what she thought was she'd die.'

Aloysius Sullivan wasn't impressed. 'The garment found on the strand was placed there in order to mislead? An act of guile, of calculated deception, we have to say?'

'Ah no, Mr Sullivan, no.'

'What then? Some pleasantry?'

Bridget had not been told – and never was – about the part played by the dog, and suggested that what had been found in the shingle had been left behind by mistake.

'What it is, sir, we were misled when it never entered our heads she'd run off. Not mine nor Henry's, nor the master's nor the mistress's, sir.'

'I didn't imagine it would have,' the solicitor drily responded.

They were in the drawing-room, the furniture still covered. Two lamps were burning. In the house the window boards were still mostly in place.

'It was the feeling there was with us, sir – that a thing happened the way it looked like it did, the way what was found –'

'I understand, Bridget, I understand.'

'What sense would it make to us, sir, that she'd set off for Dungarvan and night coming down, that she'd gone up through the woods to get on to the road and it miles off? It wouldn't have made sense, sir, any more than it does to herself now.'

'I am thankful to say, Bridget, I am not familiar with the sense or otherwise of the very young, although I grant you that in my daily work I frequently encounter limitations of sense in the mature. Where is the child now?'

'In the yard. With Henry.'

'And her condition?'

'Still quiet, sir.' Bridget lifted a sheet from one of the armchairs. 'Sit down, sir.'

Aloysius Sullivan was a big man, and welcomed the offer. The calves of his legs were aching, even though he had driven to Lahardane in his car. Some instinct told him that the aching was caused by the weight of responsibility that these new circumstances unfairly placed upon him. Ever since he had received Everard Gault's few lines from France he had been aware of nervousness of one kind or another in his body, manifesting itself in the form of a rash beneath his collar, and now making its presence felt as an ache in his calves. When, a week ago, he had learnt that the assumptions made as to the child's fate were incorrect, he had experienced the onset of a neuralgic affliction that had been quiet for years.

'My mother used to say, Bridget, you could find the Devil in a child.'

'Ah no, sir, no. She was upset in herself by what was happening. Like all of us was, sir. There was never ease in this house after the men came to murder us in our beds. If there's blame to be given out, sir, we can look for it there.'

The solicitor sighed. He understood, he said, but all the same he had to remember what Everard Gault had himself passed on: how he and his wife had gone down to the strand time and time again, how they had suffered the torments of hell by day and by night, and now, apparently, were travelling purposelessly. While all the time their wayward child had been feeding herself on sugar sandwiches.

'Sit down yourself, Bridget,' he said.

But Bridget did not sit down. She had never sat down in this room and even allowing for what had happened she could not do so now. It had put the heart across her, she said, when Henry walked in with the child in his arms. It was a terrible thing that had happened, a terrible thing the child had done: she wouldn't deny it for a minute. She'd never seen the like of the poor creature when Henry brought her in, death's door you'd have said.

'Would we send another wire, sir, in case that one would have gone astray?'

'It didn't go astray, Bridget.'

Bridget heard about the letter that had come from France. It was not her place to frown but she failed to resist the impulse; and as if he recognized that she needed a moment to herself, Mr Sullivan paused. When he continued he explained that in the communication he had received there was a reference to the furniture and belongings that were still at Lahardane. His assumption had been that removal vans would eventually arrive for them. In the letter it was stated that what had been left behind was to remain where it was.

'Your wire was received, Bridget, at the address you sent it to. Captain Gault's wire of cancellation was received there. I've naturally been in touch. Sooner or later, of course, we'll have news of Captain and Mrs Gault's settled whereabouts. It is unfortunate that we are without it at the moment.'

Lending emphasis to the inconvenience of this predicament, Mr Sullivan's oiled head moved slowly from side to side, his slate-coloured eyes morose. His sigh, coming next, was a long intake of breath, held for a moment and then exhaled.

'They said nothing to you before they left, I suppose, about the possibility of a change of heart? About what they intended?'

Anxiety flickered through Bridget's features with even less consideration for her wishes than the frown of a moment ago. Had something been mentioned? Had she not listened properly in the upset that was all around them? She thought for a moment longer, then shook her head.

'They only left the address, sir.'

Mr Sullivan's two plump hands lay lightly on the blue pin-striping that stretched over his knees. 'Would there be papers here we could look through, Bridget? In case there's anything that's a help to us?'

Bridget lifted off further dust sheets. But in the writing-desk drawers, and in the drawers of the sideboard in the dining-room, there was nothing that was relevant to the difficulty that confronted them. Nor was there anything in the dressing-table drawers when they carried the lamps upstairs.

'There's nothing only receipts here,' Bridget reported when she searched the shelves of a corner cupboard on the first-floor landing while Mr Sullivan held the lamp. Elsewhere, among other correspondence, there was a single picture postcard from the Captain's brother, with a regimental address in India and dated nearly three years ago. More recently, a note of querulous recrimination was struck in the few letters that were from Heloise Gault's aunt in Wiltshire.

'The arrangements the Captain left behind as regards the house and yourselves haven't been disturbed,' Mr Sullivan said. 'What has happened makes no difference to that.'

Expenses in the future had been provided for, emergencies anticipated. The Gaults had been meticulous, even if their departure had been more ragged than it might have been. His hope, the solicitor confessed, had been the house – some hint somewhere in it of the change that had later been effected in their plans.

'I've asked round about,' he said when they returned to the

drawing-room. 'I've asked everyone I could think of. I thought word might have reached the Mount Bellew cousins but it seems they, too, left Ireland a while back. Were they much in touch, do you know?'

Bridget didn't. Once they'd been, she remembered, but she hadn't heard them mentioned since they'd gone to England. No letters from them were discovered when the downstairs drawers were searched again; but the Mount Bellew cousins were there in a photograph album, picnicking on the grass at Lahardane ten years ago.

'If I'm not wrong about it, one of those boys went down at Passchendaele,' the solicitor recalled. 'The same regiment as the Captain's.'

'I didn't ever hear that.'

'You're worried, Bridget. It's a shock, what I've brought you. But contact will be made, there's no doubt about that. We have the regiment in India in case the Captain gets in touch with his brother and if it's no longer in the same place any communication from me would be forwarded. The army takes a pride in that type of thing.'

'It's only the child, sir.'

'Dr Carney's account will be sent to me, Bridget. We've spoken about that.' Mr Sullivan paused. 'Would it be too much to ask you to continue for a while with things as they are now? For the time being, Bridget?'

'With things as they are, sir?'

'Only for the time being.'

'Is it Henry and myself staying on in the rooms above? You're saying that, sir?'

'I'm saying that as matters stand, now that she's back here, it might be better to let the child stop in the house. If you wouldn't mind, on balance I'd say it would be better than taking her up to the gate-lodge.'

With no prediction of how long the time being he had spoken of would last, Mr Sullivan conjectured that moving out of the house and passing so often its boarded windows and locked doors would be more upsetting for the child who'd caused all the trouble than remaining in her familiar surroundings. He was aware of his own presumption that the men who had once come in the night would have by now lost interest in what they had intended. He drew attention to this in case he was imposing a degree of disquiet without wishing to.

'They'll leave us in peace is what Henry says, sir, on account of they've driven the master and mistress out. There's enough in that, Henry says.'

Mr Sullivan agreed, but did not comment. Henry had heard something, he deduced; and if he hadn't, his instinct could be trusted. Despite the wounding of the youth, the trail of events since the night of the incident might indeed be regarded as vengeance enough.

'We have the gate-lodge locked up at the minute, sir. We'll leave it till they come back so.'

'And what does our friend make of that particular eventuality?'

'Which friend's that, Mr Sullivan?'

'I mean the child. How does she view the return of her father and her mother? And will she go quietly with them this time?'

'Mightn't they decide to stop on though, once they're back? The way she was so upset in herself, mightn't they?'

'It would be my hope too, Bridget.'

'Isn't the fighting done with by what you'd hear?'

'We can have hope in that direction also. At least we can have hope.' Mr Sullivan stood up. 'I should see the child.'

'You'll notice she's docile, sir.'

Mr Sullivan sighed, keeping to himself the observation that in the circumstances docility was not out of place.

'There's a thing you mightn't know, sir. The way the bone came together while she lay there it will leave her with the limp she has.'

'I do know, Bridget. Dr Carney came in to break that to me.'

He rose as he spoke, and made his way through the darkened house to the yard. The child they'd spoken of was sitting on the

52

step of an outhouse that over the years had become Henry's own. Across the yard, beneath the pear tree on the wall, two young sheepdogs were stretched out in the sun. They raised their heads when the solicitor appeared, their hackles stiffening. One growled, but neither moved. They settled down again, with their noses flat on the cobbles.

Through the open doorway of Henry's workshed Mr Sullivan could see a bench with vices, beneath rows of carpenter's tools – hammers, chisels, planes, mallet, spokeshave, pliers, spirit-levels, screwdrivers, wrenches. Two tea-chests were crammed with short pieces of timber of different widths and lengths. Saws and coils of wire, a much-used ball of string, and a sickle, hung on hooks.

Seated on the step beside the child, Henry was painting a wooden aeroplane white. About a foot in length, with a double set of wings but no propeller yet, it was balanced on a jampot. Matchsticks joined the wings, their positioning and angles copied from a torn-out newspaper photograph that was on the step also.

'Lucy,' Mr Sullivan said.

She did not respond. Henry did not say anything either. The paintbrush – too big and too unwieldy for the task – continued to cover the rough wood with what seemed to the solicitor to be whitewash.

'Well now, Lucy,' he said.

'That's a great day, Mr Sullivan,' Henry remarked when there was still no reply.

'It is, Henry. It is. Now, Lucy, I want to ask you a question or two.'

Had she ever heard her parents speak of travels they would like to go on? Had she heard them talking about cities they would like to visit? Was there a particular country they spoke of?

In mute denial, the child shook her head, acknowledging each question with a motion a little more vehement than the last, her fair hair thrown about. The features Mr Sullivan looked down on were almost her mother's, the eyes, the nose, the firm outline of the lips. One day there would be beauty there too; and he wondered if that, at last, would be a compensation for time as it was passing now.

'You'll tell Bridget or Henry if anything comes back to you, Lucy? You'll do that for me?'

There was a plea in his voice that he knew was not related to the request he made but begged the child to smile as he remembered her smiling in the past. 'Oh, Lucy, Lucy,' he murmured on his way back to the drawing-room.

Tea was laid out for him, the lamps still burning. He drank two cups and spread honey on a scone. His reflections were painful. Now that he was in the house, the calamity that had brought him here seemed even more extraordinary in the manner of its occurrence than when he had learnt that the child was alive. What fluke had caused Everard Gault not to walk by a scrap of clothing hardly visible on the strand? What perversity had been at play when no one had thought of a friendly upstairs maid with whom a distraught child might find a haven?

No answers came. Standing up, Aloysius Sullivan wiped a smear of butter from his lips with the napkin that had been brought to him with his tea. He shook the crumbs from his knees and straightened his waistcoat. In the hall he called for Bridget and when she came they walked together to his car.

'You'll bring them back, sir?'

The engine was cranked, and spluttered into life. Yes, he would bring them back, Mr Sullivan promised with as much assurance as he could muster. He would leave no stone unturned. It would be all right.

Bridget watched the car disappear on the avenue, the smoke of its exhaust lingering a little longer. She prayed that the solicitor would be successful, and in the kitchen she did so again, pleading only for that favour, since nothing else mattered.

*

'The paint'll be dry tomorrow,' Henry said. 'We'll leave it out, will we?'

54

'He doesn't like me.'

'Arrah, of course he does. Sure, everyone likes you, why wouldn't they?'

He propped the aeroplane up on the step, using bits of wood left over from its construction. He said not to touch the paint until the morning.

'Of course he likes you,' he said again.

*

Aloysius Sullivan made enquiries all over again in Enniseala and Kilauran. He wrote to the known friends of Captain Gault, and to those English friends of his wife with whom she appeared to be in touch. He established the whereabouts, in England, of the Mount Bellew Gaults, and of distant Gault relatives in County Roscommon. No suggestion as to a place of exile rewarded his efforts – only surprise and concern that his enquiries should be necessary. The letter he had himself received from Everard Gault had been sent from the French town of Belfort, its brief contents beneath the address of the Hôtel du Parc, boulevard Louis XI. From the hotel's proprietor Aloysius Sullivan received, after a delay, information to the effect that the guests about whom the enquiry was made had stayed for a single night in *Chambre Trois*. Their destination after Belfort was not known.

The manager of Heloise Gault's bank, in Warminster, Wiltshire, was at first reluctant to release details of certain instructions he had received, but in the end disclosed that Mrs Gault had written to him from Switzerland to close her account. The balance of its funds had been forwarded to a bank in Basel, and he had reason to believe that her Rio Verde Railway holdings had been disposed of there. This particular trail ending with that, Mr Sullivan wrote to a firm of investigators, Messrs Timms and Wheldon of High Holborn, London.

It may be that my clients have taken up residence in that city, or that some indication of their present whereabouts may be discovered there.

Please forward to me an estimated total of your fees should I agree to retain your services in this regard.

Eventually, a Mr Blenkin of Timms and Wheldon was dispatched to Switzerland. He remained for four days in Basel, establishing nothing of greater value than confirmation of the shares' sale. No new investments had immediately been made; his quarries' stay in the city had been short, at a small hotel in Schützengraben; their present whereabouts were unknown. Pursuing an idea of his own, Mr Blenkin set off for Germany and spent a fruitless week in Hanover and other cities, after which he made enquiries in Austria, Luxembourg and Provence. Then, in response to his telegraphing for further instructions, and following consultation between Messrs Timms and Wheldon and Mr Sullivan, Mr Blenkin was recalled to High Holborn.

6

In the town of Montemarmoreo, in via Cittadella, they had taken rooms above the premises of a shoemaker. 'What shall we do today?' the Captain would ask, always knowing what the response would be. Well, walk a little, Heloise would suggest, and they would walk in the hills where sour black cherries grew near marble quarries now exhausted. In fits and starts the conversation would drift about – never to Lahardane or to Ireland, but back to Heloise's childhood, to memories of her father, and of her mother before she became a widow, to places and people of that safe time. The Captain encouraged with patient questions and patient listening; Heloise was talkative, for such recollections dispelled the nag of melancholy. Her beauty and Everard Gault's straight back, his soldier's stride, picked them out in Montemarmoreo, a couple who were mysterious at first and then not so at all.

Another child, so long denied them, might one day be born in Italy: for his wife's sake that was Captain Gault's hope; for his sake, it was hers. But they were wary of expectation, drew back from it as they did from what must not be spoken of. Expert now at altering sentences already begun, or allowing them to wither or smiling them away, they gave themselves to the unfamiliarity of the place they had arrived in as invalids of distress, to its rocky hills and narrow streets, to a language they learnt as children do, to the simplicities of where they dwelt. In the ways they had devised they used the hours up, of one day and of another and another, until the moment came to open the first bottle of Amarone. They were a nuisance to no one in Montemarmoreo.

7

I respond regretfully, Aloysius Sullivan was informed from the
southernmost part of Bengal, *being greatly affected by what you
report. Everard and I have corresponded but infrequently over the years. I
last visited Lahardane a year or so after the birth of his daughter, when
my brother had written to inform me of that fact. Ireland, in my own
poor view, has always been the distressful country of its renown. That
my brother and others have been obliged to leave it, as once the Wild
Geese did, is the saddest news I have heard for many a long day. Should
I hear from Everard, I will most certainly inform him of what has come
about. But I believe it more likely that you, or those remaining at
Lahardane, will hear sooner than I.*

The firm of Goodbody and Tallis, solicitors of Warminster,
Wiltshire, requested Mr Sullivan to clarify his letter of the four-
teenth inst. addressed to their client, now an invalid, the aunt of
the aforesaid Heloise Gault referred to. Replying, Mr Sullivan
revealed the circumstances in which two servants and a child found
themselves, and explained how these circumstances had come
about. The reply he received – from a Miss Chambré, companion
to the lady who was an invalid – expressed horror, and distaste for
what had occurred. There had been no recent communication from
Heloise Gault, Miss Chambré stated, nor could any of what was
presently communicated be retailed to her employer, whose delicate heart might easily not sustain the strain of learning of such
appalling thoughtlessness in a child.

*Since my employer has never been offered the courtesy of acquaintanceship
with this child, Miss Chambré continued, and has herself been long
neglected by her niece – for many years receiving no more than a card at*

Christmas – I believe the withholding of this most shocking news from an invalid is doubly justified. I would suggest the child be placed in a home of correction until such time as the parents return from their travels. Not that they themselves, from what you have imparted, are without blame in this unfortunate matter.

★

The remaining boards had been taken down from the windows at Lahardane in order to dispel the gloom they induced and to bring air into the house again. Repeatedly, Mr Sullivan had tea in the drawing-room, repeatingly bringing with him no news. But only when that autumn had passed, and most of the winter that followed, while the nervous pause in Ireland's troubles was constantly threatened, did he suggest that the future at Lahardane must be considered.

'Respecting the law,' he stated suddenly one afternoon, 'I have no position in what should next be done, Bridget. My part was to end when you closed the house. "The acreage and the cattle should keep things going," Captain Gault reiterated when last he came in to see me a day or two before their departure. Even in his great distress he did not forget that Henry and yourself should be decently provided for. But the sum he lodged with me – to cover the final expenses as regards the house – I have been obliged, with the change of circumstances, to make use of otherwise and have in fact exhausted it. So respecting the law, Bridget, that is the end of it. It is as your employers' friend – and yours, I trust – that I may in future be of assistance. I am arranging, from my own resources, to meet the expenses of the child's upkeep. On his return there is no doubt that Captain Gault will settle the debt.'

'You're good to think of us, sir.'

'You manage, Bridget?'

'Ah, we do, we do.'

Mr Sullivan shook Bridget's hand, something he had never done before and, in fact, never did again. He wouldn't desert them, he promised. He would continue to visit the house until a day of great rejoicing made that no longer necessary. He was as certain as ever he had been, he vigorously reiterated, that such a day would come.

In all this, Mr Sullivan did not touch upon his own frustrations: since he spoke no foreign languages, his enquiries in likely countries had had to be channelled through official sources in Dublin, but the confused political hiatus before, and following, an unsatisfactory Treaty made communication far from easy. A transference of power, of order and responsibility, took place at its own slow progression; chaos prevailed while it did so. Receiving no reply to his letters, Mr Sullivan had twice forwarded copies to offices that subsequently appeared to be unstaffed. And when, much later, he supposed it was understandable that a small local crisis should fail to be of import in the greater crisis of a country in upheaval, he blamed himself as much as the circumstances of which he was a victim; for the urgency he sought to convey in what he had written had clearly not registered. Nor did he trust the assurances he eventually received, but instead read into them an empty promise that was designed to soothe. Some garbled version of his pleas might one day be disseminated, stale by then and carelessly strung together, the poignancy of a family's agony reduced to nothing much. He imagined such a document filed away, in irritation or bewilderment, by foreign officials who had better things to do.

He would not cease to nag, but his helplessness, he knew, would continue to infect his solicitor's authority. His shame in this respect drew him closer to what had happened, as guilt had drawn Bridget and Henry closer when they had suspected Lucy of bathing but hadn't said.

'We must hope,' he urged again that afternoon, although he did not now believe in hope. He wished Bridget good-bye and walked to his car beneath a rain-filled sky.

*

In the kitchen, where the range was always lit first thing, the ceiling and walls were white, the woodwork green. A heavy deal table, so scrubbed that ridges stood up in the grain, had drawers with brass handles. Between the windows there was a green dresser crowded with plates and saucers and cups. Cupboards were let into the wall on either side of the doorway.

At one end of the table Lucy watched the yolk spreading out of Henry's fried egg. She liked the yellow herself but not the white, unless it was mashed up. She watched Henry putting salt on the yolk, which he smeared into his fried bread.

'Henry gets lonely,' Bridget said. 'You go with Henry, dotey.'

Every morning when it was fine Bridget said Henry would be lonely, going by himself with the creamery churns. Lucy knew he wouldn't be. She knew it was only a pretence to get her to go with him, since there wasn't much for her to do when there were holidays from school. 'Ah, Lucy! Come in, come in,' Mr Aylward had exclaimed the morning she walked into school again, and she'd thought he would put his arms around her, but Mr Aylward didn't do things like that. 'They'll get used to it,' he promised her when the handful of other children didn't want to play with her, when they eyed her and stared at her, or glanced and nudged one another, not giggling because what she had done was too bad for giggling. The nameless dog who had once run away also was her companion on the strand.

'Yes,' she said, watching Henry soaking up the last of the egg yolk with his bread. 'Yes. All right,' she said.

It was April now, early in the month. The morning was bright, clouds of fluff blowing in the sky – chasing the sun, Henry said. 'No rain today,' he said. 'Not a chance of it.' Heaven was up there, her mama used to say, beyond the clouds, beyond the blue. You made up heaven for yourself, her mama said, you made up what you wanted it to be.

The big wooden wheels of the cart rattled on the avenue, the horse ambling, the reins slack in Henry's hands. When the branches met above their heads both sun and sky disappeared. Light was filtered through the chestnut leaves and then the gate-lodge came into view. Thrown open wide, immovable by now because they'd remained like that for so long, the avenue's gates were almost lost in undergrowth. On the dusty clay road that twisted off to the right it was warmer in the sunshine.

Once she used to talk on this journey, asking Henry to tell her about Paddy Lindon, how he would appear in Kilauran once a year at the time of Corpus Christi, a wild figure with mushrooms in a red handkerchief. The priest before Father Morrissey had preached a warning from the pulpit, laying down the law: that for the sake of tranquillity in Kilauran no one should buy Paddy Lindon's mushrooms; because if Paddy Lindon sold them he got drunk, and turned wilder. 'Crowing like a fowl,' Henry said, 'up and down the pier.'

Henry had been a Kilauran boy, one of seven in a fishing family, but after he married Bridget he didn't fish again. 'I never swam in the sea,' he had often told Lucy on the way to the creamery, taking pride in that for reasons of his own. And Lucy, in the past, had told him the stories she'd been read by her mother, from the Grimms' book; or Kitty Teresa's stories.

'Where'd we be without the drop of milk?' Henry said, making conversation when they went to the creamery together for the first time since what had happened. 'Doesn't it keep us going?'

It was the best he could do. The mood there was between them wasn't right for the usual remembrances of his boyhood – the time the thatch was lifted from the Kilauran cottages in a November storm, the summer there was the horse-racing on the strand, the evocation of Paddy Lindon when he'd sold his mushrooms.

'Sure, you meant no harm, girl,' he tried when the quiet between them remained unbroken. 'Sure, don't we all know that?'

'I did mean harm.'

Lucy took the reins because they were handed to her, the rope rough on her palms and her fingers, different from the reins of the trap.

'Will they ever come back, Henry?'

'Ah, they will of course, why wouldn't they?'

The silence began again. It continued when the horse and cart turned out on to the main road, and all the way to the creamery yard, where Henry backed the cart up to the delivery platform. He lifted off the churns, smoking a cigarette while he talked to the foreman, then clambered on to the cart again. He took the reins himself, since it was sometimes difficult to steer a way through the other carts. At the gate he picked up two empty churns.

'They'll never come back,' Lucy said.

'The minute they know you're here they will. I could promise you that.'

'How'll they know, Henry?'

'A letter'll come from them and Bridget'll write back. Or Mr Sullivan will reach them. There's not a man as clever in the whole extent of County Cork as Aloysius Sullivan. Many's the time I heard that said, many's the time. Would we call in for a lemonade?'

They had to call in anyway at Mrs McBride's roadside shop for the groceries that were written in a list on Bridget's scrap of paper. But Henry made the lemonade seem like an invitation that had just occurred to him.

'All right,' she said.

Mrs McBride would try not to stare at her. Everyone tried not to. Mr Aylward had stared at first. Just once but she saw him. They stared at her for what she'd done; they stared at her limp. In the play-yard Edie Hosford still didn't want to come near to her.

'Have you a biscuit for the missy?' Henry said in the shop and Mrs McBride's big face suddenly jutted out at her. Like the wedge Henry split the logs with it was, heavy and pointed. 'A Kerry Cream is it?' Mrs McBride said, her teeth jutting out too. 'A Kerry Cream fit the bill, Lucy?'

She said it would, although she didn't understand fit the bill. The letter could be there when they went back. Bridget could be out waiting for them, waving it at them, and when they got nearer she'd tell them, and she'd be laughing and excited. She'd be red in the face, and crying as well as laughing.

'Isn't that grand weather, Henry?' Mrs McBride said, pouring Henry's stout before she did anything else. 'When all's said and done isn't it great for April?'

'It is, right enough.'

'Thanks be to God.'

Bridget would say she'd need help to get their room ready for them. They'd put flowers in it and open the windows. They'd put hot-water jars in the bed. 'We'll get the trap out,' Henry would say and he'd clean it down, ready for them too. They'd be cross with her and it wouldn't matter. All the time they were cross with her it wouldn't matter.

'Oh, I remember Kerry Creams is the favourite,' Mrs McBride said. She came round to the front of the counter, where the glass-topped biscuit tins were arranged along the counter's edge. She swung up the glass cover of the Kerry Creams and Lucy took one.

The first time she went with Henry to the creamery he lifted her up on to the counter and she sat there with her lemonade, the first time she'd seen the stout foaming when it was poured. Six she was then.

'Give me ten,' Henry said, and Mrs McBride said she had only fives and Henry said two fives then. Woodbines he always smoked. The only other cigarette he'd ever tried was a Kerry Blue. He told Lucy that once. He showed her the Kerry Blue packet, with the dog on it. Sweet Afton her papa smoked.

'How's herself, Henry?'

'Arrah, not bad.'

'Have you the list handy?'

He found Bridget's grocery list and handed it across the counter and Mrs McBride collected the items. Mrs McBride didn't like her any more even though she'd given her the biscuit. Mrs McBride was the same as everyone else, except Henry and Bridget.

'I've no strawberry jam, Henry. Only raspberry in a pound pot.'

'Will raspberry do, Lucy? Would we say it would?'

She nodded, bent over her glass, not wanting to speak because Mrs McBride was there. Mr Sullivan still didn't like her either.

'Keiller's is a good jam,' Mrs McBride said.

'None better,' Henry agreed, although Lucy had never seen

him putting jam on his bread. He smeared on lots of butter and sometimes he sprinkled salt on it. He often said he didn't have a sweet tooth.

'The greengage is good,' Mrs McBride said, and then she talked about the meat sandwiches she made for the army lads when they called in, a bunch of them going by at night. They came out from the Camp in Enniseala to go dancing at Old Fort Crossroads. They got hungry on the way, she said. 'Mike makes the sandwiches too big,' she said, referring to her husband. 'Thick as two doorsteps he has them. Sure, no young soldier could get his teeth at them.'

Not listening any more, Lucy read the advertisements: for Ryan's Towel Soap, and corned beef and whiskey and Guinness's stout. She'd asked her papa what Guinness was when they saw it written up and he said it was the stuff Henry drank. There was a bottle of whiskey they'd left behind, only a little gone from it. Power's it was.

'Thank you,' she said when they were on the cart again, when Henry had lit another cigarette. The grey paper bags that held the groceries were at their feet. Far ahead of them two other carts were bringing back their empty churns too.

'Get on there,' Henry urged the horse, shaking the reins. He pushed his hat back a bit in order to catch the sun on his forehead. Already the first of his summer freckles had come.

8

She watched the butterfly disappear and then come back, the magician's wizened fingers splayed in triumph, the butterfly's wings slowly folding away their bright pink and gold. The magician's expression never changed. There was always his pursed smile, his stare, his parchment cheeks. Only his arms ever moved.

On the stairs there were Everard's footsteps and then his key in the lock. He brought the shopping in. He'd been to the railway station as well, he said.

'How good you are to me!' Heloise murmured. For months, while she had rested, he'd read to her from books in English he'd found in a bookseller's two streets away. He had cooked her meals and washed her nightdresses, had brushed her hair and brought her make-up to her. He had listened again while she remembered moments from her childhood. From the Saturday markets he brought back cups and saucers and plates, and china ornaments that would make their rooms more their own, storing away what had been supplied.

She watched while he wound up the clockwork of the magician. He had bought it to divert her while she rested, until early one morning her baby was lost and the doctor who'd been sent for struggled to find words when he learnt about miscarriages in the past. Commiserating but firm, he instructed that what had been attempted should not be again.

'If it is what you would like,' she said when the toy was still. 'Yes, of course it would be nice.'

Fearing that her present lassitude would cling to her, the Captain had suggested that they should visit the great Italian cities. 'Just once in a while,' he had persuaded, 'to be somewhere else for a week or so.' He had read to her from the guide-book he'd bought, drawn her attention to photographs of buildings and sculpture, of frescoes and mosaics.

'Of course,' Heloise answered his further coaxing now. 'Somewhere different would be nice.'

Yet Montemarmoreo was all the difference that mattered: she might have said that too. Their small *appartamento* above the shoemaker's shop, their own possessions increasing, the walks that would begin again now: there was a kind of peace. That *cucchiaio* meant spoon, that *seggiola* was chair and *finestra* window, that every morning across the street the porter at the Credito Italiano unlocked the doors for the waiting clerks to pass into the bank, that the woman at the Fiori e Frutta had begun to say more than a few words to her, that she woke to the chiming of the bells at the church of Santa Cecilia, the saint whose courage in her tribulations had for centuries given heart to this town: all that was peace, as much as there could be.

The pale hands of the magician were raised again, the butterfly appeared, was banished and then returned. The details copied from the timetables at the railway station – convenient trains, a choice of cities – were perused.

'Shall we open the wine,' Heloise suggested then, 'a little early tonight?'

9

The visits of Mr Sullivan continued, as he had promised they would. And Canon Crosbie came out from Enniseala, to satisfy himself that Lucy was being brought up in the Protestant faith. On Sundays when they went to Mass, Bridget and Henry took her with them to Kilauran, where she waited for half an hour for the service to begin in the green-painted corrugated-iron hut where the small Church of Ireland congregation worshipped. Although he knew she attended the Sunday services in Kilauran, since they were conducted by his curate, Canon Crosbie felt he should see how things were at Lahardane for himself.

'And you always say your prayers, Lucy?' As genial in old age as his innocent smile and pure white hair suggested, Canon Crosbie twinkled at her over the tea things Bridget had set out for them on the dining-room table. 'Can you say Our Lord's Prayer for me, Lucy?'

'Our Father, which art in heaven,' Lucy began, and went on until the end.

'Well, that's grand.' Before he left, Canon Crosbie gave her a book called *The Girls of St Monica's*, reflecting privately that had things been different she would by now have been sent away to a boarding-school herself. There was no doubt in the clergyman's mind that that would have been the intention of the family, but when later he raised the subject with Aloysius Sullivan it was pointed out to him that, as things were, the funds for anything of the kind were lacking. Until her parents' eventual return, Lucy Gault would continue to receive her education in Mr Aylward's small schoolroom.

By now, the lull that had followed insurrection in Ireland had given way to civil war. The new Irish Free State was bloodily torn apart by it, as towns and villages and families were. The terrible beauty of a destiny fulfilled trailed a terrible bitterness, which haunted memories long after the conflict ended in May 1923. Towards the end of that same month, Mr Sullivan received a letter from Miss Chambré to the effect that Heloise Gault's aunt – informed, when her health was a little improved, of her niece's departure from Ireland – had been affected by a desire for reconciliation. Learning then that Heloise's present whereabouts were not known, she had confidently instructed Miss Chambré to place an advertisement in several English newspapers. That this had elicited no response was the cause of considerable disappointment. *I myself did not expect otherwise*, Miss Chambré wrote, *but for the sake of an old lady's peace of mind I feel it to be my duty to request you to inform me when you receive news of Heloise Gault. Naturally the conduct of her child is still concealed from my employer.*

Mr Sullivan sighed over that. He might have pointed out, but did not do so, that Lucy Gault's conduct had spawned its own punishment, a fact confirmed in his conversations with Bridget and in his own continuing observation. It was apparent to him also that bewilderment possessed the household at Lahardane as unproductively as did the agitation that disturbed his thoughts when he dwelt for too long on what had come about. The solicitor, who lived alone but for a housekeeper, for the most part kept the depth of his concern private, occasionally and to no avail touching upon it in the presence of his clerk.

Waking often in the night to find herself similarly affected, Bridget would lie sleepless, waiting to greet Henry when he opened his eyes with a plea to tell her all over again about the moment of discovering the bundle among the weeds and fallen stones. The dog that had been befriended had run off one day and hadn't been seen again: to Bridget, and to Henry, that seemed of a piece with all that had happened otherwise, but in time this was dismissed by both of them as fancy.

While at Lahardane there was the rawness of disorder, the story of what had brought it so dramatically to a country house came to find a place among the stories of the Troubles that were told in the neighbourhood – in Kilauran and Clashmore and Ringville, on the streets of Enniseala. The tragedy called down upon herself by a child, and what had since become her life, made a talking point, and seemed to strangers to be the material of legend. Visitors to the beaches of this quiet coast listened and were astonished. Commercial men who took orders for their wares across the counters of shops related the story in distant towns. Conversation in back bars, at tea tables and card tables, was enlivened by reports of what had occurred.

As often with such travellers' tales, exaggeration improved the telling. Borrowed facts, sewn in where there was a dearth, gathered authority with repetition. Stirred by what was told of the events at Lahardane, memories strayed into other houses, through other family archives: to have suffered so harsh a misfortune, the Gaults had surely once betrayed a servant to the gallows, had failed to stand by common justice, or too haughtily had taken for granted privileges that were theirs. In talk inspired by what was told, the subtleties that clogged the tidiness of narration were smudged away. The spare reality of what had happened was coloured and enriched, and altogether made better. The journey the stricken parents had set out upon became a pilgrimage, absolution sought for sins that varied in the telling.

*

'The Grand Old Duke of York,' sang the children at the Christmas party in Mr Aylward's schoolroom, 'he had ten thousand men . . .'

Balloons decorated the spelling charts and the blackboard, holly cheered the maps and Mr Aylward's own portraits of kings and queens. There was tea for the children, all fifteen of them on benches around the four tables pushed together – sandwiches and barm brack, and cakes speckled with hundreds and thousands. The room was darkened. Borrowed curtains hung over the two windows and Mr Aylward made shadows with his fingers on a white sheet – a rabbit, a bird, an old man's craggy profile.

Afterwards Lucy walked home along the strand, alone in the gathering darkness, the fierce winter sea unruly beside her. She kept hoping, as she always did on the strand, that the dog might have come back, that he'd rush stumbling down the cliffs, barking the way he used to. But nothing moved except what was driven by the wind, and the only sound was the wind's ceaseless whine and the crash of the waves. 'Don't come near me,' Edie Hosford had said again, not wanting to be touched by her when they were playing Oranges and Lemons.

TWO

I

On a February morning, a porter who was sweeping the railway-station platform at Enniseala found himself recalling the occasion when he had been shot in the shoulder from an upstairs window. He was drawn back to that time because in the night he had dreamed about it – about showing his wound to people, and showing them the dark mark left behind on the jersey where the blood had soaked it, and telling of how the bullet had torn his flesh but had not lodged there. In his dream his arm had again been carried in a sling, attracting on the streets glances of approval from older men, who invited him to join any one of half a dozen pitch-and-toss schools, as in his real life such men had. They had honoured him as an insurrectionist, although he had never belonged to a revolutionary organization. 'Well, isn't it shocking that would happen to you!' an old beggarwoman had exclaimed from the doorway of Phelan's bar and grocery. 'A man to take a gun to you!' The same remark was made to him on the street by the Christian Brother who used to twist the flesh at the back of his neck when his long division was wrong or when he confused the counties of Ulster with those of Connacht. He was invited into Phelan's so that he could display the wound, and the men in the bar said he was lucky to be alive. In his dream these men and the beggarwoman and the Christian Brother were there too, raising their glasses to him.

Sweeping up the railway-station litter on the day after he had this dream for the first time, the porter found it difficult to separate it from the experience that so long ago had inspired it. Unable to verify on his own what he remembered, he was aware, that morning, of a sense of solitude. His companions of the night in the past had since emigrated, one of them a while back, the other only recently. His father, who had so severely refused to accept either compensation for the injury or the apology that was offered, had died a month ago. During his lifetime his father had always taken pride in what had occurred, since it had been swiftly followed by the departure – apparently for ever – of a one-time officer of the British army and his English wife. That this couple had mistakenly believed their child to be dead amounted to no more than just deserts: often the railway porter's father had put forward this view, but when he did so in the dream it had caused the porter distress, as it never had in reality.

The February day was cold. 'There's coal wanted on the waiting-room fire,' a voice called out, and while the litter-pan and sweeping brush were deposited in the station shed, while the waiting-room fire was riddled and coal piled generously on, the porter's unease did not lessen. In his dream the curtains of the house had blown out from the windows, blazing in the dark. There was the lifeless body of a child.

That day passed. And as other days came and went it was noticed among people who knew him that the railway porter had become a quieter man, less given to casual conversation with passengers on the platforms, often lost in an abstracted mood. The same dream – unchanging and vivid in his sleep – continued to disturb his nights. Waking from it, he was invariably seized by a compulsion to calculate the age of the child who had become separated from her parents, and when he made enquiries was informed that she and they had not since been reunited. In his dream it was he who laid down the poison for the dogs; he who, before he was wounded, broke the window-glass and trickled in the petrol; he who struck the single match. One afternoon, when he was whitewashing the stones around the station flowerbeds he saw, as clearly as in his dream, the curtains blazing.

Before that year had passed he ceased to be a railway porter and learnt the trade of a house-painter. Afterwards he wondered why he had made this change and at first did not know. Then some instinct suggested to him that he imagined a house-painter's day would be busier, that graining doors and skirting-boards, fixing putty and mixing colours, would allow him less opportunity for brooding. In this, unfortunately, he was wrong.

As he worked his blow-lamp, scraped away old paint and brushed on new, it became a struggle, even more than it had been for him as a railway porter, to establish reality. After the shot was fired he had been assisted. His companions had found their bicycles where they'd hidden them and had helped him when he could not manage his. The petrol tins, still full, had been left behind, abandoned in the haste of hurrying away. All this he insisted to himself, knowing it to be the truth, but still the contradiction was there. As familiar a sight in his white overalls as he had been in his railway porter's uniform, the quiet disposition he had acquired earning him respect, he told no one of the disturbance that afflicted him, not his mother, not his employer, nor anyone who stopped to speak to him as he worked. He lived in this surreptitious way, reassuring himself that nothing more terrible had occurred in the reality that haunted him than the poisoning of three dogs. But then, again, and yet again, there was the body of a child.

2

With more time than ever on her hands when she'd left Mr Aylward's school, Lucy began to read the books in the drawing-room bookcases. All of them were old, their spines familiar for as long as she could remember. But when she opened them she was drawn into a world of novelty, into other centuries and other places, into romance and complicated relationships, into the lives of people as different as Rosa Dartle and Giles Winterborne, into bleak London fog and the sun of Madagascar. And when she had read almost all there was to read in the drawing-room she turned to the bookcases on the first-floor landing and those of the unused breakfast-room.

In the house the window boards that had briefly been in place were hardly remembered now; the sheets that had been lifted from the furniture had long ago been put to other use. When school had been finished with, Henry and Bridget were still Lucy's daily companions, offering the same friendship they had when she was a child. If Mr O'Reilly happened to be working nearby when she walked through the pasture fields he waved at her, as he always had.

Nor did the interest Mr Sullivan and Canon Crosbie had taken in a solitary child's welfare wane when childhood passed. There were still their visits, still the birthday presents and the Christmas presents they had always brought to her. And in return there was their choice of the Christmas turkeys Henry reared.

'It's only that I wonder,' Canon Crosbie confessed, 'if it's right for a young girl to find herself so much alone, so many miles from anywhere?'

Each time the clergyman wondered, he elicited the same response: this was how things were, Bridget pointed out.

'Does she ever mention making something of her life?' Canon Crosbie persisted. 'Does she ever show a preference?'

'A preference, Canon?'

'For one vocation or another? To – well, I suppose, to go out into the world?'

'This is what she knows, sir. There isn't a shell on the strand she doesn't have affection for. It is how she is, Canon. Always was.'

'But that's not the thing at all! A girl should not lavish affection on shells. It is not right that shells should be her companions.'

'There is Henry. There is myself.'

'Oh, indeed. Indeed, of course. A blessing, Bridget, that doesn't go unremarked. You're very good.'

'I'm not saying it's short of unusual, sir, the way things are. All I'm saying is, Henry and myself do our best.'

'Of course you do. Of course, of course. You've done wonders. There's no one saying you haven't done wonders.' Canon Crosbie was emphatic, then paused a moment. 'And tell me, Bridget, does she continue to believe in their return?'

'She has never stopped believing that. It's what she waits for.'

'I knew her father when he was her age,' the old clergyman continued after a pause. The vagueness in his voice sounded like defeat now, as if no matter how long they talked the conversation wouldn't advance. '"Everard Gault has married a beauty," Mrs Crosbie said, having seen Mrs Gault before I did myself. "Well, that makes up for it," Mrs Crosbie said – because Everard Gault's family had been taken from him, we all knew that. She has had a soft spot since for Heloise Gault. Well, for both of them, you have to say. And so have I, of course.'

'Henry and myself –'

'I know, Bridget, I know. It's just that sometimes in the evenings when we sit there in the rectory we think of a young girl on her own – or, not quite, of course, but still a little on her own. And we hope, Bridget, we hope.'

'She has taken on the bees.'

'Bees?'

79

'The Captain used have beehives in the orchard. We didn't bother with the honey the time he left. Henry can't be doing with bees, but she's started up the hives again.'

Canon Crosbie nodded. Well, that was something, he said. Bees were better than nothing.

*

That something had befallen Captain Gault and his wife came to be believed: that they had found themselves unexpectedly destitute, a particular plight of this time; that they had been the victims of disaster. This newspaper tragedy or that easily became another fragment of their story, which increasingly gathered interest the more often it was told. Absence made truth of conjecture, Mr Sullivan often reflected, and yet had conjectured himself, for it was impossible not to. 'It is our tragedy in Ireland,' he was heard to remark more than once, 'that for one reason or another we are repeatedly obliged to flee from what we hold dear. Our defeated patriots have gone, our great earls, our Famine emigrants, and now the poor to search for work. Exile is part of us.'

He did not himself believe that further misfortune, natural or otherwise, had befallen Captain Gault and his wife. Exiles settled in their exiled state, often acquiring a stature they had not possessed before. He had observed this often in those who came back to Enniseala only to find themselves restless in a town that was too small, feeling they belonged nowhere now, yet seeming wiser than they had been. And who could blame Everard Gault and his wife, lowered by their sadness, for wishing to begin again, where everything was different? He regretted, with the benefit of retrospect, that he had engaged an incompetent private detective to conduct a search of a Swiss city, especially when he considered that the tally of the man's expenses could not now be put to better use. It annoyed him, too, that the woman Chambré had chosen English newspapers in which to place advertisements when he had assured her that England had been specifically rejected as a country to settle in by the couple who were sought. His own professional tidiness resented the muddle he had contributed to himself by withholding his convictions: Lahardane as it was today was less awkward to live with than the memory of his saying that everything would be all right.

*

For her part, Lucy did not wonder much about the nature of exile, accepting, with time, what had come about, as she did her lameness and the features that were reflected in her looking-glass. Had Canon Crosbie raised with her the question of going out into the world, she would have replied that the nature and the tenets of her life had already been laid down for her. She waited, she would have said, and in doing so kept faith. Each room was dusted clean; each chair, each table, each ornament was as they were remembered. Her full summer vases, her bees, her footsteps on the stairs and on the landings, and crossing rooms and in the cobbled yard and on the gravel, were what she offered. She was not lonely; sometimes she could hardly remember loneliness. 'Oh, but I'm happy,' she would have reassured the clergyman had he asked her. 'Happy enough, you know.'

Presents from him, from his wife, from Mr Sullivan, came again on her twenty-first birthday. Afterwards, in warm evening sunshine, she lay reading in the apple orchard another of the novels left behind by other generations. Enough of the world it was for Lucy Gault, at twenty-one, to visit Netherfield.

3

The images of the *Sacra Conversazione* did not entirely obliterate those of an English afternoon, and English twilight gathering in December. Through the detail of Bellini's composition – marble columns and trees in leaf, blue and green and scarlet robes – there were teacups on a rosewood table, and misty window-panes, coal blazing in a fireplace: the recollections which an hour ago Heloise had lit in her husband's imagination lingered still.

He had never met the woman who was informed during that teatime that she'd been widowed, but he glimpsed her now, a shadow among the saints who surrounded the Virgin and her infant and the demure musician. These figures were a crowd yet seemed, each one of them, to be alone. Less complicated, the telegram that had come lay on the rosewood surface, the hall clock struck. 'Ladysmith,' Heloise's mother said.

The church was cool in the heat of the day, a smell of polish coming from where the sacristan worked. The holy water stoup was almost empty; on the steps outside a cripple begged. 'No, please let me,' Heloise pleaded, searching her handbag, then dropping the coin she found on to the palm that was held out.

They passed along a sunless alley, went slowly, reluctant to emerge into the afternoon's glare. She would have been sixteen that teatime, he calculated.

'Why are you so good to me, Everard? Why do you listen so well?'

'Perhaps because I love you.'

'I wish I had more strength.'

He did not say that she'd had strength enough once, nor reassure her as to its return. He did not know about that. Unable, when the distant past of her childhood was evoked, to contribute, himself, from that same time, he told instead about being a soldier, going over in greater detail what he had told already, speaking of the men he had briefly led in his modest fields of battle.

On the Riva they ordered coffee. He heard, before it came, of the household of the guardian aunt, the orphan's refuge it had been in later childhood years. 'No more than boys they were,' he said himself, and told the names of the men in his care. 'I often see their faces.'

He watched her slender fingers dipping a lump of sugar into her coffee, one lump and then another. That gave him pleasure; so much, he wondered why. Well, it was real, he told himself; and perhaps no more than that gave pleasure when artificial conversation was interrupted. He had written to Lahardane. He had expressed concern for the well-being of the servants who were his caretakers now, asked about the Friesians and the house. More than once he had written, but each time had drawn back when the moment of posting came. There would be a reply, surreptitiously received, a secret correspondence begun, the breaking of the trust that had always been there in his marriage. He kept the letters hidden, their envelopes stamped. It was as much deceit as he could manage.

'How beautiful all this is!' she said.

Near where they sat, gondolas came and went at a landing stage. Further out on the canal a steamer crept slowly in from the sea. A dog barked on the deck of a working boat.

When it was cooler they walked on the Zattere. They took a boat to the Giudecca. In the evening there was the *Annunciazione* in the church of San Giobbe. Then waltzes played at Florian's.

That night in the Pensione Bucintoro, while her husband slept, Heloise lay wakeful beside him. What riches there had been! she told herself when the sacred images of the day came back to her, with all that had been said. She did not feel deprived tonight, and resolved in the euphoria the day had nurtured to find the courage in the morning to confess that it was not enough to say a generous husband had been good to her, not enough to say that he listened perfectly to her childhood evocations. 'We are playing at being dead,' he had once gently protested, and she hadn't been able to explain why it was that she would always want to forget. But in the morning she would do better. She heard her voice apologizing, and talking then of all she didn't want to talk about; before she closed her eyes she found the sentences came quite easily. But when she slept, and woke after a few minutes, she heard herself saying she couldn't have that conversation and knew that she was right.

4

Henry lit a Woodbine and threw the match down. From the archway that was the entrance to the yard he peered at the car that had come – at its wheels, its dickey seat, its green upholstery, the little mascot above the radiator, the peaked bonnet, the number plate, IF 19. The canvas hood was down.

He had heard the car's approach, then the crunching of the sea-gravel beneath its wheels. He had imagined that Canon Crosbie had come again, or that at last there had been news enough to bring the solicitor. But the voice he'd heard calling out, apologizing, was neither's. Lucy had come out of the house, the way she did when a car arrived. 'Who are you?' she was saying now, and the driver of the car repeated his apology, then turned the engine off in case she could not hear him.

He was a young man, not wearing a jacket, and when he got out of the car Henry could see that a tie supported his flannel trousers, stripes of green and brown and purple pulled taut and knotted. Henry had never seen him before.

'I didn't realize there was a house here.'

'Who are you?' Lucy asked again, and a name was given that was unfamiliar to Henry. Lucy half shook her head, indicating that it was unfamiliar to her, too.

Leaning against the wall of the archway, the Woodbine packet still in his hand, Henry was reminded of the time when other visitors besides a solicitor and clergyman came to the house – the Morells and the people from Ringville, and people from Enniseala and Cappoquin, from as far off as Clonmel. There were summer parties, picnic baskets carried through the fields to the strand, children playing in the orchard and the garden. Lady Roche from Monatray came, and Colonel Roche, and the three Ashe sisters, and old Mrs Cronin and her flighty middle-aged daughter who once in greeting kissed the Captain. Henry hadn't seen any of them since the winter of 1920, and wondered about them now. Was this young man one of the children grown up, in spite of what he said about not knowing there was a house at the end of the avenue?

'She wants to give him tea,' Bridget said a few minutes later in the outhouse where Henry did his carpentry, coming there to ask him to set up the trellis table on the grass of the hydrangea lawn. A flush had come into Bridget's cheeks, and Henry remembered that, too, from the past – excitement engendered by what Bridget called 'society'.

He brushed grime and cobwebs from the slats of the table, then wiped them with a rag. On the lawn he brushed the seats of two of the white iron chairs that broke at intervals the curve of the wall over which the deep blue hydrangea blooms fell. The rust on the ironwork needed to be attended to, the chairs themselves repainted. One of these days he would do it, Henry resolved, knowing he wouldn't.

*

'It didn't look like an avenue,' Ralph said. 'The gate-lodge was closed up.'

He hadn't noticed the faded green entrance gates, obscured by nettles and dying cow parsley. He'd driven beneath a canopy of leaves and suddenly the big stone house was there.

'That's Lahardane you visited,' Mrs Ryall said. 'And that was Lucy Gault.'

The girl who'd come out of the house hadn't said her name. The woman who spread a tablecloth on the slatted table had arranged cups and saucers on it in silence, milk jug and teapot, brown bread and butter and a honeycomb. Her big wooden tray had a raised rim running round it and white porcelain handles. When the tea had been poured the woman came back to see if everything was all right, and returned again, with soda bread that had sultanas in it.

'IF 19 went well for you?' Mr Ryall enquired, and Ralph said the car he had been lent that afternoon had given no trouble. 'It was very kind of you,' he repeated, having shown his gratitude in this way already.

'You need a holiday from the boys.'

Mr Ryall had advertised for someone to tutor his two sons during the summer months, since according to their preparatory-school reports they were backward in all subjects. So Ralph, at a loose end that summer, not yet settled in what he intended to do with his life, had come to the house above the offices of the Bank of Ireland, Mr Ryall being the bank's agent in Enniseala.

He was a small, tidily moustached man, his wife a contrast in almost every way. Carelessly running to fat, Mrs Ryall was indulgent of herself and uncritical of other people, the generosity of her disposition reflected in her plumpness and her manner. That her boys were indolent failed to worry her. Worrying was her husband's department, she had a way of saying, vaguely implying that worrying was an enjoyment for him.

It was half past nine, dusk gathering in the Ryalls' well-furnished dining-room. A vast sideboard repeated the tortured curlicues of an equally grandiose tallboy. A set of dining-chairs matched the rosy Rexine finish of sofa and armchairs. Flowered wallpaper echoed damask curtains that did not draw across, drapes of net being permanently in place against the glass. Blue tasselled blinds obscured in daytime the windows' upper panes.

A late sustenance was laid out on a great mahogany table, for no matter what the hour Mrs Ryall wished no one to be hungry. Beneath an unlit oil lamp on a pulley, cream crackers and Galtee cheese, cake and brandy-snaps were on offer. An hour ago the boys had been packed off to bed, the dregs of their cocoa cold now in the cups that remained on the table.

'I imagine you weren't told,' Mrs Ryall said, 'what happened at Lahardane.'

Fair-haired, blue-eyed, an angular quality in features that were handsome in their way, Ralph listened while the Ryalls told the story between them, Mr Ryall factual and precise, his wife supplying emotional overtones.

'You'll find it talked about in the town,' Mr Ryall added when there was a pause in the recounting of events.

Spreading a cream cracker, his wife confirmed that. 'I have heard she grew up pretty,' she said.

When Lucy Gault smiled, a dimple came and made the smile seem mischievous. There were freckles on the bridge of her nose, her eyes were a faded azure, her hair as pale as wheat. Driving back in his employers' motor car, Ralph had been accompanied by all that, and the image was vivid again while he listened to the continuing story.

'I was approached,' Mr Ryall said, 'when Captain Gault and Mrs Gault could not be traced. There'd been a hope that he might be in touch, but there was no reason why he should be and of course he wasn't. It is the saddest thing.'

Mr Ryall lowered the lamp and took off its glass globe to light the wick. Mrs Ryall swept particles of cream cracker from her bosom and left the table to pull down the blinds.

'Would you say she's pretty?' she enquired. 'Or perhaps she's beautiful? Would you say Lucy Gault's beautiful, Ralph?'

Ralph said he thought she was.

*

Lucy Gault was beautiful all that summer. She was beautiful in her plain white dress, the sunlight catching the dots of silver in the stoneless earrings she wore. They would have been her mother's, Mrs Ryall said, probably the dress too; all left behind in a departure that had been hasty in the end.

Beneath the wide spread of a beech tree in the garden, while his pupils managed not to listen to what Ralph tried to teach them, the girl who had come out of the house he hadn't thought was there haunted every morning and every sleepy afternoon. Vaguely aware of Kildare's muttered conjugations and pretending he had not noticed that Jack was drawing animals on the inside cover of his

88

exercise book, Ralph sometimes did not trust himself to speak in case, by foolish chance, he described the solemn stare that often came before Lucy Gault's smile, and the way she had of sitting with her hands clasped in her lap, as still as marble. In his shy recall she poured their tea and said that visitors did not often come by mistake.

'There is a river, the Arar, which flows through the territories of the Aedui and the Sequani into the Rhone,' Ralph slowly repeated in the garden of the bank. '*Est flumen*, Kildare: there is a river. *Quod influit per fines*: which flows through the territories. You understand, Kildare?'

The translation came from *Dr Giles's Keys to the Classics*, which Ralph had perused as he lay in bed in the early morning.

'*Aeduorum et Sequanorum* is the Aedui and Sequani bit. You understand, Kildare?'

'Indeed I do.'

'Well, see if you can work out *incredibili lenitate, ita ut non possit judicari oculis in utram partem fluat*.'

Jack had transformed an isosceles triangle into a tarantula. Ralph drew another triangle, marking its angles A, B and C. Both boys wore floppy white hats because the sun this morning was strong.

'Now, Jack,' Ralph said.

Every Wednesday, half-day in Enniseala, was his half-day too. Mr Ryall continued to lend him his motor car, calculating that if the tutor he had found for his boys felt himself stifled by the limitations of small-town life he might do what the man last summer had done and take himself off. Ralph had driven to Dungarvan and had walked about it, had driven to Cappoquin and walked about it, had driven to Ballycotton and Castlemartyr and Lismore. He had not been back to the house near the cliffs. He had not been invited.

'So what do we know about AB and AC, Jack?'

'They're letters in the alphabet.'

'I mean the lines you've drawn. The sides of the triangle?'

Jack's toe prodded a stick one of the Ryalls' spaniels had been chewing. He kicked it gently away, ensuring that it was still within his reach.

'They're good straight lines,' he said.

'What about the angles A, B and C, Jack?'

'They're good –'

'The lines are all the same length. What does that tell us about the angles, Jack?'

Jack pondered for a moment, then for another, and another.

'Is this thing, *lenitate*, long?' Kildare asked. 'A very long river, does it mean?'

'*Incredibili lenitate*, with incredible smoothness.'

'My brain hurts,' Jack said.

The maid, Dympna, crossed the lawn with Ralph's mid-morning tea and biscuits. Both boys stood up as soon as they saw her.

'It's most interesting about the Aedui and the Sequani,' Kildare politely remarked before he and his brother ran off.

On Wednesday evenings Ralph was always asked where he'd driven that afternoon, and he sensed the disappointment when he mentioned the towns he'd walked about. It was apparent to him that the Ryalls hoped he would visit Lahardane again, even though no invitation had come. He could feel Mr Ryall thinking that this, too, could be a factor in guaranteeing the services of his boys' tutor; and, with greater sentiment, Mrs Ryall deciding that here at last was company for a lonely girl. But how on earth could he simply drive up that avenue, how could he presume that a friendship had begun? Nothing of that kind had been said.

One Wednesday, however, Ralph did drive back to where the avenue began, to the unoccupied gate-lodge and the entrance gates hidden in the summer undergrowth. He slowed down but did not turn in. Instead he drove on, and found eventually a way to the strand, where he swam and lay in the sun. No one else appeared on the shingle or on the smooth, washed sand which faintly bore his own bare footprints. No flutter of white disturbed his solitude, no slight figure on the far-off rocks that stretched like a pointing finger into the sea. Driving away, he found again the avenue and the gate-lodge. He waited, but no one appeared there either.

On other days, every evening, Ralph walked up the long main street of Enniseala, pausing to gaze into the windows of the shops, passing the time with the meat that hung in MacMenamy's, the dress dummies in Domville's drapery, the groceries in O'Hagan's and the Home and Colonial. Enormous glass retorts containing red and green liquid were the feature of Westbury's Medical Hall; furniture crowded P. K. Gatchell's auction rooms – beds and wardrobes and tables, chests of drawers, chairs and writing-desks and paintings. Scenes from films were changed three times a week in the display cases of the Picture House.

Ralph read the *Irish Times* and the *Cork Examiner* in the bar of the Central Hotel. He walked past the squat lighthouse and the railway station, by the summer boarding-houses – the Pacific, the Atlantic, Miss Meade's, Sans Souci. He strolled on the promenade among couples exercising their dogs, and nuns, and priests, and Christian Brothers. Convent girls chattered by the yellow and blue bandstand or swung their legs on the sea-wall.

Sometimes he walked past the army Camp on the Cork road, and far beyond it, out into the country. Sometimes he explored the less gracious streets at the bottom of the town, where children ran barefoot and shawled women begged, where men played street-corner pitch-and-toss and the smell of poverty oozed from infested dwellings. There was the riverbank walk to the Protestant church, close to where the swans that gave the town its name nested. One evening, among the churchyard graves, Ralph met an elderly clergyman who held out a hand.

'You teach the Bank of Ireland boys,' he said as he did so. 'I'm Canon Crosbie.'

It surprised Ralph to be addressed in this way but he covered that up by smiling. He had listened to Canon Crosbie's sermons, one of his duties being to accompany his charges to church on the rare occasions when neither of their parents wished to attend the Sunday-morning service.

'I do my best to teach them,' he said when he had given the clergyman his name.

'Oh now, I'm sure you do very well, Ralph. And I'm right in thinking you hail from County Wexford?'

'Yes, I do.'

'I was a curate long years ago in Gorey. What an interesting county Wexford is!'

'Yes.'

'Proud of its differences.'

Ralph smiled again, not knowing what was meant by that. Canon Crosbie said:

'I'm told you've been to Lahardane.'

'I drove up by chance. Mr Ryall very kindly lets me drive his car.'

'The kindest of men. And married to the kindest wife there ever was.' Canon Crosbie paused. 'You met Lucy Gault, so I've heard.'

'Yes, I did.'

'Now that's an excellent thing, Ralph. Nothing pleased me more than to hear you had called in. Nothing pleased Mrs Crosbie more. We equally rejoiced.'

Canon Crosbie's twinkling manner, the hand placed friendlily on Ralph's shoulder, the enthusiastic nodding of his head, caused Ralph to blush, and once the blush had begun it spread and deepened. There was an implication in what was being said, in the tone of voice, in an assumption that Ralph would have wished to be true but which assuredly was not.

'A summer companion for Lucy Gault is a marvel to be thankful for.'

'I've been there only once.'

'And how it would delight us all to hear that you had been again! And how delighted – oh yes, I know it – Lucy would be too.'

'I haven't actually been invited to return.'

'Hereabouts, Ralph, it is quite the thing to drop in, to lift a knocker when the spirit moves. I grant you, Ralph, there is more formality in County Wexford. I expect you are acquainted with the Dean of Ferns?'

'I'm afraid not.'

'Well, there you are. No, we take things lightly here. It's quite expected that we don't much stand on ceremony. In social ways,' the Canon added with sudden severity, 'stand-offishness has no place among us. No place at all.'

'Actually,' Ralph began, 'I'm not –'

'My boy, of course you're not. I feel that in all my bones. And Mrs Crosbie does. Has your path crossed that of Mr Sullivan?'

'Sullivan?'

'Of Sullivan and Pedlow? Solicitors, commissioners for oaths?'

Ralph shook his head.

'Mr Sullivan has searched the world for Captain Gault and his wife. And in the meantime Mr Sullivan has kept an eye on things. He has kept an eye on Lucy. In his own time, beyond all professional duties, he has been concerned – concerned, Ralph, for Lucy's well-being and livelihood, concerned about repairs and upkeep in that barracks of a house. Not much can be done, for there is no money to be spared. A few fields and the cattle on them have for generations been the outward and visible sign of the Gaults' ease of passage. Lahardane has struggled on, and it is Mr Sullivan who has arranged that it does so still. I have said to Mr Sullivan – I have stopped him in the street to say it – that he is a good man. The reply I drew was that he has taken many a dinner at Lahardane, that he has – in the Captain's day and before – spent many a night when a journey home in the dark seemed arduous. He claims no more for his humanity, Ralph, than that it's a payment for hospitality.'

Ralph nodded. The flush of colour had gone from his cheeks. He would have liked to bring the encounter to an end, but didn't quite know how to do so.

'It has reached Mr Sullivan's ears, as it reached my own, that you have been out to Lahardane. That has spelt delight for Mr Sullivan, Ralph, as it has for Mrs Crosbie and for myself. We have given thanks. We have given heartfelt thanks.'

'I mistook the avenue that day.'

'Mistake it again, Ralph. I entreat you to mistake it again. I entreat you to give a little company to a young girl who lacks the company of her own generation. I entreat you not to leave undone those things which ought to be done. I truly entreat you. Go again to that lonely house, Ralph.'

With this wordy hyperbole, Canon Crosbie offered Ralph his hand and passed on his way.

*

In handwriting that seemed strangely perfect, that followed every instruction as to downstroke and loops, and flow and style, there was a note at last from Lucy Gault. That name, so secretly cherished by Ralph, was formed with the same slant that characterized the words of the letter's content. Not all the world's poetry could capture the potency in this confirmation of a name; about that Ralph was certain. Not all the world's poetry could reflect an iota of his happiness as he taught his charges beneath the leafy boughs of the beech tree. 'Oh, we'll just read today,' he exclaimed, smiling on the morning the letter came, then reading aloud from *The Diary of a Nobody* while Kildare dozed and Jack drew gargoyles.

When the mid-morning tray came and the boys had run away there was the letter to peruse again with luxurious slowness, the taking of it from the pocket, the slow unfolding, the dappled shadows on white paper and blue ink. The envelope was kept separately; it, too, was examined now. The pleas of Canon Crosbie, the unspoken wishes of the Ryalls, were no longer at odds with the stubborn shyness that characterized Ralph's nature. And it was delight enough, in these first hours of everything being different, to gaze at a few brief sentences and at how a name was written.

Before you go away for ever come and say good-bye. Come and have tea again. If you would like to. Lucy Gault.

There was nothing else, only the address and the date beneath it, *August 5th 1936.*

5

On the day Lucy Gault's letter arrived in the house above the Bank of Ireland there was a new recruit at the army Camp that Ralph often passed on his evening walks. The officer in charge at the time saw a tall, hollow-faced man with an intensity in his dark eyes that was particularly noticeable. The impression received by the officer was that the man was troubled, but since he had been declared medically fit, since he had been interviewed in the usual manner and declared worthy of the uniform he was to wear, the officer stamped the papers that recorded such details as name and age and the period of service undertaken. The typewritten name was incorrectly spelt, the new recruit pointed out, and the officer drew two lines through the error. *Horahan* he wrote instead.

Afterwards in the parade yard this recruit stood apart. He looked about him, at huts, at latrines, at the high walls of a handball court, at soldiers idling in a corner. He had joined the army in the hope that military discipline and the noisy communal life, feet on the march and a healthy tiredness, would be more salutary in his affliction than the solitary nature of house-painting or the occupation of a railway-station porter. His mother, with whom until today he had lived, had wept when he declared his intention. She was reconciled to the change that had occurred in him while he'd still been employed at the railway station. In spite of it – or because of it, she often considered – he was a good son, clean and tidy in his habits and becoming more so as the years went by. That suddenly he'd got it into his head to join the army was as distressing a shock as ever she'd suffered. She feared the hazards that were natural in the military life, and considered her son unsuitable for exposure to them.

In the parade yard the recruit made an enquiry of the soldiers who stood about as to the whereabouts of the Camp chapel. These men were smoking and at ease, the top buttons of their tunics open. Thinking to make fun of a newcomer, as was usual at the Camp when a face was unfamiliar, they sent him in the wrong direction, so that he found himself eventually at a hole dug in the ground, half filled with the Camp's rubbish. Flies swarmed about it; a black and white mongrel dog rooted among tins and bones. The new soldier looked about him. He was at the periphery of the Camp, its boundary marked with posts and link-wire, and he walked back the way he had come. He did not ask for directions again, but found his own way to the chapel, noticing from a distance the black wooden cross on its roof.

The place was empty, its varnished benches garishly yellow in strips of sunlight. The soldier dipped the tips of his fingers into the stoup of holy water and with that same hand made the sign of the cross, addressing this devotion to the altar. He found then what he sought, a plaster representation of the Virgin Mary, before which a single candle burned. Here he knelt, and pleaded that in return for his service to his country he would be rewarded with peace of mind, that his insistent dreams, oppressing and tormenting him by night and haunting his memory by day, would cease. He pleaded for the Virgin's intervention on his behalf, proclaimed his obedience and begged for her acknowledgement of his plight. But when he finished there was silence in the chapel, as afterwards there always was in the places where he prayed.

'What's that?' another soldier enquired of him that day, but the new recruit denied that he had spoken, although he knew he had.

'You said something, man.'

'Would the trousers itch your legs for long?'

'It wasn't that you said.'

He knew it wasn't, but what he'd said was lost now and could not be found, because he did not himself know what it was. He had painted, not long ago, the window-frames of the big mellow-bricked asylum and had become familiar with its inmates. That he belonged there with them, that he would one day share their restricted existence, was his perpetual dread.

6

The yard dogs barked when the car was heard in the distance. They came loping out of their resting place on the warm cobbles beneath the pear tree and were pointed back to it by Henry, who knew there was to be a visitor this afternoon and who that visitor was. From the archway in the wall that separated the yard from the front of the house he watched the dogs obeying the gesture he had made, then turned to lean against the side of the archway he had leaned against when the car that was expected had driven up before. He felt for a cigarette, as he had then too.

When he'd heard from Bridget that the boy who had come that day was to return, Henry had said nothing. His impassive features remained undisturbed, but the lack of response seemed in no way significant to his wife, since often he chose not to comment when news was passed on to him. On occasion this reticence reflected the run of Henry's thoughts; on occasion it concealed what he did not wish to reveal. When the information came that Ralph was to return there was concealment.

He raised his left hand in a salute, answering Ralph's greeting. With his right he returned matches and the Woodbine packet to his trouser pocket. IF 19, he noticed, as he had before. A big old Renault the car was.

A few Sundays ago, after Mass in Kilauran, Henry had asked about the car. He'd asked a man who worked on the roads, who told him the car was Mr Ryall's, that once a week Mr Ryall made the journey from Enniseala to Dungarvan in it, to the Bank of Ireland's sub-office. How it was that this boy would be driving it, stranger that he appeared to be, the roadworker did not know. From what Bridget had overheard the last time the boy had been here, she said it seemed he was a teacher, but the loose ends in all that had not yet been gathered up.

'He's here,' Henry said in the kitchen, and was aware when he spoke that his wife was pleased to about the same degree that he was not.

'What it is, he's teaching the Ryall boys,' Bridget said. 'She told me that this morning. He's staying in the bank.'

'So he'll go back to where he emerged from one of these days?'

'It's why she wrote a letter to him – to say come out again before he'd go.'

'He has an easy way with him.'

'Ah, he's a nice young fellow.'

'I don't know is he.'

Bridget knew better than to take the disagreement further. She said instead:

'She has a honeycomb brought in for their tea again.'

'I'll put the table up outside.'

The boy was waiting, leaning against the side of the car, when Henry crossed the gravel with the slatted table. As he had on the previous occasion, he unfolded it on the hydrangea lawn and drew up the same two white-painted chairs. Passing by the boy as he returned to the yard, he said:

'You're over from England, sir?'

'I live near Enniscorthy. I've never been to England.'

'Arrah, why would you bother yourself?' Henry nodded a reluctant approval before inclining his head in the direction of Mr Ryall's car. 'She moves all right for you, does she?'

'I don't go fast.'

'There's a few dinges on the mudguards, nothing only that. I was noticing them the other time. She's well looked after.'

'Yes.'

'You'd like to see anything well looked after. I keep the trap up to it myself. I painted the old dog-cart a couple of years ago, but she's shaky all the same.'

The dickey was opened for him so that he could see the green-upholstered seat. The bonnet was unlatched and folded back so that he could inspect the engine. Henry wagged his head in admiration. That car would be worth a bit, he said.

'It's Mr Ryall's.'

'I heard you were stopping there. Here's the missy for you now.'

Henry walked slowly away. He felt better now that he'd had the conversation about the car. He listened to what was being said, the exchanges stuttering and nervous. The boy apologized for being early and was told it didn't matter.

*

'I thought maybe you'd have gone away already,' Lucy said. 'I thought maybe my note would have missed you.'

'I have a few more weeks in Enniseala.'

'I was glad to get your letter.'

I will come on Wednesday, Ralph had written, hurrying to catch the evening post. Six days had gone by then, during each one of which he had imagined what was happening now. While Caesar's Gallic War progressed and geometry bewildered Jack, Ralph had wondered if she would smile in that same way, and had resolved that silences should not develop. Would she tell him, this time, what others had told him since last they met? Would it bore her to hear about himself? About the friends he'd made at boarding-school? About the timber yards and the sawmills he would one day inherit? Would any of it interest her, as everything about her interested him?

'I keep bees,' she said. 'Did I tell you that before?'

'No, you didn't.'

'I didn't even tell you my name. But you know it now.'

'Yes, I do.'

'You will have heard about the Gaults.'

'Oh, not much.'

It seemed natural to deny that there was talk. Yet he would have liked to say that, far from adversely affecting his attachment, the story that was renowned in Enniseala strengthened it. But all that was impossible, since she did not know of his attachment. He could not even claim that, being still close to childhood, he sensed something of what her child's emotions had been when it was taken for granted that she should abandon without protest what she loved. He thought of her in that time and saw her clearly as she must have been, and remembered his own powerlessness in the boarding-school where he'd been assured he would be happy, his pillow drenched with tears, the home he'd been torn away from seeming like a heaven he had betrayed through a lack of the affection that was its due. How gentle in that alien dark his mother's good-night embrace had been, how musical the clatter of his father's timber mills, how cheerful his bedroom fire, how soft the carpet on the stairs! Nor was the hell that shattered his illusions yet fully spread about him: grimly spoken of were variations of discomfort and cold and discipline by disapproval; and again there'd be burnt morning porridge; again the stench of cabbage soup.

In the silence that had gathered as they stood by the car, Ralph wanted to say that he knew about the snares of childhood, and knew as well that his experience was puny compared with what still continued for the girl he believed he loved. His sympathy was part of love, as tender as his fondness.

'Would you like to see the hives?'

She was wearing a different white dress, with sleeves that came halfway down her arms, its collar different too. Her necklace was of tiny pearls or what seemed like pearls.

'Yes, please,' he said, and they walked together beneath the wide archway, into the yard and through it to the orchard. One of the sheepdogs ambled after them, the other still lazed beneath the pear tree.

'Beauty of Bath.' She named apples that were not yet ripe, in clusters on old twisted boughs. 'Kerry Pippins. George Cave.' She pointed at a row of beehives and didn't want him to go closer to them.

'It's lovely, this orchard,' he said.

'Yes, it is.'

They passed beyond it to a neglected garden, by collapsed glasshouses and raspberries gone wild. They came out on the other side of the house, where the railing that bounded the field they were in began.

'Shall we go for a walk?'

Ralph thought of her as Lucy when she said that, the first time he had in her company. *Lucy Gault*, he saw written down, as she had written it. No other name could be as right.

'Yes, of course.'

They passed from one field to another, then along the edge of one in which potatoes grew.

'The O'Reillys',' she said.

She led the way down the cliffs, and over the shingle to where seagulls stalked possessively on smooth, wet sand. Thongs of sea-weed had been left behind by the tide. Shells peeped up from where they were embedded. She said:

'"The girl is lame!" you're thinking.'

'I wasn't thinking that.'

'You noticed before, of course.'

'It isn't what you notice much.'

'Everybody notices it.'

Her limp made her more herself, he'd thought. He knew how it had come about. He'd told Mrs Ryall when she'd asked that it wasn't in the least unattractive. He might have said so now, but shyness held him back.

'That's Kilauran.' She pointed at the distant pier and the houses beyond it, her extended finger so slight and delicate that he longed to seize the hand and clasp it into his.

'I think I was there one day.'

'I went to school in Kilauran. Our church is a tin hut.'

'I think I saw it.'

'I never go into Enniseala.'

'Don't you like Enniseala?'

'I have no reason to go there.'

'I thought I might see you in the streets, but I didn't.'

'What do you do in Enniseala? What is it like where you are staying?'

He described the house above the bank offices. He told about his wandering the streets when he was free to do so in the evenings, how he often sat reading on the bandstand or in the empty bar of the Central Hotel, or walked on the promenade.

'Did you mind my asking you to come to tea again? Is it a bore?'

'Of course I didn't mind. Of course it isn't a bore.'

'Why "of course", Ralph?'

That was the first time she called him Ralph. He wanted her to again. He wanted to be for ever on this strand because they were alone here.

'Because it's how I feel. It couldn't possibly be a bore. It was lovely, getting your letter.'

'How many are the few weeks you have left?'

'Three, before the boys go back to school.'

'What are they like, the boys?'

'Oh, they're all right. I'm not much of a teacher, the trouble is.'

'What are you then?'

'Nothing, really.'

'Oh, you can't be nothing!'

'My father owns a sawmills. I'll end up owning it too. Well, I suppose so.'

'Don't you want to?'

'I have no vocation for anything else. I've tried to want to be all sorts of things.'

'What have you tried to want to be? An actor?'

'Oh, heavens, I couldn't act!'

'Why not?'

'I'm not the kind.'

'You might be.'

'I don't at all think so.'

'I would try everything. I would try for the stage. I would try marrying into riches. What are they called, the boys you teach?'

'Kildare and Jack.'

'How odd Kildare is! How odd a name!'

'It's in the family, I believe.'

'Earls of Kildare there were. And there's the county.'

'A town as well.'

'I have an Uncle Jack in India. My father's brother. I don't remember him. D'you know how many books there are at Lahardane?'

'No.'

'There are four thousand and twenty-seven. So old, some of them, they're falling to bits. Others have never been opened. Do you know how many I've read? Can you guess?'

Ralph shook his head.

'Five hundred and twelve. Last night, for the second time, I finished *Vanity Fair*.'

'I haven't read it even once.'

'It's very good.'

'I'll read it one of these days.'

'It has taken me years to read all those books. I began when I left school.'

'I've read hardly anything compared with that.'

'Sometimes there are jellyfish washed up here. Poor little creatures, but they sting if you pick them up.'

They walked among the pools in the rocks where anemones and shrimps were. The sheepdog that had followed them prodded the clumps of seaweed with a paw.

'Do you think it strange that I counted the books?'

'No, not at all.'

He imagined her counting, a finger passing from spine to spine along a bookshelf, and then beginning again on the shelf below. When he'd come the last time he hadn't been invited into the house. He wondered if today he'd see the rooms, and hoped he would.

'I don't know why I counted them,' she said, and added when a silence lengthened, 'I think we have to go back now. Shall we walk somewhere else after tea?'

★

103

She wished she hadn't said about the books. She hadn't meant to. She had meant only to mention *Vanity Fair*, perhaps even to draw attention to William Makepeace Thackeray as a name because Makepeace was as unusual as Kildare and she liked the rhythm of it. It sounded peculiar, counting four thousand and twenty-seven books. And yet he'd shaken his head decisively when she'd asked if it seemed strange.

She cut the sponge cake Bridget had made and wondered if she should have bought a Scribbins' Swiss roll, which you could sometimes get in Kilauran. The sponge cake felt clammy, the knife not slipping through as effortlessly as it might. Bridget's hand was heavy with cakes, though never with bread.

'Thank you,' he said, taking the slice she had cut.

'It may not be very nice.'

'It's delicious.'

She poured his tea and added milk, then poured her own. What should she say when they went quiet? This morning she had thought of questions to ask, but had already asked the ones she could remember.

'Are you glad you came to Enniseala, Ralph?'

'Oh, yes. Yes, I am.'

'Are you really not much of a teacher?'

'Well, I haven't taught the Ryall boys much.'

'Perhaps they don't want to learn much.'

'No, they don't. Not in the least.'

'Then it's not your fault.'

'I have a conscience.'

'So have I.'

She hadn't meant to say that, either. She was determined not to talk about her conscience. It wasn't interesting to a stranger, and she would say too much.

'I could not teach boys,' she said.

'Probably you could. As well as I can.'

'I remember Mr Ryall. With a moustache.'

'The Ryalls have been nice to me.'

'There's a man in Domville's I remember. A stringy man, very tall, his tie tied tightly in his collar. I knew his name but I can't remember it now.'

'I've never been in Domville's.'

'There's a little railway above your head and wooden balls that bring your change. Do you wonder why I wear white dresses?'

'Well –'

'It's my favourite colour. It was my mother's too.'

'*White* your favourite colour?'

'Yes, it is.' She offered the sponge cake again but he shook his head. She would have cut the Scribbins' roll into slices and arranged them herself, a chocolate roll with vanilla filling, or just jam if that was all there was. 'Tell me what Enniseala is like,' she said.

That kept things going – the convent on a hill, the Picture House, the long main street, the little lighthouse. And after that she heard that Ralph, too, was an only child. His father's timber yards and sawmills were described, and the house his family lived in, not far from the sawmills, near a bridge.

'Shall we walk down to the glen again?' she asked when they had finished having tea. 'Like we did the last time? Would it be a bore?'

'Of course it wouldn't.' And then he said, 'Your limp's not much to notice. It's hardly anything.'

'Will you come again next Wednesday?'

The brass band played in the wide piazza of the Città Alta, the outside tables of the piazza's single *ristorante* shaded by a green and white awning. *Il Duce* had come, *Il Duce* was on the way: there was confusion before the cheering began below, in via Garibaldi and piazza della Repubblica: *Il Duce* had arrived.

'*Tosca*,' the Captain said, but then the music from the opera stopped. The conductor waved a hand over the whole piazza, commanding silence, although mostly the piazza was empty. *Il Duce*'s song began.

'*Ecco!*' a slow old waiter murmured, as if from sleep. '*Bene, bene . . .*' he whispered, pouring the last of the Barolo. And in the new town below, the same tune played, amplified from a record, so that everyone, everywhere, knew that *Il Duce* was here at last.

Heloise hadn't spoken since they had been led to their table beneath the awning, nor while the dishes of the lunch they had ordered were brought to them, nor while she had played with hers, leaving most of the food untouched. It was a bad day, the Captain said to himself. In her eyes there was the nagging of what lay at the depths of her melancholy, as always there was on a bad day. She tried to return his smile but could not and, too well, he knew she saw their child allowing the waves to have their way, without resistance because that was their child's choice. His intuition was sharp on bad days; he always knew. His denial of her dread was in the pressure of his fingers, but there was no acknowledgement, no flutter of life in the hand he had reached out for and still held, no sign that this time he had succeeded in dispelling the worst that might have been.

A yellow dog crossed the piazza, the only creature there but for the bandsmen and the waiter and the occupants of a single pavement table. The waiter had loosened the stud beneath his black bow tie. Skinny and seeming ravenous, the dog scattered the contents of a waste-bin. No more than weekend musicians lazily playing their opera arias, the white-uniformed bandsmen had acquired a strut of arrogance in how they played now, as if already they marched through conquered lands.

'*Va' via! Va' via!*' the old waiter shouted at the dog. '*Caffè, signore?*'

'*Si. Per favore.*'

He loved her, more than he could ever have loved anyone, but today, as so often before, she made on her own the effort he could not help her with. How long would it be before Italy was no longer a country to find refuge in? Calmly she asked that.

He shook his head. Somewhere there was cheering and when it ceased a voice echoed through the loudspeakers, noisily excited, its message often punctuated by what might have been the smack of a fist on a palm. *Morte! Sangue! Vittoria! Vittorioso!* The same exhortations were repeated, like punctuation also. Across the piazza the yellow dog was scratching out its fleas.

'Yes, Italy soon may not want us, either,' he said, and thought again how much he loved her. They lay in one another's arms, they talked, she read out to him something she liked in a book, they were companions on their journeys; and yet on days like this one, she belonged only to herself.

'Please don't ask me to go back,' she whispered, her tone so soft, so much without expression, that the words were hardly there.

8

When Ralph had twice again visited Lahardane on Wednesday afternoons, when he had been shown the house, had gone from room to room, had seen the books in the several bookcases, the bagatelle in a corner of the drawing-room, the billiard table on the upper landing, Lucy said:

'Won't you stay a while when you finish with the boys?'

'Stay here?'

'It's not as though there isn't room.'

It was the end of the first week in September when he finished his tutoring. On the evening before the day the boys were to return to school Mr Ryall paid what was owing, then carried Ralph's two suitcases to the car while Ralph said good-bye to Mrs Ryall and to the boys. On the way to Lahardane Mr Ryall said:

'It's good of you to befriend her.'

'It isn't befriending, really.'

'Well . . .'. And at Lahardane Mr Ryall said, 'I haven't seen you since you were a little girl of eight or nine, Lucy.'

She smiled, but did not say if she remembered that last occasion or not, and when the car had driven off she led the way up the wide stairs to the room that was to be Ralph's. It was square and spacious, with a mahogany wash-stand in one corner, a wardrobe and chest of drawers, a white quilt on the bed, darkly framed engravings of Glengarriff on all four walls. Its windows looked out over the fields where the cattle were, to the sea.

'Nothing'll happen,' Lucy warned, 'if you pull that bell knob.'

Bridget had brought the dining-room back into use for the visit, had aired it and polished the long dining-table, covering it with a tablecloth she had folded away years ago. There was an excitement in her hurrying about with trays and cutlery, her cheeks flushed, starched white aprons clean every day.

'Bridget enjoys a fuss,' Lucy said, and Ralph said he had noticed that.

He loved their mealtimes. When the dining-room door closed behind Bridget he imagined it would be like this if they were married. He loved everything about Lahardane, where it was, the house itself, going to the strand in the early morning, being shown the trees on which *L.G.* was carved. He loved it when they lay on the grass by the stream and when they crossed it on the stepping stones. He loved what she loved, as if it would be unnatural not to.

'I'll show you something else,' she said, and brought him to the ruined cottage high up in the glen. 'Henry'll tell you about Paddy Lindon.'

Ralph knew without being told that it was the place she had hobbled to as a child and he imagined her there, terrified and hungry and alone. He wanted to ask her about that time but could not, since she had never in any way referred to it except to mention her limp. When they were on the strand she talked about the nameless dog who'd run away again in the end, but didn't touch upon the part it had played in what had happened. When he turned the pages of the photograph album in the drawing-room he saw, through a brown mist, a couple standing by a pram among the apple trees. His scrutiny was more intent than it usually was when he paused at one of the album's photographs, but Lucy did not comment.

One day in the woods she suddenly said, 'We must go back,' as if she sensed his longing to hear what she might have said, as if she feared it. But the longing that had begun did not go away, and Ralph wondered if it would ever be more than longing, and wondered too if he would ever take her into his arms and touch with his lips her smooth, pale hair and her neck and her cheeks, her freckled arms and her forehead and closed eyes, her lips. He wondered if his wanting to would be all there ever was.

'You mustn't leave Lahardane,' she said, 'until you have finished *Vanity Fair*.'

'I haven't begun it yet.'

'When you've finished it we must talk about it. And that will take time, too.'

Sometimes when they walked, the backs of their hands brushed for a moment, or their palms met and were grasped as the stepping stones were crossed. There was a stone wall that was difficult and there was closeness then too.

'There are six hundred and forty-two pages,' she said.

*

They would not have met if he had not lost his way: Lucy tried to think of that, of their never meeting, of not knowing that Ralph existed. It seemed to her that he had come out of nowhere, and she wondered if when he left Lahardane he would return to nowhere and not come back. She would never forget him. All her life she would remember the Wednesday afternoons there had been, and the time that was passing now. And when she was old, if she began to believe that Ralph had been a figment, and this summer too, it would not matter because time turned memories into figments anyway.

'In all the world, Ralph, what would you wish for most?'

He stooped to pick up a pebble from the sand and skim it over the water. Twice, then three times, it touched the surface and bounced on. His manner was less shy now because, she supposed, he knew her better, or imagined he did. His feeling shy and his gentleness were what she liked about him.

'Oh, I suppose, you know, that every day was doing nothing.'

'That is something I have.'

'Then you are lucky.'

'I'll miss you when you go. I doubt you'll ever come back.'

'If I'm invited –'

'You have things to do.'

'What things have I to do?'

'Well, everything, when you think about it.'

They bathed, as they did twice every day, and then they walked to Kilauran. They clambered over the rocks to the pier. No one was about there or on the village street. Lucy said:

'That's where I went to school.'

They looked through one window and then the other. The shiny maps and charts still hung on the walls, with Mr Aylward's portraits of kings and queens, William the Conqueror, Queen Maeve, the Emperor Constantine. *Let x = 6* was the writing on the blackboard.

'Now I have shown you everything,' Lucy said.

That day Ralph kissed her. On the way back to Lahardane he reached out for her hand and clumsily drew her closer to him on the shingle at the bottom of the cliffs. They did not speak.

Afterwards they climbed up by the familiar jagged path. The potato crop in the O'Reillys' field had been harvested. Only the withering haulm lay about.

'I love you, Lucy,' Ralph said then. 'I am in love with you.'

She did not reply. She looked away, and after a moment said:

'Yes, I know.' She paused again. 'It's no good, loving one another.'

'Why isn't it?'

'I'm not someone to love.'

'Oh, Lucy, you are! If only you know how much you are!'

They had not stopped and did not now. Slowly they walked on, and when Ralph again reached for her hand Lucy didn't take it away. He said:

'I have loved you since the first time I came here. I have loved you more every instant I have known you. I never loved anyone before. I shall never love anyone else. I could not.'

'You didn't tell me you had finished *Vanity Fair*. We haven't talked about it. We must before you go.'

'I never want to go. I never want to be without you, all my life.'

*

Ralph knew when Lucy shook her head that it was not in denial of what he'd said, that it was not a way of doubting the passion in his tone and in his eyes. She shook her head in protestation at the folly of his unbridled hope: none of this could be, her wordless response reiterated, repeating in that manner her statement that she was not someone to love.

'You're the first friend I've had, Ralph. I haven't made friends as other people do. Or as people in novels do.'

'I would do anything for you.'

'Tell me more about where you live, the house and everything else. So that I know, when you have gone.'

'Oh, Lucy, it's just ordinary!'

'Tell me all the same.'

Confused and unhappy, Ralph did so. He described the house and, beyond the bridge he could see from the windows of his bedroom, Logan's Bar and Stores, where hardware was sold as well as groceries. He had never assumed he would do anything other than inherit the sawmills and go on living in that two-storey roadside house, creeper-covered and compact. In a field near the bridge there was some kind of abbey, not much of it left.

'How much?'

'Only a tower, or part of one. Hardly anything else.'

'What a pity that is!'

'I think there are monks' graves as well. So people say.'

'Do you go there, Ralph?'

'There's nothing much to go for.'

'To look for the graves.'

'No, I don't do that.'

'I would.'

'Lucy –'

'Do they know you in Logan's Stores?'

'Know me?'

'Know who you are.'

'They have always seen me about.'

'Tell me about your boarding-school.'

'Oh, Lucy –'

'Please tell me. Please, Ralph.'

'There were two.' And Ralph described the first, where he was homesick: the grey house in a Dublin square, crocodile walks through empty streets on Sundays, the cabbage soup.

'It couldn't have been cabbage soup. You can't have cabbage soup.'

'We called it that.'

'And did you have it at the next school too?'

'The next one was better. I didn't mind it.'

'Why didn't you?'

'I don't know.'

'Tell me about it. Tell me everything.'

'It was outside Dublin, in the mountains. We wore gowns. Scholars wore special ones, more voluminous.'

'Were you a scholar?'

'Oh, no.'

'What were you good at?'

'Nothing much. They wouldn't remember me there now.'

'Did you play games?'

'We had to.'

'What were you good at?'

'I wasn't bad at tennis.'

'Is that why you didn't hate that school so much?'

'Yes, perhaps. Did you mind my kissing you?'

'We must go in now. No, I didn't mind.'

★

The meal Henry sat down to every evening in the kitchen was similar to his breakfast and always the same: fried eggs and fried bread, a rasher of bacon. Tea accompanied it, which Henry took strong and sweet and milky.

On the evening of the day when Ralph had confessed his love nothing was different about this meal except what was said during it. An hour ago Henry had noticed a change in Ralph's manner, and Lucy's too, when they passed through the yard. They'd been abashed, affected by what was clearly a privacy between them, neither saying much. Henry wondered if there had been a quarrel;

113

but Bridget, who later caught that same mood also, had several times noticed Ralph's glance across the table in the dining-room and had surmised the nature of his feelings: the difference now would be that he had spoken of them.

In the kitchen Bridget passed this speculation on, at a loss when she tried to guess what would happen next. Their visitor would leave Lahardane and the autumn days would shorten as the season gave way to winter. Christmas would go by, the worst of the weather in the first months of the new year. Would he come back to Enniseala when another summer came? Would he again be here, at Lahardane? Or would time, fickle in its arrangements, slip him away from them?

There were often moments at Lahardane when Bridget would still have comforted Lucy, as she had comforted her in her infancy, as she had in her childhood. Always so close and yet not close at all, there was the solitary figure reading by lamplight or in the apple orchard, or wandering alone in the woods of the glen and on the seashore, her friends a stout solicitor and an elderly clergyman. When a letter arrived in the house there still was expectation, still a hope, but only for the instant before the envelope was scrutinized. The envelope always told.

'You're right enough,' Henry agreed, nodding each word into place, his hindsight stirred by Bridget's perceptions. He finished his tea and pushed his cup away. 'And it's maybe not a bad thing at the heel of the hunt.'

Clearing the table of dishes, Bridget was not surprised to hear this: she'd known that sooner or later she would. But she did not respond to the change of sentiment in her husband, for what could be said except to repeat what already she had herself declared? What had come about this summer was where hope flickered now.

'They're lost to her,' she said. 'Even if they'd come back tomorrow.'

Saving a match, Henry lit his Woodbine with a spill from the range. He did not know his feelings were that of a father, was aware only that he felt protective of the Captain's child and, as a father might be, suspicious of a stranger's fondness. Yet while Ralph had been staying in the house Henry had continued to like him more than he had at first. And in saying that what had happened was not a bad thing he had meant more than the assertion stated. It was not bad that the Captain's child should be taken from this place, separated at last from the dark that clung to it.

*

It rained in the night and all the next day. They played bagatelle, and Lucy began the conversation she wanted to have about *Vanity Fair*. Then they played bagatelle again. Ralph said:

'I love you, Lucy.'

Lucy did not remind him that he had told her so already and more than once. Gently she stroked with her fingertips the back of his hand. She stroked his hair.

'Dear Ralph,' she whispered, 'you must not love me.'

'I cannot help it.'

'One day, when you marry, will you write and tell me? So that I know and can imagine that too. And will you write when each child is born? And tell me your wife's name and give some slight description of her? So that I can always see you and your wife, and children, in that house beside the sawmills. Will you promise, Ralph?'

'It's you I want to marry.'

'You'll forget me. You'll forget this summer. It will fade and turn into shadows, and voices will be murmurs you cannot hear. Now – this present as we sit here – is a reality that will not last and is not meant to. You'll see this room no more clearly than I see the faces described to me in novels. You'll dream of Lahardane, Ralph, once in a while, or perhaps you never will. But if you do I'll be a ghost by then.'

'Lucy –'

'Oh, I shall dream of you, of all the times you came here, of these days that are passing now, of this very moment when bagatelle has bored us because we have played too long, of my saying in the moment that comes next, "Shall we play Twenty-one instead?"'

'Why do you say I must not love you?'

'Because loving me will make you unhappy.'

'But it doesn't. It makes me happy.'

'Shall we play Twenty-one? It's going to go on raining.'

'We could walk in the rain. At least on the avenue.'

The trees sheltered them a little. The air was fresh; delicious air, Lucy called it. They dawdled on the avenue, and dawdled again, standing in the porch of the gate-lodge.

'Of course I love you too,' Lucy said. 'If you are wondering about that.'

*

Bridget lit a fire in the drawing-room, feeling that something cheerful must be done. The rain was heavier now, drops rolling down the windows, and then the first gusts of wind made its falling different. The wind was slight when it began, but within an hour had changed the character of the day. It brought the leaves down, swirling them about before they became sodden and still. It rattled the hall door and the windows. It drove sheets of rain against the panes, disrupting the drops that had earlier accumulated, before sliding monotonously down the glass. The sea would be a sight, Henry said.

In the drawing-room they made toast at the fire, poking their slices of bread into the red ashes of the logs. They sat on the hearthrug, reading. 'Who's that?' Ralph asked about the only portrait in the room, above the writing-desk, and Lucy said it was some Gault she didn't know about. She wound up the gramophone, then put a record on. John Count McCormack sang 'Down by the Salley Gardens'.

They went to look at the sea, the wind so strong now that they could scarcely hear one another speak. The waves reared up like wild white horses, spectral forms exploding into foam, one chasing another as they broke. The thrash and crash of the sea sucked in the wind's whine, a seashore sound that belonged nowhere else.

When the two embraced at the sea's edge, each tasted the salt on the other's lips. Drenched, Lucy's hair was straggly and matted, Ralph's pressed tight on to his scalp. The excitement of the storm held them in thrall, as completely as their love did. Would there ever again in her life, Lucy wondered, be such happiness as this?

'How can we forget today?' she whispered and was not heard.

'I could never not love you,' Ralph said, and this was lost as well.

They dried themselves in front of the drawing-room fire. Bridget brought in a tray, since it was warmer here than in the dining-room. Seeing them happy, she remembered that in a few days Ralph would be gone. She did not pray; it was not a subject for prayer. Instead, she willed a time in the future and saw them smiling in one room and then another, and heard them speaking of love, and saw them together always.

'Look, it's tinned salmon!' Lucy cried.

It would have been on Henry's list for Mrs McBride, John West's red salmon, a treat because it was expensive. And there were the tiny, sweet tomatoes that Henry cultivated in the cold frame he had resurrected a few years ago. They made a salad, with lettuce and little onions, and slices of hard-boiled egg.

'Shall we have wine?' Lucy suggested. 'White wine? I think I've never tasted wine except the bitter red in church.'

She went away and a moment later returned with a bottle and two glasses. There were many bottles left, she said, red and white, untouched on the pantry racks.

'Look in all the drawers for a corkscrew. Somewhere there is one. Oh, now nice this is!'

They pulled two chairs up to a table they moved closer to the fire. Ralph poured the wine and he wanted, then, not ever to leave this house he had come to. He wanted, then, not to take Lucy from it but to be here with her, since she belonged here and tonight he felt he did also. On the gramophone the needle scratched through the Londonderry Air.

*

Two fishermen from Kilauran were lost at sea that night, caught earlier by the sudden storm when they had pulled their nets in and were beginning to row home. There was mourning in the village, a melancholy that affected Lucy when she and Ralph walked there on the day before he was to leave. The sound of keening came from a cottage around which people had congregated. A fiddler had come, to play a dirge if one was called for.

'How could I have run away from them?' Lucy said on the strand as she and Ralph walked back to Lahardane, with wicks for the lamps and the newspaper they'd bought. 'I made them suffer as those women are suffering now. I long for their forgiveness. That will not just go away.'

These revelations came suddenly, and Ralph did not say anything as they walked on.

'I was in love then, too – with trees and rock pools and footprints on the sand. Was I possessed, Ralph? I have always thought I was.'

'Of course you weren't.'

'Like poor Mrs Rochester! Whom nobody had sympathy for!'

'You were a child.'

'A child can be possessed. Did I hate them when I made them suffer? Was that why so very soon I was ashamed?'

'Please, will you marry me, Lucy?'

Slowly, she shook her head. 'My father shot a man and did not kill him. My mother was afraid. I did not understand. Shall I tell you, Ralph?'

And he listened and was told what he knew already, and saw what so often he had seen: the figures on the shingle and the sands, the light brought from the house, darkness giving way to dawn.

'I have found a little courage,' Lucy said.

'You are courageous, Lucy.'

'Dear Ralph, how could I marry you?'

Her lips reached up for his and lightly touched them. The sea was as calm as a pond, waves softly breaking. The sky was a deeper blue than it had been all this hot summer. White, bunched-up clouds hardly moved on it.

'I don't care about what you did. I swear I don't, Lucy.'

'I have to live with it until they return.'

'No, no, of course you don't.'

'You must go back to your contented life. Not be a visitor in mine. For you could only be that, Ralph, although I love you. When we love one another we are stealing what does not belong to us, what is not our due. Darling Ralph, we must make do with memories.'

'We need not and I cannot. I cannot make do with memories.'

'Oh, memories aren't bad, you know.'

'They're nothing.' There was an edge of bitterness in his tone. They walked in silence then, until he said:

'I wouldn't take you from Lahardane if you don't want to go.'

She seemed not to hear. She drew with the point of her shoe on the sand. She looked up when their names were written. She said:

'What do they think, Ralph, and do not say? Why do they not come back?'

But when Ralph began to answer he felt that what he said was hardly heard, and so desisted. They walked on slowly, and Lucy said:

'I did not hate them, yet how do they know it, any more than they know all they so easily might? One day – today, tomorrow, some day a year away – they'll find the strength to make the journey, and it will never be too late for that.'

'Oh, Lucy, long ago they have forgiven you and now would want your happiness. Of course they have forgiven you.'

'Memories can be everything if we choose to make them so. But you are right: you mustn't do that. That is for me, and I shall do it. I shall live a life that is all memory of our love. I shall close my eyes and feel again your lips on mine and see your smiling face as clearly as every day I see the waves. What friends we've been, Ralph! How we've longed for this summer not to end! Another summer would be different – we both know that.'

'I don't know it. I don't believe it for a moment.'

'I wish it could always be there, stopped in time, this summer we have had. Don't let's be greedy now. I used to be afraid of their returning. Sometimes I used to think I didn't want them to, for what good to them was my awful, sore regret? There was too much for them to forgive: how could I hope for forgiveness? Yet if they came now, if they were there when we climbed the cliff, if they were astonished while Bridget told them, how marvellous it would be! And you and I would not make do with memories.'

Two days later Ralph left, taken by Henry in the trap to the railway station in Enniseala. Lucy might have accompanied them, might have stood waving on the railway platform as the train took Ralph away. But she said she didn't want that, and waved instead from the hall door, and then from the avenue.

THREE

I

Prayer continued to be the solace of the man who had become a soldier. But his expectation that the rigours and severity and the communal nature of military life would discipline his confusion had been denied. When his mother lay dying he had thought to share his trouble with her, for as things were she would have passed it on to no one. But each time he tried to he was seized by panic, fearful of eavesdroppers he knew could not be there.

He was an old hand at the Camp now, his hollow countenance and the intensity of his averted gaze familiar to all who came and went around him. Some had carried to other Camps a description of his lanky, quiet presence, had spoken of his strangeness, his regular, lone attendance before the chapel statue. He had made no friends, but in his duties was conscientious and persevering and reliable, known for such qualities to the officers who commanded him. He had dug latrines, metalled roads, adequately performed cookhouse duties, followed instructions as to the upkeep of equipment, was the first to volunteer when volunteers were called for. That he bore his torment with fortitude was known to no one.

In such a manner further years of Horahan's life went by. When rumours of war in Europe began he was aware of anxiety and uncertainty at the Camp, but that mood did not concern him. There was talk of invasion. In preparation for what might occur in the years ahead, sandbags and other equipment of defence made their appearance. On occasion, the hours of training were longer.

Horahan fell in with this hastily arranged regimen. Hardly knowing the reason for it, he was obedient to all that was required of him, and questioned nothing. By day, instead, a funeral that was repeated in his sleep possessed him. The hearse passed through the streets of the town he knew and, when he had himself dug the grave, the clay closed in on top of him. He lay beside the coffin, but when the child called out from within it he could not reach her.

In the town he asked about the house that in his dreaming blazed and was destroyed. He was told, yet again, that it had never been set on fire, that the child who was dead in his dreams had been left solitary by her parents, the victim of an error. But still there was the funeral, the hearse drawn through familiar streets, the horse hooves echoing; still he awoke, his body wet with sweat. He rose often in the night from his narrow cot to creep through the darkness, his feet still bare. In the chapel, where he dared not light a candle, he knelt before the Virgin he could not see, begging for the gift of a sign, a whisper of assurance that he was not abandoned.

2

Captain Gault and his wife left Italy. Unreliable portents had kept them for longer than the Captain had anticipated: embracing his people with the warmth of his promises and his architecture, Benito Mussolini declared himself for peace. But when he had mulled that over he decided it would be more advantageous to declare himself for war.

They crossed the frontier into Switzerland, going back the way they had come, seventeen years ago now. They went regretfully, taking with them as many of their possessions as they could manage. They settled in the modest town of Bellinzona, where the language they had become used to was spoken.

3

We often think of you, Mrs Ryall wrote, *and wonder how you are. How many times have I said, 'Today I shall write to Ralph', and yet again do not do it! But then there is always something – when the boys are here the house is upside-down, when they are not there is jam to make and something for them to take with them when they go away again. They are growing up more sensible than you'll remember them. Quite lanky now, Kildare is, quite the young man! Jack wants to be a horticulturist, though I believe myself it is just the word he likes! Both of them speak of you often, and we are grateful for the months you spent here. Lucy Gault, whom you'll remember, I'm sure, is still at Lahardane. There has been no change there. All of us here are well.*

★

It was nice of you to write, Ralph replied, *and I am glad to hear the boys are settling down. I do not forget your kindness to me and often think about those long warm mornings in the garden. Do please remember me to Mr Ryall, and to the boys when next they're home. Perhaps one day our paths will somehow cross again. It's good to hear that all of you are well.*

He could not imagine the Ryalls otherwise. He could not imagine them unhappy or dispirited. They would have known, of course, that he had not been back to Lahardane.

★

I have found another book, Lucy wrote. *'Florence Macarthy' by Lady Morgan. I didn't think it would be good. But it is far better than I could have guessed.*

Yesterday there were cormorants on the rocks. I thought of you

particularly then because – do you remember? – we watched them one
afternoon. How long ago it seems, our summer, and in another moment
seems hardly any time at all!

And often Lucy read, for yet another time, the first of all Ralph's
letters since he had gone.

. . . I add up figures and lose my way in them. I look down through the
paned glass of an office to the hubbub of activity below and in my
melancholy feel its mockery. What does it matter if the machinery rattles
on or stops? What does it matter if the elm is only fit for coffins or that
the oak has warped while seasoning? The belts are tightened on their
wheels, the cogs connect. I watch a tree trunk carried into place, planks
lifted away when they are sawn. Sunlight catches the dust in the air, the
men are silenced by the engines' clatter. You stand in white in the wide
doorway. You wave and I wave back. But how little comfort there is in
the ghosts of daydreams!

Always she touched that letter with her lips before she tied it
away with the others that had come. It was not difficult to see the
scene described, to hear the machinery's noise, to smell the freshly
sawn wood. *I have been a nuisance to you,* she read as well. *I have*
disturbed the vigil you keep. I blame myself for hours on end and then do
not blame myself at all. Do you know how much I love you, Lucy? Can
you possibly guess?

One day they would not write, Lucy supposed, for all of it was
repetition now. *Ralph, you must live your life,* she wrote herself.

*

In wrenching off the worn sole of a boot, Henry found it did not
come cleanly, held by a few remaining brads, which he loosened with pliers. Some time in the past, well before his own time
at Lahardane, a Gault had gone in for shoe-making. All the tools,
the knives and the last, were still in the outhouse that even then
had been a workshop. Leathers still hung there, and on a shelf

beside them were tins of brads, metal half-heels, cobbler's thread.

Twice before, Henry had repaired the boots he was repairing now. He had taught himself the knack of this work, guessing at first what each knife was for, eventually finding that the skill required came naturally, with patience. Cutting a new sole, he found himself reflecting, as he often did, on how it would be now if this remote house had been forgotten in the vengeance of 1921, if a threat in the night had not engendered such fear and such distress. Another man, different in nature and temperament from the Captain, might not have heeded the nervous premonitions of his wife, might have dismissed them as unwarranted and foolish, might not have considered it a wife's place to be upset. That three callow youths, hardly knowing what they were doing in their excitement, had exercised such power still seemed to Henry to be extraordinary.

He trimmed the edge of the leather until the sole perfectly fitted the boot, then cut the second one. The time he'd made Lucy a pair of shoes they hadn't been comfortable, but she hadn't said. 'Arrah, throw those old things away,' he'd urged her when he noticed she was hobbling, but she wouldn't. When he had been against her marrying that boy, when he had been against the friendship, he hadn't understood what Bridget had, she being quicker than he was in ways like that. 'It's the lonesomeness would worry you,' Bridget had said.

It worried both of them now. The letters that were exchanged were what was left, but the postman's bicycle, free-wheeling on the last few yards of the avenue, scattering the gravel pebbles in front of the house, came less frequently now, sometimes for months on end not at all. One day, when it had not been for almost the whole of one winter, Henry saw a distant figure on the strand and wondered who it was. He saw the same figure again, much later and at a different time of year. It might have been anyone, for Henry was not one to rush to conclusions, but when he told Bridget she said of course it wasn't anyone. Henry watched, but the solitary visitor did not return, and a day came then which seemed – for

128

Henry at least – to bring to an end all that had begun when, years ago now, Mr Ryall's Renault had first tentatively appeared between the two stately lines of the avenue's trees. 'She says he's after joining up,' Bridget reported when the war in Europe began and, to Henry's confusion and surprise, she added that it was an ill wind that blew no good. For couldn't it happen, Bridget argued, that the separation, and the danger there'd be, would straighten things out? Wasn't it often the case when a man came back safely from a war that there was a different way of looking at things?

Henry tapped the second sole into place and filed down the leather instep. Not saying so, he had dismissed these prognostications at first as the wishful thinking to which Bridget was prone; but there was no doubt about it, this was an outcome that yet might come about. The young fellow would come back, and in the relief he brought with him the question would be asked: where was the sense of waiting any longer for what would not occur? It would be Lucy then who would say close the house up, as her father had before. Stored away were the window boards Henry had taken down, and none the worse for that. One of these days he'd fix the slates on the roof of the gate-lodge so that he and Bridget could go back to where they belonged. With the doors and windows open, he'd get rid of the damp that had begun there and slap on a bit of paint where it was needed. He'd dig over the patch at the back. When the time came he'd secure the packing-cases that had never been sent for, and Bridget would find new sheets to put over the furniture. No matter how things happened, Henry guessed this would be what Lucy would want when the marriage was fixed, before she was taken away to County Wexford. As Bridget herself said, something in you knew when a thing was meant.

Henry darkened the leather where it showed, and stitched into one of the boots a new tongue, which he darkened also. Children would be born, Bridget said, and now and again they'd be brought to look at the old house, calling in at the gate-lodge on the way. One by one Henry stowed away the tools he'd used, on the rack above his workbench. He reached down his polishing rags from a nail in the wall and smeared polish on to the leather, taking his time, since he had plenty of it.

*

The war that Ralph had gone to fight in impinged on Ireland's chosen neutrality. The precautions against invasion that had already been put in hand at the army Camp near Enniseala became general throughout the country, while armies advanced in Europe and distant cities were bombed. A nightly blackout was enforced; gas masks were issued; there was instruction in the use of the stirrup pump. Familiarly known as the Emergency, the war brought short- ages – of petrol, of paraffin for the lamps that still illuminated Lahardane and houses like it, of tea and coffee and cocoa, of clothes made in England. Crops that had not been cultivated before – fields of sugarbeet and tomatoes – were grown. More wood and turf were burnt. Bread was less white.

Every day Lucy walked to Kilauran to buy an *Irish Times* and read about what was happening. Parts of the few letters she now received from Ralph were blackly smudged out, or so cut away by the army censors that both sides of a page were de- prived: for any information that was available, or permitted, she relied on reports in which death was spelt out in numbers – in the count of Spitfires that did not return, in the casualties of evacuation and retreat. And she knew that there were losses left unmentioned and uncalculated. Every Sunday evening on the wireless she had bought for the drawing-room there was the playing of the Allies' national anthems, now and again a new one added, and that at least was cheerful.

But cheerfulness was brief. For Lucy, on the strand and in the woods, Ralph's features were as death had arrested them, his limbs gone rigid, the sprawl of his body awkward. Someone had pressed his eyelids down over his unseeing stare, and then passed on. Dirt was thick on the uniform she had never seen.

These images haunted her until another letter came to contradict

130

them, another brief reprieve before her fears began again. It was then, when reassurance had been too temporary a dozen times, that Bridget's intuition became Lucy's resolve. If Ralph returned she would go to him as soon as she heard.

4

'*Signore! Signore!*' the caretaker called up the staircase. '*Il dottore . . .*'

The Captain called back, and then there were the doctor's footsteps on the stairs.

'*Buongiorno, signore.*'

'*Buongiorno, dottor Lucca.*'

The Captain made coffee while he waited. Outside, it was still freezing, the coldest winter they had known in Bellinzona for a generation, so it was said. From the window he watched people going to work, to the post-bus depot, to the clock factory to keep the machinery turning over in case it became defective through lack of use: during Switzerland's isolation in the war years there had not been much trade in fancy clocks. The baker who had a short left leg stomped back in his lopsided manner from his night's work, his overcoat pulled close around him. The road-clearers dug their spades into the snow.

'If she does not wish to live,' the doctor said in Italian, 'she will not live.'

He said it again, less confidently, in English. The Captain understood both times. It was what dottor Lucca always said. Less than five minutes his examination had taken and the Captain wondered if, this time, the stethoscope had even been taken from his bag.

'My wife has influenza,' he said, speaking in Italian also.

'*Sì, signore, sì.*'

They drank a cup of coffee together, still standing. The influenza was an epidemic now, the doctor said; hardly a house in the neighbourhood did not have a case. In the circumstances the spread of any epidemic was understandable and must be expected. The melancholy of *la signora* was a more pressing matter, more serious.

'It is the truth, *signore*. With illness as well, to make a complication . . .'

'I know.'

The doctor shook hands before he left. He was a humane man, who charged little for his services, who wished only that all his patients might recover from their ailments and be happy in their good health. Life, he never tired of reminding them in a sensible Swiss way, was short, even when it went on a bit.

'*Grazie, dottore. Grazie.*'

'*Arrivederci, signore.*'

He left behind the prescription he left for everyone. It would bring the temperature down and clear the headache. He instructed the Captain to keep his wife warm.

The hopelessness in dottor Lucca's eyes remained with Everard Gault after the doctor had gone. He made a jug of weak tea and carried a cup of it to the bedroom. During the many years that had passed since their exile began, he and Heloise had become used to making tea in a jug, no teapot being supplied either in Italy or in Switzerland, and they had never bought one.

'Let it cool a minute,' Heloise requested when he pressed the cup on her. It was a cup with a motif of leaves and blue flowers, one of the two they had brought from Montemarmoreo and which had always reminded the Captain of the hydrangeas at Lahardane. He had often, at first, regretted the reminder and had considered putting these cups and saucers away, pushing them to the back of a cupboard, but then it seemed absurd that he should indulge a weakness, so he resisted the urge.

'Do you think Montemarmoreo's St Cecilia survived the war?' Heloise murmured while they waited for the tea to cool.

Often, aloud, she wondered that. In the church of Santa Cecilia there had been Montemarmoreo's single image of the saint the town honoured. Had that been lost in rubble, violently destroyed, as the saint herself had been?

'I would not have known that St Cecilia had ever existed if we had not come to Italy.'

'Yes, there's that.' He smiled, and held the cup out, raising it to her lips. But nothing was drunk from it.

'I would not have stood before Piero della Francesca's Risen Christ.' Her voice had weakened to a whisper that was scarcely audible. 'Or Fra Angelico's Annunciations. Or Carpaccio's terrified monks.'

The Captain, who often didn't remember what was so easily remembered by his wife, held her hand by the bedside and sat with her a while longer. They were the marvels in her life, she said after a moment, and slept then, suddenly falling into a doze.

The Captain pulled the bedclothes up to keep her warm and settled her among her pillows. She did not wake while there was this attention, nor did the trace of a smile that had touched her lips when she'd spoken of Carpaccio's monks slip away. Disposing of the tea she hadn't drunk, he wondered if she was dreaming of them.

When he left the room he closed the door softly behind him and stood for a moment in case there was anything to listen for, then moved away when there was not. How little difference it made to his love that at the heart of his wife's every day there had been for so long the dread she had been unable not to nourish: the reflection was a familiar one as Captain Gault drew on his overcoat and gloves and set out on his habitual afternoon walk. For nearly a month, ever since the illness had begun, he had been solitary in this. People he met and who knew him enquired about his wife, assuring him that she would be better soon, since that was so in other instances of the local influenza.

The air had not yet thawed and did not as the afternoon wore on. He remembered the day of their wedding, how she had laughed away the disapproval of her aunt, and someone he didn't know seeking him out to say how lucky he was. In all the time since, he had never believed he'd been anything less. Their lives, conventionally joined that day with words, were locked together now, impossible to separate. He turned back soon, for he could not leave her long, although always she begged him to. Frost still glistened in the lamplight when it came on. In the café by the church he had a brandy and felt the better for it.

'My dear,' he murmured from the doorway of the sick-room when he returned, and knew before he went to her that she would not reply.

*

All that night the Captain wept, wishing he could be with her, no matter where she was. His shoulders heaved, his sobs were sometimes noisy, and between his bouts of grieving he went again to stare at the features he had loved for so long. He had been faithful in his marriage, never wishing to be otherwise, and he remembered how often Heloise had said she was happy – even during their last years together, here in Bellinzona, and before that in Montemarmoreo and on their excursions to Italy's cities and busy towns. She had made herself as happy as she could be, and it seemed not to matter how she had done it. In mourning her, the good moments came back, the pleasures, her laughter and his own, their discovery of one another when first they were married, when love was untouched by shadows. And there was now a blankness as empty as the snow on the streets.

'How steadfast you were!' the Captain murmured, reaching again into the past, the time he had had to leave the army. He had known it then, but he knew it differently tonight: so quietly and so gently, with such self-effacement, she had supplied the strength for both of them. She had demanded no acknowledgement of that, would have denied it as absurd. Yet that truth from so long ago was what, more vividly than all the rest, she left behind.

He remained by the bedside until the next day was well advanced, until bleak winter daylight settled again over the mountains and the town. Then he made the arrangements for the funeral.

*

When the coffin had been lowered, words in English were softly spoken. Heloise Gault was buried among stern Swiss graves, some decorated with artificial lilies beneath domes of glass, some with a photograph of the deceased on a polished granite stone. Among them, one day, there would be recorded also a stranger's death.

People who felt they had known this English woman a little, who had liked her in that distant way, attended the occasion in the church, a few going on to the cemetery. 'Bella, bella,' a woman whispered to the widower, not having to explain: his wife had been beautiful even as she aged, even when the blur of wearying pain had come into her eyes. In mentioning only beauty, the woman comforted more than she knew.

*

. . . for I believe you were Heloise's only remaining relative of any closeness. Influenza, with complications, was too much for someone who was no longer young. All of it was peaceful.

But Heloise's aunt had died herself. The Captain's letter was received by her long-time companion and the inheritor of her property and possessions. To Miss Chambré, that a niece existed or did not was neither here nor there. She reread what had been written before tearing the single sheet of paper into small, square pieces and dropping them into the fire.

5

On a grey December morning when a letter from Ralph again came with an Irish stamp, Lucy learnt that one of his wartime barracks had been in Cheshire, another in Northamptonshire. Modestly he recounted what the army censors had removed: he had fought in Africa, he had been present when the garrisons were captured on Corfu. His pleas, which had not ceased from wherever he'd found himself, were renewed from County Wexford.

But Lucy's promise to herself, lasting fearfully for so long, faltered: that Ralph was safe drew tears of gratitude from her when she saw his handwriting on the envelope with its safe Irish stamp. Not at once but gradually, over days, her good intentions were washed away in a continuing sea of relief. The war had everywhere spread change; all over Europe, all over the world, nothing was the same. Was it not likely that the hiatus in her parents' lives had run its course, that six years of war, and the peace that had come, were enough to bring them back to an Ireland in which there had been change also, which had itself been peaceful for a generation? She heard their voices as she remembered them. She saw the suitcases that had been bought in Enniseala, the shiny leather scuffed and battered now, clothes folded, already packed. *My heart is not stone,* she wrote to Ralph, begging him to understand. *And oh how happy I am that you are no longer in danger! I think of you in all the places you have told me of and now at last at home again.* But afterwards, when she had posted it, she thought that letter sounded false; and it was too much, the reference to her heart. She wrote again to say she had been overwrought.

'Ah, but you couldn't know,' Henry consoled his wife when Bridget's intuition failed with the failure of Lucy's promise to herself. Bridget said nothing. She might have spoken to Lucy, might have touched upon her own misplaced optimism as to the beneficial debris of war, might have spoken of Ralph's devotion, of the warmth of the companionship there had been, of the letters that had kept a friendship going. But nervous of doing more harm than good, she said nothing.

When the last of Ralph's letters came, Lucy didn't know it was the last. But mulling it over when another did not arrive, she discovered in it a mood she had earlier missed, a meaning in statements and declarations that was imprecise, as if the wording had been reluctant to be otherwise; as if, beneath the ordinariness of what was related, despair was spelt out too, a futility at last accepted. A single line from her would have changed what could so easily be changed. That she felt betrayal within herself for not honouring love which had grown more intense with her fear for Ralph's safety was a confession that was his due, and might be added to that single line. In fairness it belonged there; yet it seemed like betrayal, too, to lose faith with the hope that war and its ending might allow. Her insistence, again, that Ralph must not muddle his life with her distorted one was as painful as it had been before. That she felt she must trust some twist of fate – that all there was was fate – seemed hardly an explanation she could offer, and she did not do so.

A new generation of summer visitors in Kilauran glimpsed from time to time a solitary woman on the strand or among the rocks, and heard with pity the story that still was told. They did not condemn, as a previous generation of strangers had, a wayward child whose capriciousness had brought it all about. The wayward child belonged to the immediacy of the occurrence; what strangers made of past events was influenced in the present by the observation of a lonely life. Lucy herself was aware that this opinion was as temporary as the one that anger and distaste had once created: the story had not yet passed into myth, and would not be cast in permanence until her life was over, until it was reflected in time's cold light. It did not greatly interest her that she was talked about.

She took up petit-point embroidery, discovering she had a natural skill for it when she began to teach herself the stitches. The silks, and the linen she decorated with them, came by post from a Dublin shop, Ancrin's, which specialized in domestic crafts. She had found one of their catalogues, sent for by her mother, forgotten in the pages of *The Irish Dragoon*. Between the two long windows of the first-floor landing there was a framed embroidery of a turkey on pale grey cloth, which very faintly she remembered her mother stitching. 'It pained her eyes,' Bridget said. 'She gave up the embroidering after the turkey.'

Ancrin's sent linens with designs already marked on them, but Lucy preferred to ignore what was suggested in that way. The first embroidery she attempted was of the pear tree in the yard, the second of the crossing stones she and her father had arranged at the shallow part of the stream, another of the pinks that thrived on the cliffs. In time, she knew, there would be Paddy Lindon's cottage, entirely a ruin now.

'Well, I never!' Mr Sullivan exclaimed with genuine admiration, seeing this work for the first time. 'My! My!' Recently retired from his legal practice, he had resumed his visits to Lahardane, petrol again being available. Canon Crosbie – though now in his late eighties – was still active in Church matters, but corresponded instead of making the journey.

Mr Sullivan, also, remembered Heloise Gault stitching the speckled feathers of the turkey, its scarlet head and gobbly throat. But he kept that to himself, for the display spread out for him on the dining-room table – the pear-tree embroidery complete now, the stepping-stones just begun – made the occasion Lucy's own. If something had developed in her friendship with Ralph – whom he had known on the streets of Enniseala in much the same way as Canon Crosbie had – Mr Sullivan might at last have begun to consider Lucy as more than a child. But his outsider's eye saw Lahardane, and the small household that had come about there, as something petrified, arrested in the drama there had been. Lucy was stilled too, a detail as in one of her own embroidered compositions.

'We must have them framed,' he said, taking off the reading

glasses through which he had been peering at the intricate stitching.

'It's just a pastime.'

'Oh, but they're beautiful!'

'Well, they are something.'

'Things are easier, you know, now that the Emergency, thank God, is over. Goods are coming back in the shops. If ever you'd like a lift into Enniseala, Lucy, you've only to say.'

The rubber boots she went for walks in through the rain came from the general store in Kilauran. Once in a long while shoes were sent on approval from Enniseala. When the white summer dresses her mother had left behind had worn out, the dressmaker in Kilauran had begun to make her ones that were quite similar. The hairdresser who came to the village cut her hair.

'I manage well enough with Kilauran,' she said.

For Aloysius Sullivan she quite eerily resembled her mother, and not just because she wore the dresses. Often he was struck by intonations in her voice that startlingly recalled Heloise Gault's: it seemed as though in the early years of her life she had absorbed, and never forgotten, her mother's Englishness, an emphasis on certain syllables, a choice of phrase. 'Well, I am probably imagining that,' Mr Sullivan often remarked to himself, driving away after his visits. Yet the next time he closed his eyes and listened it was the same: he was listening to the Captain's wife.

'Please have this,' he was offered when again he admired the embroideries, and took away with him the one of the pear tree in the yard. He had it framed, and after that when another one was ready he took it in to Enniseala to be framed also, and returned it when next he visited.

On Thursday March the tenth 1949, he read in the *Irish Times* – as Lucy did too – that Ralph was to marry.

FOUR

I

Restless in Bellinzona, the Captain travelled. Because he knew it would sadden him, he had not returned to live again in Montemarmoreo, as he and Heloise had planned to when the war was over. Nor, for the same reason, had he revisited the cities of their many Italian journeys. At the end of the first year of being on his own, he went instead to France, disposing of his household possessions before he left Bellinzona, since he did not intend to come back: nostalgia dogged him there too. He arrived in Bandol when the mistral was blowing and took a room on the front.

When spring and summer had passed he moved on, to Valence and Clermont-Ferrand, to Orleans and Nancy. He found himself in landscape he half recognized, passed through towns and villages with names that had a familiar ring. In the war before the last one he had led his men through Maricourt. There was a recollection of emerging at night from a copse that ran along a railway line, of a farmhouse that was found to be deserted, the bread in the kitchen not yet stale, milk in a saucepan on the stove. They had slept there, in the farm sheds and in the house itself, marching on again when dawn came.

As a child, Everard Gault had imagined war, had invented for himself its discomforts and adventures, had been attracted by the formality and traditions of army life, inspired by tales of the Crusades. It was an inspiration compounded by his father's repeated return – always suddenly – to Lahardane; when the gleam of his boots, his wide leather belt, the rough material of the tunic that smelt so of tobacco, his deep, quiet voice, were again a presence in the drawing-room and the garden. The honour associated with his father's profession and with his father himself, and with the heroes of history books, had always attracted Everard. Later in his life he did not know – and never came to know – if he might privately claim honour as a quality in himself; or if other people considered him an honourable man. It was not a word his wife had used and he had never prompted her in that regard, had never confessed that the quality had influenced him in his choice of vocation or that he valued its possession. There was too much, the Captain considered now, they had not said. Because love nourished instinct, and instinct's short cuts and economies, too much had been too carelessly left.

All this occupied his thoughts when he revisited the places of his war. Tramping over soil fed by the blood of the men he had led and whose faces now stirred in his memory, it was his wife's response that came – as if in compensation for too little said before – when he wondered why his wandering had led him back to these old battlefields: in his sixty-ninth year he was establishing his survivor's status. He nodded that into place, feeling it to be true, and being a survivor was something at least, more than it seemed. He had been much less of a soldier than his father, was sure he had felt fear more often, was sure he had experienced less courage. It was a mockery that death for his father had not been marked with gallantry on a battlefield, but had crept in upon him through disease, the kind of domestic death that belonged to wives and children. Everard had been twenty then, had stood with his brother in the little graveyard at Kilauran while the three coffins were lowered. It was his brother who, years later, had brought Heloise to Lahardane, as his fiancée. 'Please write and tell him,' she had begged when first they decided to leave Ireland, and he had promised that he would. But during that unsettled time he had put off doing so and later, in Montemarmoreo, had procrastinated further, fearing that a letter would bring – as readily from India as from Ireland – a reply that would have to be suppressed. But everything of course was different now.

The next day he travelled on, to Paris. A woman stopped him as he was crossing the Place de la Concorde to ask the time. His French being uncertain, he displayed for her the face of the watch he took from his waistcoat. Smilingly she admired the watch and then his waistcoat, before drifting into conversation with him in English. She had been to Folkestone; she had been to London; she had lived for a time in Gerrards Cross; she was a *couturière*.

'Madame Vacelles,' she said, holding out a well-tended hand.

They went to a café, where Madame Vacelles drank absinthe. '*Vous êtes triste*,' she murmured, her ready smile for the moment subdued. 'You are in pain, monsieur.' It was a statement, although the tone implied a question, and he shook his head, not wishing to share his mourning with a stranger. He spoke instead of the war he had taken part in and of his experience of her country at that time, and playfully Madame Vacelles denied that he was old enough to have fought so long ago. In a friendly way she seized his arm, as if confident of finding beneath her grasp a young man's muscle.

The Captain returned with Madame Vacelles to her rooms, which were high up in a corner house, above a baker's. But when the moment the *couturière* had been waiting for arrived he apologized and shook his head. It disappointed him to have to go away, and so hastily. The drag of his solitude was not easy to overcome and the hour he had spent in Madame Vacelles's company had not been disagreeable. '*Cochon!*' she shouted after him, leaning dangerously over the banister.

That evening the Captain wrote to his brother. The detail of his letter was copious, the Irish side of things no doubt already known, for of course his brother would have heard.

> I wonder if Ireland is now a country you and I would recognize. I wonder if you have been back and know more about it – and Lahardane – than I do now. Ireland of the ruins I have heard it called, more ruins and always more.

He related a little of his feelings, and Heloise's, after the incident in the night. He wrote of the years in Italy, of Switzerland and the deprivations of the war, of Heloise's death. There had never been resentment that Heloise did not continue to return his brother's feelings, only disappointment; no one had been to blame, no bitterness lingered. *Well, there you are*, the Captain's lengthy missive ended. *I wonder how you are.*

There was nowhere to send that letter, no recent regimental address that would ensure its safe reception. The Captain kept it in his luggage, resolving when the opportunity arose to make enquiries about the fate of his brother's regiment following Indian independence. A month later he made the long journey to Vienna, for no other reason except that he had always hoped to see its grandeur one day. But what he saw was a broken city, its great buildings looming like spectres among the ruins, a brash night-life enlivening shabbiness and corruption. He did not stay long.

War had sucked the heart out of Europe: everywhere there was weary evidence of that. There had been too much death, too much treachery, too great a toll paid in the defeat of greed. He thought of Ireland, drained of its energy by centuries of disaffection, and the feeling he had experienced at the beginning of his exile came back – of punishment inflicted for those sins of the past to which his family might have contributed. Had it been greed that the Gaults had held their ground too long? While penal laws were passed there had been parties at Lahardane, prayers said in church for King and Empire, the aspirations of the dispossessed ignored. Had such aspirations at last been realized? Had Ireland in his absence remade itself, as Europe was doing now?

In Bruges he put up at a house that took in visitors, near the Groeningemuseum. Heloise had stayed in this town, had described the brick and grey stone of its buildings, its gilded figures and window displays of chocolate, its cafés and jaunting cars. She had talked about a tea-room that wasn't there any more, a convent lawn where a sign begged that the nuns should not be photographed. 'Oh, how I loved that little city!' Her voice floated through the Captain's musings as so often it did, and when, in Ghent, he looked up at the painting of the Adoration of the Lamb he imagined her as awestruck as he was now.

'You are English?' he was asked in his guest-house and for a moment he hesitated, not knowing in that moment what he was. Then he shook his head.

'No, I'm an Irishman.'

'Ah, Ireland! How beautiful Ireland is!'

The enthusiast was an English woman, younger by maybe twenty years than he was, not at all like the woman who had accosted him in Paris. He wondered if it happened that lone old men on their travels were naturally the subject of such attention and although, again, he welcomed it, he was more cautious than he had been in the Place de la Concorde. He had noticed the woman in the dining-room, sitting with another, whom he presumed to be her mother, a deduction that was later to prove correct.

'Yes, it is beautiful.'

'I have visited Ireland only once, but I have not forgotten.'

'I haven't been there myself for close on thirty years.'

The woman nodded, not curious. She was fair-haired, her prettiness a little faded but attractively so. She wore no wedding ring.

'I hope I did not offend you,' she apologized, 'by assuming you were English.'

'My wife was English.'

He smiled to disguise the weight of his bereavement, for murmurs of sympathy, however kind, were trivial in spite of their intention. Travel had not rescued his spirits as he had hoped it might, and he began to doubt that he would ever throw off the mourning that possessed him or that, somehow, he was ever meant to. The least demanding of wives, in death Heloise demanded more than he could sometimes bear.

'My country has treated Ireland badly,' the woman said. 'I've always thought so.'

'Well, it's over now.'

'Yes, it's over.'

There was a loss, too, in this woman's life, a wedding the war had stolen from her: he sensed the common ground they did not stray on to, and was aware that she did also. Idly, they conversed through an afternoon – about Bruges and cities that seemed like it, of Ireland again, of England. They were companions for half a day, their exchanges still impersonal, keeping private what they wished to. Before he had a chance to meet the mother the two were gone.

A few weeks later the Captain went himself. He crossed from Calais to Dover, then rattled through Kent to London. There he made his enquiries about the regiment in India and was told his brother had years ago been killed in action. The sense of being alone, of being more than ever a survivor, filled the Captain then, and in the drab post-war capital, where victory seemed more like bad-tempered submission, he found little to cheer him. Dreariness was everywhere, in every face, in every gesture; only the street-corner spivs and the multitude of sweetly scented tarts were jolly.

2

The morning was fine, bright March sunshine warm on Lucy's arms and face. The bank of the stream might have been grazed by sheep, the grass was so short, but no sheep ever came here. It was a mystery that this grass, green throughout the longest heatwave, its springiness a pleasure to walk on, never seemed to grow at all. Lucy lay on it, staring up at the sky, her shoes kicked off, the book she had been reading face down beside her. She wasn't thinking about it, neither of its people nor its cathedral places, not of Mrs Proudie or Mr Harding or the sun on the bell-tower. 'Will you write and tell me?' she had asked, but realized now that she had asked too much: of course Ralph hadn't written to say what the wife he had married was like. He'd forgotten or was embarrassed; not that it mattered, and perhaps it was as well. In her reverie Lucy saw a pretty, capable face, and sensed a manner that went with it. A window of the creeper-covered house by the sawmills opened and tendrils of the creeper were cut away: tidiness was a quality too. When the saws were silent, husband and wife walked in the balmy evening air, across the bridge by Logan's Bar and Stores. 'How peaceful it is here!' Ralph's happy wife remarked.

Lucy sat up and reached for the book beside her, its red cover marked where rain had fallen on it once. Aloysius Sullivan had bought three lots of books at an auction a year ago and had brought them to Lahardane, a present, since he knew that reading novels was so much her pleasure. *Alfred M. Beale* was inscribed on the fly-leaf in dark ink, and Lucy made herself wonder who that had been. *Monkstown Lodge, 1858.* Only Canon Crosbie of all the people she had ever known would have been alive in 1858; musing through names and faces, she could think of no one else. Affectionately, she remembered the old clergyman – how concerned for her he had been, and Ralph's saying he had been approached by him in the churchyard and how he had spoken of her. Canon Crosbie had lived into his ninetieth year.

Mr Harding had never been so hard pressed in his life. Drawn back at last to her novel, she read and was absorbed, and did not for ten minutes wonder about Ralph, his marriage or his wife.

*

A car brought him, and on the way from the railway station he said nothing to the driver. He had asked to be driven to Kilauran and would walk the distance that remained: he wanted to do that. Twice the driver spoke during the forty minutes the journey took, and then was silent.

At Kilauran the Captain remembered easily. There was a woman who used to search for shellfish in the rock water below the pier, and he wondered if the woman he saw searching there now might be her daughter. It seemed likely that she was, for in the distance there was some resemblance, or so he imagined. On the sands the fishermen had almost every day looked for the green glass floats that had slipped their nets. No fisherman was there today.

He walked by the sea. The cliff face was familiar, the jagged edge at the top, the crevices in its clay; only the clumps of growth seemed different. The smooth, damp sand became powdery when he turned to make his way to the shingle. The easy way up the cliff was as it had been.

Once or twice he had thought the house would be burnt out, that the men would have come back and this time been successful, that only the walls would be there. When the Gouvernets left Aglish they sold the house to a farmer who wanted it for the lead on the roof, who took off the slates and gouged out the fireplaces, leaving what remained to the weather. Iyre Manor had been burnt to its foundations and the Swifts had stayed at Lahardane while they thought about what to do. There'd been talk of the remains at Ringville becoming a seminary.

The Captain paused, remembering a procession through the

fields he had reached, his father with the tea basket held formally in front of him, his mother with rugs and a tablecloth, his sister carrying all their bathing-dresses and wraps and towels, he and his brother trusted only with their wooden spades. Then Nellie came running after them, shrill in the sunshine, her apron and the skirts of her black dress flapping, the ribbons of her cap floating out behind her.

For a moment Everard Gault thought he was a child again. He thought he saw the sunlight glinting on a pane of a window, but he knew that could not be so, because the glass was behind timber boards. Walking on, he counted the cattle he had made over to Henry, twice as many now as he had left behind. One cow was curious, lumbering close to him, head stretched in his direction, sniffing. Lazily, the others followed, shuffling along. There was a crop of mangolds in the O'Reillys' field beyond the pasture land.

Again, the sunlight glinted on glass. Walking on, he saw a curtain fluttering. 'You left your parasol!' Nellie had cried that day, waving it above her head. 'You left your parasol, ma'am!'

He had read once, in the *Corriere della Sera*, of a cattle disease in Ireland, and had worried at that threat to the herd. 'We always have our little herd at Lahardane,' his father had said, showing off the cows to someone who'd called in. Seen closer now, not a single window was boarded.

Lost in bewilderment, he passed through the white-painted metal gate in the railing that separated the fields from the gravel in front of the house. Again he stood still, his gaze held for a moment by the deep blue of the hydrangeas. Then slowly he walked towards the open hall door.

*

In the yard Henry lifted the churns off the trailer and rolled them over the cobbles. In the dairy he ran the water, filling each churn to its brim before he hung the hose on the hooks again. He could have done it in his sleep, he used to say to Lucy when she was a child, making her laugh when she imagined that. 'Lucy, Lucy, give me your answer, do!' he used to sing, making her laugh then too.

Bridget called him and he called back, saying he was in the dairy. She'd have known that, seeing the pick-up and the trailer not put away yet. He wondered why she didn't know, why she just called out.

'Leave off,' she shouted and from her tone he knew that something was wrong. 'Leave off and come in.'

The sheepdogs were settling down again at the foot of the pear tree, having been roused by the rattle of the churns. Another few weeks and the daily journey to the creamery wouldn't be necessary; the milk lorry would come to the head of the avenue. Nearly a year back he had completed the platform that was necessary.

'Henry! Will you come on in!' Bridget shouted again, not appearing in the back doorway.

There was a man's voice speaking when Henry reached the dog passage, but it was so low he couldn't hear more than a mumble of words. 'Glory be to God!' Bridget was whispering when he walked into the kitchen. As red in the face as she used to go when she was a girl, she was sitting at the table. The tips of her fingers kept touching her lips, drawing away, then touching them again. 'Glory be to God!' she kept whispering.

Henry guessed before he recognized the man, and afterwards wondered why he hadn't been at a loss for words, why he was able to say at once:

'Have you told him?'

'She told me, Henry,' the Captain said.

He'd been there a while. There was tea poured out, Bridget's not touched, the Captain's finished. Henry went to the range for the teapot and poured the Captain another cup.

*

Lucy came back by the strand, walking close to the sea as her father had, coming from the other direction. Her footprints, though, remained, as his had not, for the tide was going out now. She turned towards the cliffs, carrying a shoe in either hand, dawdling on the damp sand. She sat down when it became dry and softer. *The great family characteristic of the Stanhopes*, she read, *might probably be said to be heartlessness; but this want of feeling was, in most of them, accompanied by so great an amount of good nature as to make itself but little noticeable to the world.*

She could not for a moment remember much about the Stanhopes and then remembered perfectly; as foolish to forget, she told herself, that Mr Harding was the Precentor or Mr Slope chaplain to Bishop Proudie. She read again, but no sense came from the sentences of one long paragraph. 'How lucky I am!' Ralph's wife remarked as they turned back on their evening stroll.

★

In each upstairs room he entered the Captain went first to a window to look out. He saw his daughter in the pasture fields and in a moment of confusion thought she was his wife.

When she was in the hall and he looked down from the turn in the stairs, he could not prevent himself from imagining so again. In her walk she had a way of hesitating almost imperceptibly and he realized that she limped. She had her mother's features.

'Who are you?' she asked, her voice her mother's also.

Unsteady on the stairs, Everard Gault reached out a hand to the banister and slowly descended. What he had learnt in the kitchen – and, so soon afterwards, this encounter with his daughter – had weakened him.

'Don't you know me?'

'No.'

'Look at me, Lucy,' the Captain said, reaching the bottom of the stairs.

'What do you want? Why should I know you?'

They gazed at one another. Her cheeks had gone as white as the dress she wore and he knew that she recognized him then. She did not say anything and he stood still, not going closer to her.

★

When first she had heard the Captain walking about the house Bridget had crossed herself, seeking protection from the unknown. She had done so again in the dining-room when she saw a stranger standing by the sideboard. She had done so again in the kitchen, seeking guidance.

'I doubted it was him at first,' she said. 'He's gone to skin and bone, but it wasn't that.'

'Oh, it's him all right.'

'The poor man was shocked out of his wits when I told him.'

'She'll be, herself.'

'What'll happen, Henry?'

Henry shook his head. He listened while it was explained why it was that the Captain was alone.

*

He wanted to embrace his daughter, yet did not do so, sensing something in her that prevented him.

'Why now?' It was a whisper he heard, the words not meant for him. And then, as though regretting them, Lucy called him papa.

3

In the village of Kilauran and the town of Enniseala people were on the look-out for Captain Gault. A glimpse of him was anticipated as keenly as that moment in a play when an offstage character of significance first appears. He had thought – so it was said in speculation – to walk through the darkened rooms of his house and then to go away. Instead, there was his living daughter.

In Lahardane itself the events since the night he had aimed his rifle from an upstairs window had not become a chronicle as they had elsewhere. They had not ever been tidily put together for the sake of their retailing, but in memory remained haphazard, as they had happened. Nor was the upheaval occasioned by the Captain's return, and the news he brought of his widowing, taken to be the completion of a pattern of events, as they were assumed to be elsewhere. At Lahardane there was the rawness of a shock and, more ordinarily, the smell of the small cigars the Captain smoked and of the whiskey in the bottles he opened. It was remarked upon between Bridget and Henry that his voice had grown deeper with the years. His footsteps on the stairs were not quite a stranger's, but almost so; his shirts seemed alien, hanging out to dry in the orchard.

The Captain himself was still affected by confusion, occasionally by disbelief. Was this some perpetuating dream – that his daughter should be alive, that there should seem to be in all he had imagined for this place a greater veracity than in what was now around him? His instinct when in his daughter's company was to reach out for her hand, seeking the child she'd been, as if in touching her he would somehow find what had been lost to him. But the instinct was each time stifled.

'Lahardane is yours,' he clumsily insisted instead, any statement seeming better than none at all. 'I am a visitor.'

Her response came full of protest, but was no more than words. Forgiveness for a child's silliness was at least what he could offer, not only his own but her mother's too. His daughter would have been absolved of her small transgression within an hour of its perpetration: reassurance as to that tumbled sincerely from his lips. That a child's anxieties had been impatiently ignored was the cruelty that remained.

But in spite of all he said in terms of contrition and regret, the Captain was aware that he could not say enough. His daughter's brooding years had created something of their own that long ago had possessed her, wrapping her like fog that chilled. So at least it seemed.

The two sat at either end of the long table in the dining-room, which was where their conversations mostly occurred, although as often as not nothing at all was said. During meal after meal, the Captain watched his daughter's slender forefinger drawing on the polished surface of the mahogany patterns he could not identify from the finger's movement. When politeness demanded it, she sometimes said what she had done that day, or would do if it was still early. There was honey to gather, there were the flowers she grew.

*

In time, Ralph heard.

His marriage was more than a year old but had it taken place only a day ago it would have made no difference. Not quite as she was imagined, Ralph's wife was brown-eyed and tall, with dark hair drawn tightly back, a natural slenderness now returning after the birth of her first child. It happened that she was, as imagined, capable and tidy: advancing tendrils were indeed clipped back from the windows of the creeper-covered house that had become Ralph's on his marriage, his parents moving to the nearby bungalow they had begun to build when they realized the house would one day be too much for Ralph's ailing mother.

It was in the middle of a Monday morning that Ralph learnt of Captain Gault's return. Years ago he had discovered that a lorry driver who often picked up a load of timber at the sawmills came of a Kilauran family and kept in touch with his sisters there. He and Ralph had talked about the village and the neighbourhood, Ralph often speaking of the house on the cliffs, though not of his intimate connection with it. A secrecy had always influenced him where Lucy Gault was concerned. During his six years in the army he had been reticent, not once revealing what by then had seemed inevitable: that he and Lucy Gault would never marry. Nor had he spoken of her, or of his time at Lahardane, to the wife he had married in her place – a circumstance that in no way indicated, in the marriage, an absence of love or that Ralph had settled for second best. The impossible had simply been retreated from.

'Surely not?' he said, calm when the lorry driver told him.

'Oh, I'd say it's right enough, sir.'

The man was certain. There was a sureness in his tone that made Ralph want to close his eyes and look away, that stabbed him somewhere, and he imagined in the heart. But his heart was throbbing, for he could feel it, more than he ever had before. A dryness had come into his mouth, as if some bitter fruit parched it. The lorry driver had to shout when the motion of another saw began, adding to the snarl of beech planks slowly cut.

'A while back, sir.'

They went outside.

'Mrs Gault too?'

'They're saying Mrs Gault died.'

Ralph gave the man the invoice that had been prepared. He guided him when the lorry was backed out of the mill-yard on to the road. Still simulating calm, he waved good-bye and went away to be alone.

*

When he'd heard of the return, Mr Sullivan had been nonplussed. In his view Everard Gault was a simple man to whom a complicated thing had happened, and further complications were added now:

Aloysius Sullivan didn't know whether to be pleased or apprehensive.

'Well, you'll see a change or two in Enniseala, Everard,' he remarked in the back bar of the Central Hotel when eventually the two men met again. He considered it advisable to keep the conversation to the surface, as he remembered so much talk with Everard Gault had been in the past. 'Would you have guessed we'd be manufacturing mackintosh coats in Enniseala?'

'There's that?'

'Oh, indeed, indeed. There's not much in Enniseala that's the same.'

Some of this the Captain had seen for himself. Certain boarding-houses he remembered were gone, the main-street shops were different. The railway station was in decay, the doors of Gatchell's auction rooms were closed and it was said would not open again. Familiar shops were no longer familiar when he stepped inside, the faces that came forward new to him.

'To be expected, of course,' he remarked now in the Central Hotel. 'A different Ireland everywhere.'

'More or less.'

'I must apologize for not suggesting that you and I met sooner. It has taken a bit of time to settle in.'

'It's understandable that it would.'

They were the only drinkers in the small bar, where no one served unless summoned. The Captain stood up and crossed to the wooden counter with their two glasses.

'The same,' he said when a squinny youth appeared. They were drinking John Jameson.

'We would not have gone, you know,' the Captain said when he returned to the table they sat at. 'Had we searched the woods and found her we would not have gone.'

'Best not to dwell on that, Everard.'

'Oh, I know, I know.' He lifted his glass and when there had been a silence he imparted what he was fearful of relating in his dining-room. 'Heloise believed her child took her own life.'

The conversation had crept beneath the safety of the surface the solicitor preferred. He made no effort to check that, knowing he would not be able to now. The Captain said:

'But graceful in all things, she was as graceful as it is possible to be, living with that.'

'Heloise could not be otherwise.'

'The outward sign of her beauty was always there.'

Aloysius Sullivan nodded. He said he remembered the first occasion he had met Heloise Gault, and as if he had said something different, or nothing at all, the Captain went on:

'She loved Annunciations. She wondered about the nature of St Thomas's doubt. Or if Tobias's angel had taken the form of a bird. Or how on earth St Simeon managed on his pillar. We looked a lot at pictures.'

'I'm sorry, Everard.'

The solicitor remembered the demure eyes of the girl he saw when the woman she had become was spoken of. He had often considered she was someone who in all her life had not sought to hurt a soul. Aloysius Sullivan, who never regretted that he had not experienced the intimacies of marriage, for a moment did so now.

'You were a good husband, Everard.'

'An inadequate one. We left Lahardane when we could bear the days no longer. I should have resisted that careless haste.'

'And I should have set out myself to search for you. We could go on for ever.'

'Is it necessary for Lucy to know what I have told you?'

'It would be kinder if she did not.'

'I think she should not know.'

'And I am certain of it.'

The two men drank. Their talk loosened, sprawled, was easier for both. On the promenade a little later, their gait sprawling a bit also, they were again the friends they had been once. The solicitor – the older by eleven years and still as Everard Gault remembered him – spoke on their walk of people they were both acquainted with, his clerk, and the housekeeper whom he had had for so long.

He came no closer than that to his private life, all he said still giving the impression, as in the past, that this was shared with no one. The Captain talked about his travels.

'Heloise had a photograph that must have been taken hereabouts,' he said, interrupting something else. 'Faded brown and torn a bit and creased. I doubt she knew it was still among her things.'

He pointed to where the promenade had been built up when high waves had broken through. Lucy stood among the old breakwater posts that staggered out to sea in her mother's photograph, and some of the rotting posts were still there. The breakwaters were to be replaced, Aloysius Sullivan said, and one of these days perhaps they would be.

They had stopped by a seat but did not sit down. Listening to what he was told about the breakwaters, the Captain stared out over the sea, to the splashes of gorse that dotted the far-off view. A silence gathered when the local news was exhausted, before he said:

'You've seen to it that she had money. All these years.'

'She has not spent much.'

'Lucy does not talk to me.'

He spoke of the moment of their encounter, his embrace resisted, and of the silences in the dining-room, her finger tracing its patterns on the surface of the table, his euphoria so often shattered.

Mr Sullivan hesitated. It was not his place to be expansive, yet his affection for both father and daughter made it necessary that he should be now.

'Lucy might have married.' He paused, then added, 'But she believed she had no right to love until she felt forgiven. She never doubted, when the rest of us did, that your return would come about. And she was right.'

'This was some time ago? That she might have married?'

'Yes.' There was another pause, and then, 'He has married since.'

They walked on at the same slow pace, and Aloysius Sullivan said, 'It's good you're back, Everard.'

'How like the rest of our domestic tragedy it is that I have come too late!'

The two men on the promenade were watched from far away.

The soldier who had been disturbed by delusions was no longer a soldier: when his period of service ended it had been put to him that he might consider continuing for a further spell, but he had declined to do so. Even though it had failed him, Horahan bore the army no ill-will and he had gone about the last of his military duties with his usual care and perseverance, brushing polish into his boots, shining his buckles and the buttons of his tunic. When his final day came he rolled up the mattress on the springs of his narrow cot. A black suit hung waiting in his locker.

He wore it now. He was temporarily out of employment, living in a room he rented in a house not far from the one where he had been a child, where his mother had continued to live until her death. Hearing of Captain Gault's return, he had been on the look-out for him on the streets of the town. He had followed him today and, as he continued to observe the two figures on the promenade, tears that were not tears of sorrow or dismay welled behind his eyes, spilt out on to his hollow cheeks and ran down into the collar of his shirt. He knew, there was no doubt. This was, at last, Our Lady's sign: at her holy intervention, Captain Gault had come back to bring the torment to an end.

Three Christian Brothers going by noticed the rapt expression on the ex-soldier's face. When they had passed they heard him cry out and when they turned they saw him on his knees. They watched until he stood up again, until he mounted a bicycle and rode away.

5

'They lived on alms,' Ralph said when he was asked about the monks whose graves they walked on. 'Augustinians were always beggars here.'

Was there impatience in his tone when he said that? Some sign he had failed to disguise as tiredness after his day's work? He smiled at his wife, an apology she would not know was one. The air was soft, without a breeze. Somewhere a pigeon cooed, not finished yet with the day.

They talked about the monks, wondering if all of them had been dedicated equally to simple goodness, driven equally by what gave their cloistered lives a meaning. Did faith such as theirs, she asked, make people the same? Had all of them been that, as their dress would have implied?

'Hardly.' Again in his tone there might have been impatience, a trace of unfair irritation, and again he was ashamed. More gently he said:

'What's left here is a bit of their church. Where they lived would have spread over all this field, and beyond it – their cells, their refectory, the garden they must have had, their fishponds.'

There was a single stone, its purpose not established, upright in a corner of the field. Damaged carving at its base was unidentified. It might have been the broken perpendicular of a cross, the jagged breach rounded, incisions of decoration added. But that was not known for certain.

'Shall we go back now?' Ralph suggested.

Their child was asleep. Through the open window, safely barred, a cry would reach them. In the still evening they listened for a moment.

'Yes, perhaps we should go back.'

When she had hesitated about marriage he had pressed her. He had listened to her doubts, allaying them with laughter that was genuine and fond. It had not been humility that had held her back, not lack of confidence in her ability for what lay ahead – more like caution that, without quite knowing why, she felt wasn't out of place. All this Ralph remembered now, as if time had waited to make sense of it.

'A pity they've been let go.' She looked back at the untended ruins. Among them the cows that grazed the field sought shade when the sun was hot, trampling the growth of nettles. It seemed odd to Ralph that that was what she said, and yet of course it was not.

'Yes, it's a pity.'

They climbed over the gate on to the road because that was easier than struggling with its rusty bolt. Bicycles were propped against the shiny pale-blue wall of Logan's, its shop open in the evenings for as long as there was trade in the bar.

They talked about the day, what news had been passed on in the sawmills. When first they'd met he had confessed that once he couldn't see himself a timber merchant for the rest of his life. Often she had brought that up and as if she had now, he said:

'It's what I am.'

Bewildered, she frowned, and smiled when he explained. They smiled together then.

'I don't want anything else,' Ralph said.

It slipped out easily; he didn't have to look away, could even take her hand. In her deep brown eyes was all the love that made their life together pleasurable.

'How nice you are!' she whispered.

They crossed the narrow bridge and then there was the bungalow where his parents lived, a smell of tobacco in the air. Bulky and grey-haired, his pipe gripped tightly in the centre of his mouth, Ralph's father was unhurriedly watering his flowerbeds. He waved and they waved back. 'It's just you'd maybe be interested,' the lorry driver had said.

What had never felt like deception had felt like it ever since. Keeping his own secret, obscuring it with vagueness when ages ago someone had asked too much about that summer in Enniseala, had been no more than protecting what was precious. It was more now. Past and present had somehow become one. What was Lucy thinking in this moment? What did she think when each morning she woke to another brightening half-light? That he had heard the news? That he would know what to do, that he would find some way?

The child lay undisturbed. No dream had frightened her, no sound shattered her empty peace. One cheek was a little reddened from where she'd rested it on her curled-up fingers.

*

When the Captain realized that since his wife's death he had lost something of his military bearing – that with an old man's carelessness he had let himself go, that he shambled when he was tired – he made up for these lapses in the care he took, for his daughter's sake, with his dress and his appearance. He had his hair cut regularly in Enniseala. He clipped his fingernails close; he knotted his tie with care. Unfailingly every morning he polished his shoes, and had the heels replaced before it was entirely necessary.

But conversation was still easier with Bridget or with Henry than with his daughter. For them he recalled how he had wandered so aimlessly in the early days of his mourning, drifting on to this train or that, his movements dictated only once in a while by some half-lost sentiment or predilection. He recalled, too, idling one day on a seat in a park and thinking of the caretakers he had left behind in Ireland. Smoking one of his slim cigarillos, he had found himself reflecting that they would have become as old as he was, had worried that the herd might not still support them, and about their circumstances if it did not. He had wondered – but did not say it now – if they were still alive.

'We could fix the gate-lodge up,' he offered Bridget. 'If you would like to return there.'

'Ah no, sir, no. Not unless you'd rather that yourself.'

'It's not I who should rather one thing or another, Bridget. My debt's to you.'

'Ah no, sir, no.'

'You brought my daughter up.'

'We did what any people would. We did the best we could. We'd rather stop on in the house, sir, if it's the same. If it's not a presumption, sir.'

'Of course it's not.'

It was Bridget who had told him how his daughter's limp had lessened with the years and how a stoicism had developed in her as a child when those same years failed her, how faith had still been kept, love shattered. Cutting away the brambles in the orchard or sealing the perforations in the lead of his roof with dabs of Seccotine, the Captain reflected that it was humbling to hear in this way about his own child, to have light thrown on her disposition as it had become. Yet it would have been surprising had he and she not been strangers, and he accepted that. He tried to imagine her at fourteen, at seventeen, at twenty; but his memory of her as an infant in his arms, or when he had been concerned about her as a child too much on her own, more potently intervened. Now, there was her seclusion in this gaunt old house, and it concerned him that she never went in to Enniseala, that as an adult she had never walked in its long main street, that she hardly remembered the swans on the water of the estuary, or the promenade, or the bandstand, or the squat little lighthouse she had known in childhood. Did she not wish to shop in better shops than the general store in Kilauran? How did she manage for a dentist?

In the dining-room, when he asked, he learnt that a dentist came once in a while from Dungarvan; that Dr Birthistle kept up a weekly practice in Kilauran, as Dr Carney had before him; that on Sundays a bright-faced young curate came out from Enniseala to the corrugated Church of Ireland church. But it was Bridget who recalled for him the days in his long absence when something out of the ordinary had happened: the icy morning when the pump in the yard froze, a Sunday when her nieces came to show her their First Communion dresses, the sunny afternoon when Canon Crosbie reported that France had fallen. It had been sunny in Bellinzona too; without an effort he remembered that.

'I still have these,' he said in the dining-room, and when Bridget came to collect the plates and vegetable dishes the table was strewn with picture postcards of Italian towns and landscape. Politely, so Bridget reported in the kitchen, Lucy nodded over each in turn before making a little pile of them.

*

Electricity came to Lahardane because for his daughter's sake the Captain felt there should be that convenience. He bought an Electrolux vacuum cleaner from a salesman who came to the door, and one day brought back to the house a pressure-cooker. Bridget took to the Electrolux but put aside the pressure-cooker as dangerous.

From Danny Condon of the garage at Kilauran the Captain bought a motor car. It was a pre-war Morris Twelve with the sloping back of the period, green and black. The car that had been left behind in 1921, with solid rubber tyres, had even then been something of an antique and hardly ever used. In a shed in the yard robins had since nested between the folds of its hood, their droppings darkly staining its brasswork, dust dulling its gloss. Danny Condon took it, reducing the price of the Morris by a little.

The buying of the car was another attempt on the Captain's part to rescue his daughter from her isolation. On the avenue and on their journeys to the cinema in Enniseala he taught her how to drive. 'Today, the races?' he suggested and they would set out for Lismore or Clonmel. He took her to the Opera House in Cork, dinner first in the Victoria Hotel, where an old woman once stood up and in a quavering voice sang the last few lines of an aria from *Tannhäuser*. The diners applauded and the Captain was reminded of the afternoon in the Città Alta, the tunes of *Tosca* before military music was commanded. He spoke of that afternoon and was listened to politely.

★

For Ralph, it was always easier in the sawmills. Practicality brought relief; emotion was belittled by the hum of the saws and the rasp of planes, the men intent and careful, the smell of sweat and resin and dust. He was in charge and had to be in charge. But too readily, when he climbed the ladder-way to the office that looked down on the machinery and the men, when the noise fell away but still was there less loudly after he had closed the door, his thoughts escaped. Attention to orders and invoices and the columns in account books, concern about signs of wear in a driving belt or a saw gone blunt, the counting of the weekly wages, were tasks that suffered unintended interruption; and as from sleep, he would return minutes later to where he was, to stare in bewilderment at what he held in his hand or what was open before him.

Often his father came to the office, to share what had to be done that day. His father did not remark upon these moments of abstraction, the sudden crossing of the bare-boarded office floor in an attempt to disguise them, back turned for too long. Guile was not Ralph's way: his father would say that. The men would say it when the saws went quiet at midday, when they sat with their sandwiches, outside in the sun if it was warm. People would say it in Logan's bar, the evening drinkers, the women who came to shop in the grocery, people who had known Ralph all his life. Not for an instant was he doubted, as he was not in the house he had brought a wife to; not for an instant in the bungalow that had been built for his mother and his father.

Yet what became a habit began. 'I'll walk to Doonan,' he would say when he returned to the house in the evenings, and would walk in this direction or that in order – so he knew it seemed – to ease away the rigours of the day, the worries left behind when things had not gone well, when a part for a machine was not yet available or there was failure again to deliver what had been promised.

Lies that were not quite lies – slight deception, hardly there, the bluster of pretence – coloured every day. He had always despised all that.

'Were Cassidy's heifers out?' his wife would ask when he returned from his evening walks. Or, 'Have they begun the tarring at Rossmore?'

And he would say, although he hadn't noticed. He could not bear to hurt her, yet her contentment seemed unnatural. Why did she feel no pain, since so much pain was there?

'You used to tell me more.' She would smile away what might have been mistaken for a complaint and he would say the tinkers were back at Healy's Cross. Or say that Mrs Pierce had cut her fuchsia early. Or that the stream was running over at Doonan.

She was particular about the house, and he liked that quality in her, the care she took, not being slapdash. He liked the food she cooked; he liked the rooms kept clean, the way she so easily comforted their child. If ever he had told her what he had suppressed she would have listened in her careful, serious way, not interrupting. 'In fact, I told nobody,' he might have ended his confession. 'It wasn't only you.' But it was too late for confessions now, too cruel that she should see a girl in a white dress, and Mr Ryall's car, and tea laid out; too cruel that she should be there on the shore when the high waves splattered the rain with foam.

'I'm thinking I should buy Malley's slope,' he said one evening.

'The field?'

'If you can call it that. Waste land more like.'

'Why would you want waste land, though?'

'I'd clear it to grow ash on. And maybe maple.'

An investment, he said. Something to take an interest in, he did not add; something to keep him where he belonged; a stake in the future that would give the future shape before it happened.

'Is Malley wanting to sell?'

'I doubt he ever thought anyone would want those few acres.'

It had become almost dark in the room where they sat and he sensed more treachery in not wanting to put on the lights. It was she who did so. Her happy face was there then, her dark hair loosening, as it sometimes did at this time of day. He watched her drawing down the blinds before she came to sit near him.

6

'You should have better clothes, lady.'

Her mother had had a coat made in Mantua, pearls strung for her at a stall on the Ponte Vecchio. Her mother was never less than smart, and had acquired Italian ways and taken to Italian fashions. Her mother had delighted in the cherubs of Bellini, was kind to waiters and hotel maids, and spoke Italian with a natural ease. Her mother was recognized by beggars on the streets, her generosity famous in Montemarmoreo.

In the dining-room Lucy listened, and nodded now and again. 'I used to wear her dresses,' she said.

'Well yes, of course.'

'They're all worn out now.'

'Will we buy you a few new ones?'

She shook her head. Her clothes were what she chose to wear. She looked away, at the unlit fire in the grate, the black mantelpiece above it, the familiar blue stripes of the wallpaper. She pushed about on her plate food she didn't want to eat. What terrible folly had possessed her? All these years to have so stubbornly waited for no more than an old man's scattered words?

'There was a balcony,' he said, 'and the people passing on the street below would call out *"Buon appetito!"* when the tablecloth was spread for lunch.' The magician's butterfly disappeared and then came back. There were processions on St Cecilia's day. 'All that,' he said.

She drew her knife and fork together. The images she might herself have conjured up were too fragile to be talked away in dinner-time conversation over plates and dishes on a table, too precious to be offered as a triviality. She had come to terms with what was there to come to terms with; she had managed, but could not now. She could not grieve; no more than a fact it felt like that her mother was not alive.

'The Mitchelstown Caves?' her father said.

'I've never been there.'

'Shall we go?'

'If you would like to.'

*

A few days later the Captain passed into his seventy-first year but did not say so, although he would have liked to. He wanted to share with his daughter what was sometimes considered to be a milestone in a life, but as that day advanced the inclination slipped away. He could not comfort her and it mattered more than the milestones of ageing that he could not.

He suffered for her. He understood the trait in her that had forbidden her to draw someone else into her disquiet: for that, she was remarkable but did not know it. Nor would there have been consolation if she had.

In the evenings after dinner they sat together in the drawing-room, her company dutifully there. She read. He smoked a single cigarillo and drank a little whiskey. Every evening it was the same.

But once, restless, Lucy put her book aside, sat for a moment doing nothing, and then lifted out her embroidery drawer from the sofa-table and placed it on the floor. She knelt beside it to sort out skeins of silk, needles, drawings on scraps of paper, stubs of pencil, linen pieces, pencil-sharpener, rubbers. As her father watched, she unfolded a wide rectangle of linen on which she had drawn one of her sketches. She spread it on the hearthrug, quite close to where he sat: seagulls were only just discernible as such, little more than specks on the sand; a curve of broken lines indicated the shingle beneath the cliffs. Two figures stood by the spit of rocks that poked out into the sea. The embroidery had been abandoned and her tears came while he watched her rearranging the drawer's disorder; other sketches that had lain there were examined and bundled away, this one kept.

'Lady,' he murmured, but she did not hear.

The Captain lay awake that night, thinking that Heloise would have ordered all this better, would have been wise in what she said to their daughter and how she said it. Her practicality came into that. It was she who had wallpapered their bedroom when first she came to Lahardane, she who had insisted that the smoking of the breakfast-room fire could be cured and had been right, she who gave their summer parties and in December had a Christmas tree in the hall for the children of Kilauran.

He turned on his bedside lamp to look at the faded roses of the wallpaper, then turned it off again. In the darkness he got up and stretched out on the sofa beneath the windows, which he sometimes did when he couldn't sleep. He might tiptoe across the landing, as once or twice he had, to gaze down at the soft fair hair spread on the pillow, eyes gently closed. But tonight he didn't.

He dozed, quite easily in the end, and then in some Italian church the woman sacristan read the evening lesson. In the shaded corner of the piazza men played cards. 'Love is greedy when it is starved,' Heloise reminded him when they walked across the difficult paving. 'Don't you remember, Everard? Love is beyond all reason when it is starved.'

*

She would rather be anywhere but here, Lucy thought, and wished she hadn't agreed to explore the caves at Mitchelstown.

On a damp morning she and her father were the only visitors. The way lit by their guide, they clambered over slippery rock beneath the stalactites, while the different caves were named for them: the House of Commons, the House of Lords, Kingston Gallery, O'Leary's. They waited for the spiders that were peculiar to the place to creep out from the crevices, and afterwards they walked about the town that gave the caves their name. Its great, wide square and the Georgian elegance of a refuge for impecunious Protestants were its main attractions. Nothing remained of the once stately Mitchelstown Castle, burnt and looted the summer after petrol cans had been brought to Lahardane.

'Eccentric family,' her father said, 'those poor mad Kingstons.'

They drove away, through rain that turned to mist. Men clearing out a ditch saluted them as they went by. They met no one else until they stopped in Fermoy, a town familiar to her father since his army days. 'D'you know Fermoy?' she remembered Ralph asking and of course she didn't. He had driven to it in Mr Ryall's car on a Wednesday afternoon before he'd ever been to Lahardane. He had driven to half the towns in County Cork, he'd said, before he knew her, and she imagined being with him, being with him now.

'Nice old town,' her father said.

They walked together on an empty pavement, the mist still falling. Turf smoke was cloying in the air. Cattle were being driven on the street.

'Would we try for coffee here?' her father said.

In the quiet lounge of a hotel a clock was ticking softly. A waitress in black and white stood by a window, the lace of the curtain pulled back a little. They took their coats off, piling them with their scarves on an empty sofa. They sat in armchairs and when the waitress came to them they ordered coffee.

'And something – biscuits perhaps?' Lucy's father said.

'I'll bring you biscuits, sir.'

The clock struck twelve. The waitress returned with a coffee pot and a jug of milk, and a plate of pink-iced biscuits. An elderly couple came in, the woman holding on to her companion's arm. They sat near the window where the waitress had been standing. 'We need more nails,' the man remembered when they were settled. 'And Keating's Powder.'

Lucy broke a biscuit in half. The coffee had a scalded taste; the sweetness of the icing was a help. Marriage was not for ever any more. Marriage could be set aside, as often these days it was: in Ireland too it could be set aside.

'That guide didn't know much,' her father said.

'Not much.'

The waitress brought tea for the couple who had come in. It was fair day in Fermoy, she said, and the old woman said they knew: you couldn't not, the state of the streets. Oh, something shocking, the waitress agreed. Six o'clock in the morning the cattle started to come in: she was watching them earlier. She came from Glanworth herself, she said before she went away; she often used see the cattle driven on the roads all night, going to the Fermoy fair.

'We're old familiars here,' the old woman called across the lounge and Lucy tried to smile. Her father said he'd known the hotel a long time ago.

'Everything's long ago now,' the old woman said.

Teaspoons rattled on their saucers. The clock ticked in a silence; then the old man's whisper became loud because his companion had indicated that she couldn't hear. He was ashamed that they had fleas in the house, he said. Coming in off the fowls or not, he was ashamed.

'Lady.'

Already, a moment ago, her father had tried for her attention; she'd been aware of that.

'Sorry,' she said.

'Early on, I wrote letters I didn't post.'

She didn't understand; she didn't know what letters he meant. She shook her head.

Enquiries had been natural in the circumstances, her father explained, and told how he had stamped each envelope, how he had afterwards kept the letters by him. Years later he had dropped them, one by one, into the fire and watched the blackened paper curling before it fell away.

'All that,' he said, and there was something about her mother not wanting ever to know the news from Ireland, and how his love had caused him too assiduously to protect her and take from her a greater marvel than she saw in pictures. He sought no sympathy but blankly laid out these facts as if apologizing for some failure in himself.

She nodded. In novels people ran away. And novels were a reflection of reality, of all the world's desperation and of its happiness, as much of one as of the other. Why should mistakes and foolishness – in reality too – not be put right while still they might be? The pleas there'd been, the certainty that this was what mattered most, everything so often repeated, the longing, the begging: word for word, spoken, written, all became a torrent in Lucy's head while her father was silent and she was silent too. She heard the old man complaining that when people went away from the house they noticed they had fleas in their clothes. You couldn't hold your head up.

'I can't not tell you,' her father said, 'that the guilt your mother felt was a bit too much for her.'

'I'm glad you've told me.'

The old man stood up. The rain had stopped, he said, and the two gathered up their belongings. Coins were left on the table before, slowly, the old couple went away, clinging to one another again. The Captain and his daughter sat in silence then.

*

Back and forth, back and forth, the digger crossed Malley's slope, prodding at the rocks, lifting one to the pile when it was loose enough. Against the rabbits, every inch of the fencing would have to be renewed, the mesh at the bottom dug six inches in. Yesterday Ralph had ordered the saplings. Ashes and maples would change the landscape, seen for miles around when they strengthened and spread.

From where he stood at the edge of the steeply sloping field he could see a rabbit, and then another one, scuttling into a clump of undergrowth. *So often you have wanted to come back to Lahardane. So many times I was foolish.* Already, perfectly, he could remember where each word fell, how the lines broke on the single page that had been his for only a day. *How could it be wrong of us?*

How could it be? To sit down at the slatted table on the lawn, to walk once more on the strand, to meet her father and then to drive away? The digger's engine spluttered before it gathered strength again. Undisturbed, the rabbits ran about.

Another Wednesday afternoon; by chance it would be that and they would notice and would say it. There'd be the sunlight through the chestnut branches, the white hall door half open. There'd be the silence of the cobbled yard, the rooks as still as stone on the high chimneys. There'd be her laughter and her smile, there'd be her voice. He wouldn't want to go away. In all his life remaining he wouldn't want to.

The digger's driver clambered down and crossed the slope to say he'd come back and shoot the rabbits. Catch them in his tractor's headlights and then begin to pick them off, maybe a hundred you'd catch in a night. A lifetime otherwise it would take to rid the place of them.

Ralph nodded. 'Thanks,' he said, and the man lit a cigarette, wanting to talk about the rabbits, wanting to have a break. 'Come over any time,' Ralph said. Next week, the man promised, and ambled back to his machine.

Even for a few minutes, even just to look in. How could it be wrong? 'Lemybrien,' he could say. 'There's been a felling of old oaks at Lemybrien.' Casually at breakfast over the last cup of tea, the dishes not yet gathered from the table, he could say he should maybe go over and take a look at what there was. 'While we're still slack. I wouldn't want to miss that timber.' And sandwiches would be made to see him through the journey, and he'd wait for them, a flask filled too. Clonroche, then Ballyanne, not in a hurry passing through Lemybrien, because it would feel wrong to be in a hurry. He'd have no appetite for the sandwiches when he stopped and he'd wonder what to do with them and would throw them down for the birds before he drove on. Her father's hand would be held out when he drove up and she wouldn't be there at first and then would come from the house. He closed his eyes, yet none of it went away, and when it did he didn't want it to.

Still playfully, the rabbits scampered. Back and forth the digger went. Another rock was added to the pile.

'Oh, God!' Ralph crunched the invocation out and felt tears warm behind his eyes. 'Oh God, where is your pity now?'

7

Henry saw the visitor and wondered who it was. From among the trees high above the hydrangea lawn, where he was breaking twigs for kindling and tying them into bundles, he saw the figure at the hall door as hardly more than a shadow. While Henry watched, it passed through the open door, into the house.

Later that afternoon when Lucy brought mushrooms to the kitchen, Bridget said:

'There's a man come.'

Lucy had gathered the mushrooms in the orchard. She emptied them from a battered punnet on to the draining-board.

'Who is it?'

Kneading dough for the bread she baked, Bridget shook her head. The front-door bell hadn't sounded, she said.

'Your father called down from the hall for me to bring in tea when I'd be ready with it.' Whoever it was, she said, had maybe just walked in. 'Your father was asking were you around.'

'Me?'

'He asked were you about.'

Visitors weren't frequent. More than a year ago Mr Sullivan had ceased to drive his car. The man who'd arrived one morning to demonstrate the vacuum cleaner the Captain later bought had been the first stranger for months. When O'Reilly's man came, or Mrs O'Reilly with a bottle at Christmas, or the E.S.B. man to read the meter, it wasn't to the front door. Sometimes, not often, the postman didn't arrive until late in the day, but the postman wouldn't have been invited into the drawing-room for tea..

'I have the kettle on to boil,' Bridget said, wiping her floury hands on her apron.

'I'll take in the tea.'

She didn't trust herself to say more. Had Bridget heard a voice? Had any bit of conversation reached her from the drawing-room before the door was closed? Lucy didn't ask. Shivers of excitement, cool and pleasurable, came and went all over her body, gently pricking her skin. Who else would just walk in?

*

Henry carried his bundles of twigs into the shed that had been the feed shed when hens and turkeys were kept in greater numbers. He loosened the string he'd used to bind them and slipped it off. He stacked them tidily with those he'd stacked already.

'Who's after coming?' he asked in the kitchen, picking shreds of brushwood from the sleeves of his jersey.

Bridget said she didn't know. She didn't pause in her task of filling two tins with the mixture she had prepared.

She opened the oven door. The tray of tea things for the drawing-room was ready, the kettle beginning to sing on the range.

'Good mushrooms, those,' Henry said, picking one up from beside the sink.

*

Brushing her hair in her bedroom, Lucy didn't hurry. From her dressing-table looking-glass her eyes stared back at her, so bright and so intent they seemed almost to belong to someone else. Her lips were parted in the beginning of a smile; her hair hung loosely, the ivory-backed brush still raised to it. Both heads would turn at once when she carried in the tray. 'Well, we have met at last.' The words were what she heard, not which voice said them; but it would be her father's.

It could not spoil everything to look from the window, to see the car that had come, not that the sight of it would tell her anything; and not of course that it could be the old car with the dickey. But when she looked there was no car.

She changed her skirt and jumper for a dress. Would he have come by train to Enniseala? Or to Dungarvan, which would be a shorter journey? She tried to remember if there was a railway station at Dungarvan. More likely, he would have come by bus to Waterford and then on to Creally's Crossroads. He would have walked the rest; more than an hour that would have taken, but quicker in the end than taking a train even if there was one.

She tied the belt of her dress and found a necklace. Again at her looking-glass, she smeared away the lipstick she had applied and changed it for a different shade. Would he be shy of her father? Would her father take to him? No one could not take to him; in spite of the trouble his presence brought, her father would want her happiness. Her father would want everything to be all right again.

She touched her cheeks with powder. She had been flushed but that was gone now. She wondered if Bridget guessed what had come into her thoughts, if she had noticed those moments of confusion. She wondered how he'd have changed.

She closed the door softly behind her and went downstairs. They looked at her, surprised, when she walked into the kitchen. Bridget had just replaced on its shelf the big brown bowl she used for mixing her bread ingredients, Henry was standing with his back to the range.

'Did you wet the tea yet?' she asked Bridget and Bridget said she hadn't.

'I'll do it so.'

It would shock them, his coming to the house. And dressing up for him, for a married man, was more shocking still. She hadn't thought of that, of how in their simple, uncomplicated lives they would feel.

She made the tea. Bridget had buttered bread and put more jam into the filling of a cake that had been bought in Kilauran, only half of it left. There was a bicycle outside the front door, Henry said, and Lucy imagined the conductor handing it down from the roof of the bus at Creally's Crossroads, and Ralph's hands reaching up for it. Of course he would have come with a bicycle. Knowing how long the journey from the crossroads was, of course he would have.

'That's lovely, Bridget,' she said, picking up the tray. She carried it from the kitchen, along the passage to the hall. The front door was still open; her father had a way of leaving it like that, even when the weather was cold. She caught sight of the back wheel of the bicycle as she put the tray down on the long hall table that had become cluttered since her father's return. It was his place for the white hat he wore when it was sunny; he threw his tie down there when he took it off on his way to work in the orchard. Bills had accumulated there, their torn brown envelopes beside them. Loose change and keys were scattered.

In the mirror that hung in the alcove at the bottom of the stairs she straightened the collar of her dress and pushed a strand of hair into place. Then she opened the drawing-room door, the tea-tray balanced on her free arm.

*

'I saw the bicycle there and I coming down out of the woods,' Henry said in the kitchen. 'Sergeant Foley's, I said to myself.'

'What's Foley want?'

'It wasn't his at all. When I examined it, it wasn't.'

Henry described the bicycle: its dull black ironwork, mudguards peaked, the springs of the saddle a heavy coil, jutting out in front. Bridget didn't listen. He'd thought it was the sergeant's, Henry said, because it had the look of a Guard's bicycle.

'The next thing I thought it was maybe young O'Reilly's. Until I looked in the window.'

Bridget paused in the washing of her baking board. 'It's never who she thinks?'

Slowly Henry shook his head. 'I'll tell you who it is,' he said.

*

'Come in, come in, lady,' her father said.

The man in the armchair by the bagatelle table didn't look in her direction. His manner was nervous, the fingers of one hand rubbing the knuckles of the other, his head held at a slant. His suit was of black serge, the badge of the Pioneer temperance movement in one of the lapels. A tie was knotted tightly into a shabby collar. Bicycle-clips still gripped the turn-ups of the dark serge trousers.

'Tea.' She dragged the word out of herself, and was aware that the man had raised his head to look at her. His eyes were empty of expression; a hollowness in his features gave him a distinctive look. His hands reached down to pull his bicycle-clips off.

'Ah, tea,' her father said, and there was the rattle of the cups as they were settled on their saucers. 'Or would you prefer a glass of whiskey, Mr Horahan?'

He couldn't take whiskey, the man said, and seemed not to notice that tea had been brought in. Her father was saying that the man's shoulder was all right, telling her that he had asked about it, that he'd been told it had never been a hindrance. He hadn't recognized their visitor when he'd found him in the hall, her father said, but he remembered the name as soon as he heard it. 'Mr Horahan,' he said, and added that he'd just been telling Mr Horahan that bygones were bygones.

She didn't understand. She didn't know who the man was. She didn't understand what was being said. She'd never seen the man before.

'A mineral if you'd have it,' he said, touching the badge on his lapel.

She turned and went away then. She heard her father calling after her. He opened the door she had closed. He called out again in the hall, saying it was all right. But she was outside by then, running over the gravel.

*

'But in the name of God,' Bridget distractedly repeated, 'what's he want? Why's he come here?'

She reached up to the mantel-shelf for the rosary beads she kept there. She closed her eyes, leaning against the wall where she stood, her face as white as the flour that still powdered the black material of her dress.

From a chair drawn out from the table Henry watched her fingers working the beads, her lips silently beseeching. Then the drawing-room bell shook on its coiled spring, summoning attention. Bridget opened her eyes. She couldn't enter that room, she said, and Henry went instead. It was the first time any bell except the hall-door bell had sounded in the house since the Captain and his wife had left it twenty-nine years ago. That registered in Bridget's consciousness, slipping through her perplexity and her outraged sensibilities.

'He's t.t.,' Henry said when he returned. 'He wants lemonade.' He rooted in one of the wall cupboards for lemonade crystals.

'They're old,' Bridget said when he found a bottle in which there were some left.

'They'll do.' Henry tipped what there was into a glass, which he filled up with cold water from the tap. It should be hot, Bridget said, in order to dissolve the crystals.

'But Mother of God,' she suddenly cried out, 'what are we thinking of to be giving the man lemonade?'

*

'I'm afraid you've upset my daughter,' the Captain said in the drawing-room. 'To tell you the truth I still didn't know who you were when I brought you in from the hall.'

'These times I've no employment, sir. The day you were out on the promenade with Mr Sullivan, sir, I was after finishing at the Camp.'

'You were a soldier?'

'I had no employment the day I seen you, sir. I got employment with Ned Whelan since. He took me on with him on account I would have experience with laying roads up at the Camp.'

Henry came with the lemonade, but it seemed to the Captain that it was not required after all. The loquaciousness of the man who'd been wandering about in the hall ceased abruptly. He shrank back into his chair when Henry approached him. Not knowing what to do, Henry put the glass of lemonade on the floor.

'We're in the kitchen, if you'd pull the bell again,' he said before he went. He had taken his hat off. He glanced back apprehensively before he closed the door.

'Who's that man, sir?'

'Henry works for us.'

'I'm careful with a stranger, sir.'

'Mr Horahan, why have you come out here?'

'Ned Whelan let me go two days back, sir. What I'm telling you is in case you wouldn't know it, sir. How it is with me, sir.'

The Captain drank the cup of tea he had poured for himself. Then he said he was at a loss.

His visitor was welcome, he added; bygones were bygones, he repeated; in no way did he wish to be inhospitable. All the same he was at a loss.

'Time has settled our hash for us, Mr Horahan. But for all that it might have been better if you hadn't come out here again.'

It occurred to him as he spoke that the man had come looking for work, since he had said he was unemployed. It was extraordinary that he might have, that having once attempted to burn the house down he should now return with such an end in mind. It seemed impossible, but even so the Captain said:

'I'm afraid we've nothing to offer you here. If you were thinking of work.'

There was no response to this, neither a denial nor otherwise. Nothing was said for several minutes, and then the visitor said:

'The three of us was smoking butts down at the bandstand and I said why wouldn't we fix them? It was myself says it and the next thing is aren't we asking Mr Fehilly would he give us advice.'

'All that's a long time ago.'

'"Dose the dogs," he says. "The first thing you'll do is dose the dogs." Mr Fehilly has the dose put by. He'll have the bicycles got for us, is what he says. "Get the lie of the land," he says. "Don't set a foot in till it's dark." Mr Fehilly was a cripple for Ireland, sir. He had broken bones in his back. He had two fingers gone off of his hand. "Wait till we see what have we in the petrol line," he says, and the tins were out the back, down a drain that'd gone dry. "Cover anything you'd have over," he gives us the instruction again. He has an old waterproof to obscure the tins when they'd be secured to the cross-bars. "Don't call in anywhere, take care if you'll stop for a smoke." You'd repeat the whole thing back until you'd say it right. Smash a pane, reach in for the catch. Raise up the sash, pitch in the juice. Pitch it in on the curtains. Pitch it in on any cushions would be lying around so's you'd get the feathers to go up. Pull the bell chain, rouse up the house. Wait for a lamp to be lit upstairs before you'd strike the match. Bring back the matchbox. Don't leave the matchbox lying around.'

'Drink up your lemonade, Mr Horahan, like a good man. All this is better left.'

The Captain stood up.

'There's things wouldn't be known to you, sir,' his visitor said.

'Well, yes, there would be, but all the same maybe they're better left.'

'There was a Brother used say to us the big house is the enemy. Did you hear tell of the Whiteboys, sir?'

'Oh, indeed.'

'Then again, the Ribbonboys. Then again, the hedge schools. That Brother would lay it out for us. How the Whiteboy would take a name for himself – Slasher or Cropper, Fearnot, Burnstack, anything he'd like. How the name would pass on when one boy'd be finished with it. I was a good few years at the Camp, sir.'

'I see.'

'I signed up in the army on account of the way I was with the dreams I'd have.'

'Ah.'

'I was never settled at the Camp. I was never settled since, sir, although it was quiet with me one time. The only commotion there'd be at the railway station was when the Cork train would be late with the August outing on it. Mr Hoyne would have his pictures made on the sand and the colours would get washed off by the sea before the August children would see them. The same month of the year, the Pierrots had a wicker basket with a lid hinged on to it and I'd wheel it on the trolley up the platform for them and they'd give me a few coppers. Another time again it was the Boys' Brigade parading down the platform and I'd stand there watching and nobody'd mind. Only a half-dozen of the boys there'd be, with their little drummer caps on. I never saw a cap the like of it since, sir. Is it gone altogether?'

'Maybe it is.'

'I was grand at the railway station the first while, sir. I was going out with a girl and we used walk down to where the swans would be. There was a little white dog would come running out of the hut where you'd buy cigarettes and he'd be snapping at her heels and she'd scold him like he was an infant. "Wait till you'll see this," I says to her and I showed her the shoulder. Doing the big fellow, the way you would with a girl you'd be gone on. Oh, I was gone on her all right. "Where'd you get that?" she says, and when I told her she says she didn't know I was one of the lads going out on that game. To tell the truth of it, you could hardly see the old scar, but however it was the next thing is I was never walking by the swans with her after. I'd look out for her and she wouldn't be around. If I'd locate her at Mass she'd scuttle off from me.'

'Oh. I'm sorry.'

'I didn't get the truth of it until the dreams. I knew the truth of it then, sir. I was never easy since. I'd be frightened of the dreams, sir.'

The Captain wondered if this man had come to the house before, if during the years of his own absence he had ever been a visitor. If this was so, it had never been mentioned, and for a moment he wondered if it had been kept from him, or not spoken of, as sometimes the activities of the disturbed were not. But neither his daughter's manner while she had been in the room, nor Henry's, suggested that any of this was likely.

The ex-soldier's awkward occupation of the armchair he had hunched himself into was confirmation of the unease he referred to. From time to time, while silences gathered or his fragmentary talk continued, his hands touched his clothes in different places, appearing to search for something. Abruptly, they would become still and then the knuckles of one were again rubbed by the fingers and palm of the other. His eyes squinted perpetually to the floor, to the rugs that covered most of the wide floorboards, to the corners of the wainscoting.

'You mightn't have known it, sir. That the two lads moved away altogether.'

'Which lads are these, Mr Horahan?'

'They're gone this long time, sir.'

'The boys who came out that night, is this? They'd have emigrated, would they?'

The Captain remembered the gasp of regret and fear that had caught in him somewhere when he realized he had wounded one of the youths who were standing on the grass, the relief there'd been when the boy hadn't fallen down. The boy had stumbled forward a few paces before his companions reached for him.

'It was an accidental thing,' he said. 'There was no intention to wound. I'm sorry it occurred.'

He lit one of his small cigars and, feeling in need of it, crossed the room to pour himself some whiskey. On the way, he caught a glimpse of the bicycle that was propped near one of the windows and he wondered if it was the one that had been ridden to the house twice before. He wondered how Horahan's two companions had got him back to Enniseala on the night he had been injured. Three bicycles between them could not have been easy to manage. He poured more whiskey than he'd intended. Slowly he went back to his chair.

'There's no one would say it, sir. The girl you were going with wouldn't say it to you on account it was too terrible to say to any man. The same as there's people in Enniseala wouldn't say it yet. In a shop they wouldn't. Nor my mother herself in her lifetime, God rest her. Nor the lads above at the Camp. There isn't a man working for Ned Whelan would say it out, sir.'

'And would you tell me what they won't say, Mr Horahan?'

The Captain spoke softly, estimating that he might do better in this conversation if he did. He remembered the mother who'd been referred to – stony-faced when he visited the house, drably dressed, with carpet slippers. She'd been as hostile as her husband, although she hadn't spoken.

'The lights would go up in the Picture House, sir, before you'd hear the Soldiers' Song. In the crowd going out nothing'd be said, sir. Not by a man or by a woman. You'd be done drilling in the barrack yard and it'd be the same the whole time. You'd be taking your grub and not a word said. It was Our Lady brought you back, sir.'

With a pity that came so suddenly it startled him, the Captain imagined this afflicted man at the army Camp, strange and solitary in a drill yard, the butt of whispers behind his back, struggling in his sleep against dreams that frightened him. He glimpsed him standing properly to attention in Enniseala's picture house while the national anthem was played. Did the empty screen he stared at fill with whatever were the figments of his torment? Were they there again on the streets, by the sea, on the banks of the estuary where the swans were?

'The day I seen you out walking on the promenade I was addressed by Our Lady, sir.'

*

A few bees hovered about the hives, most of them at work inside. The bees never stung her, but once a wasp had been in her shoe when she put it on and her mother had rubbed something cold on the place and read to her for the whole morning from the green Grimms' book. And a long time later, when her mother wasn't there any more, Henry had found a hornets' nest in a crack on the pear-tree wall. 'Sometimes I think the strand, or where the crossing stones are,' she'd said when Ralph asked her which her favourite place was. 'Sometimes I think the orchard.' They'd picked the Beauty of Bath and they were ripe again now, streaked pink and red like Hannah's cheeks when last she'd seen her. In the sunny corner Bridget's tea-towels were thrown over the blackcurrant bushes to dry. Stiff as card they had become. She picked them up in case it would rain later.

One of the sheepdogs ambled over to her in the yard. She stroked the smooth, dark head and felt it pressed against her thigh. When a fire was kept going in the feed shed she used to sit by it in winter, as Bridget once told her she had too when she was a child. Lucy went there now, into its shadowy dark. There hadn't been a fire there since, years ago, its purpose had changed. 'Will we store the wood here?' Henry had asked her, pretending that her opinion was valuable. Eleven she'd been.

She sat there, on a chair that had been in the kitchen until its back fell off. The sheepdog had not come in with her, turning away at the doorway from the cold air. She heard Henry's footsteps in the yard and he said it was Horahan who had come. She didn't know who Horahan was, only that it was the same name her father had said. She asked Henry and he told her. He took the tea-towels from her, saying he was on his way to the kitchen.

'Those days Horahan's not the full shilling,' he said.

She stood in the doorway of the feed shed, watching Henry cross the yard to the house. It seemed neither here nor there that the man who was to blame for everything had come back to Lahardane, neither here nor there that he wasn't the full shilling. Would Ralph have set out? Would he have driven just a little way? Today, this afternoon? Would that have accounted for the intensity of her intuition? Was, even now, a car backed into a gateway on an empty road, then turned around to go away?

'Oh yes,' she whispered, certain about what was left of a reality that hadn't lasted. 'It was today.'

She walked again in the orchard and in the garden that was overgrown. She felt a weariness in her body, as if suddenly she had become old. He would know. He would know that she suffered for her foolishness. One day a sorrowful reply to her letter would come, and she would want to write again herself, and would try and perhaps not be able to.

She wondered if the man who'd come in his place had gone by now, but when she passed from the garden into the yard and through the archway to the front of the house, the bicycle was still there. In the hall she could hear the voices. She might have turned away; she might have gone upstairs. But something seemed unfinished and she didn't.

'A drink?' her father offered in the drawing-room. 'Or the tea's still warm, I'd say.'

She shook her head. She could tell from his glance that he guessed she'd been told who the man he'd found in the house was. She wondered when he had realized himself. She wondered why he hadn't told him to go away.

'Mr Horahan has been a soldier,' her father said.

The unfinished embroidery of the figures on the strand was on the arm of the sofa, a pale-blue thread trailing from the eye of a needle. Colours she was waiting for were missing, blank patches here and there. She rolled the linen up, securing it with the needle, and returned it to her embroidery drawer.

'Stay with us, lady,' her father said.

She watched him pouring himself another drink. He poured her one even though she had declined a drink a moment ago. He carried it to her and she thanked him. A bird flapped against a window-pane, its wings beating in agitation before it recovered itself and flew off.

The man was muttering.

*

The time he was painting the windows at the asylum an inmate would suddenly be there, maybe two or three of them and they'd shake your hand through the bars, asking was there putty to spare and he'd roll them a few balls and put them on the inside window-sill. 'Oh, I know who you are,' one of them said one time and the others made a clamour, wanting to be told. 'Don't I know who you are?' the sergeant in the drill yard said, and a man coming out of Phelan's said it, bleary after drink. 'Another cripple for

Ireland,' one of the lads said and the curtains blew out, blazing against the sky.

'Every day I light the candle for the child.'

He raised his eyes to look around the room that hadn't been repaired in any way, not even to put new panes in the windows, not even to clean the blackened walls. Charred nearly to nothing, the furniture was there, and splinters of glass all over the floor, the rags of the curtains hanging down. 'Jeez, hurry on,' the lads said. 'Jeez, don't look back.'

The splinters savaged him when he knelt. Droplets of blood were warm on his legs when he stood up again, and he said he was sorry for bringing more blood into the room.

'No more than shadows,' he said, and explained because it wouldn't be known. No more than shadows in the smoke when he looked back and people were carrying the body.

*

'This is my daughter, Mr Horahan. My daughter is the child who was here then.'

Upstairs a door softly banged, the way doors sometimes did when a breeze blew in from the sea, its handle rattling because that handle was loose. In the quietness of the room Lucy tried to say that she might have married the man she loved, that her father and her mother had been driven from their house, that her mother had never recovered from her distress. It was the truth; she had come to the drawing-room to say it because it was all that was left to say, but the words would not come. The flowers she had earlier arranged, white campanulas, were pale against the sun-browned wallpaper. Smoke curled lazily from her father's cigarillo.

'That's a lovely evening for your journey back,' her father said.

She thought she had misheard, so extraordinary did that politeness seem. Again there was the urge to speak of the destruction in their lives, of fear and chaos where there had been happiness once, of pain. But again her anger collapsed, unable to break out.

'Well, now,' her father said, and crossed the room to the door, opening it and standing there. 'Go safely now,' he said in the hall.

She went with him, as if he'd asked her to, but he hadn't. Outside, the sun slanted over the gravel and the front-door steps. The sea in the distance was quiet. She might have wept but she had not and she did not now; she wondered if she ever would again. For a moment she looked into the features of the man who had returned after so long and saw there only madness. No meaning dignified his return; no order patterned, as perhaps it might have, past and present; no sense was made of anything.

'Every day I light the candle,' he said.

'Of course,' her father said. 'Of course.'

Bicycle-clips were carefully put on and then the afternoon's visitor rode off, a gangling figure on his big iron bicycle. They watched the bicycle disappear on the avenue, and when her father said he was sorry she knew from his tone that he realized why she had dressed herself up.

They walked a little way on the avenue, not saying anything before her anger broke, fiercely wrenched from her tiredness with an energy of its own. She cried out after the man who had gone, her anguish echoing in the trees of the avenue, her tears damp on her father's clothes when he held her to him.

'There now, there now,' she heard his voice, the two words murmured, again and then again.

8

Henry and Bridget had not yet begun seriously to suffer from the elderly ailments that were later to incapacitate both of them. When their aches began – Henry's knee, Bridget's shoulder when it was damp – they trusted to Providence; when in his workshed one day Henry was aware of a tightening in his chest, he stood still and felt it go away. Bridget had become deaf in one ear, but maintained that the other would see her out.

A greater, and unexpected, calamity was the creamery's declaration that the Lahardane milk was infected. It was discovered later that tuberculosis had spread in the herd: after the mandatory slaughter only eight cows would be left. Since the Captain's return he had assisted Henry with the milking, in which he was not skilled. This and all it otherwise involved – driving the cattle in twice a day to the milking parlour, scalding the churns, hosing out the dairy – was already becoming too much for two old men, as it had been for Henry on his own. He had struggled on, managing better with the Captain's assistance, but it was he who pointed out that the eight cows they were left with were too many if they ceased to send milk to the creamery and too few if they did not. The three with the best yield were kept, the others sold.

An end came with this. It would have been a similar finality, Bridget considered, when generations ago the greater part of the Lahardane acreage was lost playing cards with the O'Reillys. It grieved Henry that his work had been taken from him by misfortune, even though the work had begun to weary him, even though it was a comment of his that had brought about the reduction of what was left of the herd. As it was now, three cows would not manage, season after season, to consume the grass at their disposal. The fields would become ragged, thistles would seed themselves unchecked, nettles would spread. Helplessly, he would watch all that, without the heart or the strength to tackle matters with his scythe. 'Leave it,' Bridget's orders were.

There was no sense in doing otherwise, no sense in catching his death out in the rain the way a young man never would. Drenched through his clothes, Henry had time and again returned from these fields to the kitchen, where Bridget had hung his sodden garments on the pulley rails. From five o'clock in the morning until dark he had worked on summer days with his sickle or his long-handled hook, trimming back the hedges. Every March when the grass of the hydrangea lawn began to grow, he had scraped away the lawnmower's winter rust and oiled the axle. He did so still.

'Ah no, sir, no.' Bridget had refused the Captain's suggestion that he could arrange for a woman to come over from Kilauran to help her in the house. As Hannah used to come over in the old days, he had urged, but Bridget said a strange woman about the place would be more trouble than she was worth. 'Ah, sure, we're getting on grand,' she'd said.

The Captain knew they weren't. They were obstinate in their ways, an obduracy nourished by pride. They were proud of Lahardane as they had maintained it, of the continuing part they had played in it, of managing it, of improvising, of making themselves more than the caretakers he had left behind. It was Henry who suggested how the pasture might be saved from neglect and deterioration in the future: for a small annual rent, and undertaking to maintain the fences, the O'Reillys agreed to have the grazing.

Of the visitor who had come again to the house one afternoon, more than a year ago now, it was only said that, being insane, strictly speaking he was not responsible for his intrusion. Henry said it reluctantly and Bridget, after prayer, reluctantly agreed; but in neither was resentment entirely dissipated. The Captain said it more wholeheartedly.

Lucy did not, again, write to Ralph, as she had known she wouldn't, not even when a note came from him, as also she had known it would. The confusions of an afternoon, so strangely happening, calmed in retrospect, and yet for Lucy the afternoon had not dulled to greyness but had kept its colours as fresh as in a painting. Images of reality and of illusion still were there. The car stopped, and turned back. She lifted the tea-towels from the bushes. The man who'd come, whose presence was incidental and yet was not, knelt down to pray. Her father held her.

It is how things have happened, Ralph wrote. *No one is to blame.* What she had willed was not his way: that it was not was why first she'd loved him and still did. She had not known it then but only now: that all the letters in the world, all the longing, would not have made a difference. Until her life ended she would love a man who was married to someone else.

'Tell me about Montemarmoreo,' she asked at breakfast one morning, as if her father never had, and he repeated what he had told already. There were, again, the journeys to the races and to the Opera House, and Lucy was aware that her father hoped for what would never be: that out of a racecourse crowd or a theatre audience a man would step, as so long ago Ralph had stepped out of nowhere. Her father did not speak of this, but Lucy sensed such aspirations in his solicitude.

Their companionship – on Lucy's side once edgy with resentment, on her father's anxiously seeking too much – settled for what there was. She had rejected him was how it seemed to Lucy now, as it must have seemed to him at the time. She felt ashamed of that, and ashamed that she had not mourned her mother, that love's selfishness had so unkindly got the upper hand. Circumstances had shaped an emptiness in her existence; and love's ungainly passion belonged, with so much else, to the undemanding past. On her thirty-ninth birthday she and her father saw *Nicholas Nickleby* in the smart new cinema in Enniseala that had replaced the Picture House. They sat together far into the night when they returned to Lahardane, as sometimes now they did.

A few weeks later, on a fine November afternoon, they tended together the family graves at Kilauran, which Lucy in the past had always done on her own.

'We are among our people,' her father remarked, clipping away grass that had grown rank.

The stones were laid flat, as by tradition the Gault stones were, and the grass around them had grown high. Buttercup shoots sprawled in places over the lettering, clover softened the limestone edges.

Lucy rooted out herb Robert and ragwort and docks. In the time that had passed she had often reflected on the equanimity with which her father had listened to the ravings in their drawing-room. Simple man that he was, he might have gone that afternoon to find the rifle that had been fired from an upstairs window and with a soldier's instinct might have threatened its use again. Instead, he had withdrawn from an occasion that was beyond him; and he had done so since.

'One day, of course,' he predicted now, 'there'll be no one here to do all this. Not that it'll matter, since we do it for ourselves, don't you think?'

She nodded, digging out another root. Their people would end when they did, all duty to them finished, all memory of them dead. Only the myths would linger, the stories that were told.

'Oh, yes, all that,' he agreed.

She swept away the grass cuttings that were scattered on the smooth grey surface of a gravestone. Sometimes she wondered if the races weren't too much for him; it was ages since he had spent a morning with Aloysius Sullivan in the bar of the Central Hotel. 'He's slow, you'd notice,' Lucy had heard Henry say. Slow on the stairs, less agile than he had been once, when he'd clambered through the trapdoor to the roof. Slow with his scythe in the apple orchard, with his spade when he dug the brambles. It was she who drove the car now, leaving him in it when she went away to shop, to pass from counter to counter in Enniseala with Bridget's list, the steady handwriting unchanged since the days when Henry used to pass it over to Mrs McBride on the way back from the creamery. There had been a *For Sale* notice outside Mrs McBride's shop for years, but recently it had been taken down. No one came to live there.

'Well, it's better anyway.' Her father turned away to grimace when he ceased to kneel. 'A bit better, lady?'

There was a place in a corner of the graveyard for depositing weeds and grass. She carried her debris, already withering, to it.

'Much better,' she said when she returned, and began to gather together the tools they'd used.

They drove into Enniseala then, since they were on the way there. She bought what she had to, known and greeted in all the shops. Often she wondered if she caused a nervousness in the people of Enniseala, since strange events must have left her strange: they could not be blamed for thinking that. But even so she always dawdled there now, for she had come to like a town she had been indifferent to in the past.

This afternoon she watched the swans swimming back and forth, or less gracefully parading on the banks they had made their own. She admired the reddish-pink valerian that hung from the high walls she passed on her way to the promenade. She noticed what her father had drawn her attention to when he first returned: the royal insignia still there beneath the green paint of the letter-boxes. She gazed down at the children playing on the rocks below the sea-wall; she watched the loads of seaweed drawn away. Sometimes she sat in the café of the bread shop next to the abandoned auction rooms, sometimes she sunned herself on the bandstand, but today she passed these places by, returning instead to the car, where her father was dozing over the *Irish Times*.

That same evening he talked about the Enniseala regattas and summer carnivals that were no more. And she remembered how Mr Sullivan had once brought news of the Blueshirts who had marched up the long main street, and of the racing cars that had roared through the town in the middle of the night, their circuit of Ireland half completed.

'Remember how we went that evening to say good-bye to Mr Aylward?' her father said. 'How you looked for the deaf and dumb fisherman?'

On his way to bed he stood by the cluttered table in the hall, a scuffed leather-bound book he had picked up from it in his hand.

'He taught me how to talk to him,' she said. 'Did I tell you that? He'd be waiting when I was going home from school.'

'You can talk with your fingers, lady?'

'Yes, I can.'

From where she stood, in the open doorway of the drawing-room, she showed him. The fisherman's hands had been rough and scarred, freckles spreading on the backs of them when he was old, and yet the movements had made her want to make them herself. Their conversations were what infants might have said to one another, and often she had thought that no more should be demanded of an old man and a child who did not know one another well.

'You were lonely then,' her father said.

'It doesn't matter, being a little lonely.'

'Well no, perhaps not.'

Vaguely, he put the book back on the table, the leather of its spine flapping where it had given way. Le Fanu's *Irish Life* it was, his bookmark in it an electricity bill. For a moment his hand rested on the tattered leather, his thoughts not showing in his face, although often they did. He had been aware of her jealousy of a wife; he knew it was less painful than it had been. But none of that was ever said.

'One day, lady, will you visit the cemetery in Switzerland? And Montemarmoreo too?'

'Might we not go together to Montemarmoreo?'

'You would like to?'

'Yes, I would.'

'During those years she was not always unhappy, you know.'

'You're tired, Papa.'

'It's difficult to explain. I only knew it.'

She watched him go, without the book he had picked up and then put down again. There had never been the convention of wishing one another good-night in this house and there was not now.

'The bees have not left Lahardane,' he said, looking down from halfway up the stairs. 'I wonder if they ever will.'

In the drawing-room Lucy sat alone for a little longer, then drew the fire-guard in front of the embers that still glowed in the grate. She tidied the cushions and the chairs, closed the doors of the corner cupboard, easing them where they stuck and had to be pushed a little. Passing the bagatelle board, she set the marbles going among the pins. Two hundred and ten was her highest score, achieved when she was six, and she did not better it tonight.

For an instant when she looked back to see that everything was all right she saw the room as, once upon a time, fire might have ravaged it, and heard again the tormented voice. Often when she awoke from early-morning sleep she took with her from some unquiet dream the figure in bleak, black clothes crouched terrified in an armchair, the empty eyes. Once she'd seen the big old-fashioned bicycle propped against the wall near the lighthouse and, far away on the sands, the lanky form of the man who believed he was a murderer. She had watched him for a moment, not knowing why she did, not knowing why so easily she remembered and saw again the restless shuffle of the hands, the agitated fingers groping to touch each place of agony. On the sands he hadn't moved from where he was but all the time stood staring at the sea.

*

Propped up on his pillows, the Captain listened for his daughter's footsteps and heard them pass his door. For a moment in the night he was glad that they had tidied up the graves. Later he was aware of pain. It did not wake him.

FIVE

I

Long after the funeral, when another year had begun, Lucy went through her father's belongings and his clothes. Nothing she came across was a surprise. Folding away shirts and suits, she wondered if drama was finished with at last in the house that now was hers. He had drunk his whiskey to the end, she had not stopped him. He had known that death was creeping up on him; more than once he had remarked that nothing was more certain than that it should. He had smiled through this acceptance of nature's strict economy and she had too, keeping company with him in his dismissal of morbid anticipation, remembering him as he had been while she made the slow journey of loving him again, forgiven for her unspoken reproaches.

Some of his belongings she kept: his sets of cufflinks; his watch; the stick he had taken to using when, once in a while, he accompanied her on her walks; the wedding ring he'd worn. She drove into Enniseala with his clothes, to give them to the women who collected for the charity of St Vincent de Paul. She put away the picture postcards he had kept. The bedroom that had been like a grave during its unoccupied years was a grave again, its door closed, never entered.

A certain formality passed from the house with the Captain's death, a way of proceeding that belonged to his past, that he had valued and cherished, that had fallen into place as a matter of course on his return. 'No. It is not necessary,' Lucy laid down, not wishing either Bridget or Henry any longer to carry trays of dishes back and forth between the kitchen and the dining-room. It was she who now, more and more, looked after them rather than they who attended her. She took her place at the kitchen table again, as she had during her childhood and for years after it. In the adjustments that were made it was they whose convenience she saw to, not her own. Without complaint, the trays would have been carried to the dining-room and from it, had her father still been there: Lucy knew that nothing he or she could have said or done would have altered that.

Bridget continued to cook; Henry split logs in the yard, and milked, and did his best with the long grass in the orchard. On Sundays Lucy took them with her when she drove to Kilauran, arriving half an hour early for church so that they could go to Mass, all three of them remembering how years ago this, too, had been the other way around. Henry bought his cigarettes and then they waited for her outside the shop. Attending Mass, and seeing people afterwards, was an occasion Bridget had enjoyed since her girlhood, and she still did. That the gate-lodge was derelict now wasn't mentioned when they passed it on their Sunday journeys. In the kitchen the talk was more about how Henry, when he'd married into Lahardane, had missed the sea and how, when he hadn't settled for a while, Bridget had been unhappy, believing she had deprived him of his way of life. 'But, sure, you get used to anything,' Henry said, and he had, and it had been all right. A pedlar used to go about the roads at that time, with little floor rugs that came from Egypt, and buttons of all sizes and colours, and skewers for roasting that he made from the ash he cut, and sticks of chalk and brown jars of ink. You'd never see the like nowadays, you hadn't for maybe thirty years. Another man had called at Lahardane selling lamp mantles, and every year the *Old Moore's Almanac* man had come. Tinkers mended the saucepans in the yard, the horses were taken four miles to be shod.

That was the talk now, and Lucy listened, hearing that on the day she was born it had been misty all morning, and that she might have been called Daisy or Alicia. The drawing-room chimney had gone on fire the first Christmas Eve she was alive. The wren-boys made up something about an infant for St Stephen's Day. Going home once on the strand, Hannah heard a banshee.

'No more than the wind,' Henry said, 'moaning down through the hollow in the cliffs.'

But Bridget said Hannah had seen a wispy form not a yard from where she stood.

*

The Captain's wish was honoured. On a bright March morning in 1953, Lucy looked down at her mother's grave.

Heloise Gault in her 66th year. Of Lahardane, Ireland.

The dark letters shone out from unpolished granite, and Lucy tried to see the face she remembered as it must have become with age. The cemetery in Bellinzona was small; no one else was there. She knelt and prayed.

Afterwards she ordered coffee in the café opposite the railway station. Everything was strange to her: never before had she left Ireland. The long train journeys in England and France and Switzerland had spread before her a foreignness she had encountered only in the novels she read. The language spoken by the waiter who brought her coffee was a language she had never heard spoken before, every word of it incomprehensible. Swiss walkers came in a bunch to fill the tables around her, their sticks and haversacks piled on to the unoccupied chairs. Somewhere in this town there was a kindly doctor.

Another journey took her across the Italian border. That evening in a small room in Montemarmoreo's one hotel she unpacked the blue suitcase she had once been assured was particularly her own, even though there hadn't been an opportunity to have her initials pressed into the leather. She ordered food not knowing what would come.

In the early morning she found via Cittadella and the house of the shoemaker, whose wares were displayed in the downstairs windows. On the first-floor balcony that overlooked the street there was just enough room for a table and two chairs. She did not disturb the shoemaker, either then or later, only wondering if he was the son of the shoemaker of the past or if someone else had bought the business.

She walked about in cramped, congested streets. There was an altarpiece in the church that honoured St Cecilia. The public lighting was being improved, new lamp posts settled into the holes that had been excavated at the pavements' edge, traffic diverted. She learnt her first Italian words: *ingresso, chiuso, avanti*. She found a restaurant her father had told her about, modest in a back street. Outside the town she found the finished marble quarries.

Her mother had belonged here. More than England, more than Lahardane, she had made this ordinary small town her own, and Italy her country. For Lucy there was still a shadow and the distant echo of a voice remembered, but in the bustle of the streets and on the road to the marble quarries she sensed a stranger. *I shall remain a little longer,* she wrote on a postcard to Bridget and Henry, and wondered if she too – through some new quirk of chance – would stay for ever.

She heard the story of St Cecilia. A woman in the church told her, a slight, gently spoken woman she had seen there before, who approached her from among the empty pews. The miraculous, the woman pointed out in English, was in the eyes of the altarpiece's image. Together they looked at the pale-blue eyes and at the tresses of fair hair, the halo finished in gold leaf, the dress so light it seemed almost colourless, the lyre held delicately. As a child, the woman said, St Cecilia had heard all the world's music that was yet to come.

Lucy guessed that her mother – perhaps from this same source – had learnt that St Cecilia had been born to be a martyr, had been murdered when she mocked the ancient gods, becoming after death the holy patron of musicians, as St Catherine was of saddlers and Charles Borromeo of starch-makers, as St Elizabeth sought mercy for all sufferers from toothache.

Alms were begged for the church's repair and then the woman went.

*

Lucy left Montemarmoreo reluctantly, yet knowing she would not ever return. Hers was a different allocation of time and circumstance from her mother's, from her father's. She could not pretend.

When winter came that same year, when the memory of her long journey had begun to lose its vividness, she read again – methodically in order of their composition – the letters she had received from Ralph. They stirred the love that still affected her, but the people of the letters were other people now, as her mother and her father were. She took the unfinished embroidery from her embroidery drawer and wrapped Ralph's anguished pleas in it, tying the bundle with string she made from her coloured threads.

2

One afternoon in Enniseala Lucy looked for the black bicycle. She looked for it near the lighthouse where the fishing boats came in and in the poor part of the town. She thought she saw it once, outside the League of the Cross Hall, and again in MacSwiney Street, but when she went closer she realized she'd been mistaken. She took to sitting by one of the windows in the café attached to the bread shop. She did not know what she would do if the bicycle went by or what she would do if she saw it propped up against a shop window or a wall, as she had before. Her compulsion came from nowhere that she knew about, and seemed to feed on the very failure of her efforts. In the end she asked, and was told that the man she sought had been admitted to the asylum.

She brought that information back to Lahardane, but it elicited neither interest nor much of a response. It was a suitable thing, the unspoken opinion seemed to be; and Lucy imagined it voiced in the kitchen when she wasn't there, with a note of satisfaction in whatever exchanges there were. She drove out to the asylum when she was next in Enniseala and drew on to the verge by high iron gates. The brick building on a hill had an empty look, as if there were no inmates, but she knew that wasn't so. The locked gates were intimidating. A chain trailed down one of the pillars, a bell suspended from an iron bracket on the other side.

She drove away again.

*

On the dining-room table she stretched out another piece of linen, each corner weighed down with a book. Carefully she copied on to the cloth the watercolour sketch she had made: poppies on an ochre ground. She chose the silks and laid them in a row.

She wondered how many times she had done all this before; how many times she had said when an embroidery was finished, 'You might like to have it?' She had never found a better way of not appearing to presume that there was merit in what she offered. The giving was a pleasure, her exaggeration part of it when she said there was no room left on the walls at Lahardane.

She stitched in single threads to mark the colours: the orange and red of the poppies in half a dozen shades, four different greens for the spiky leaves, the ochre frilled with grey. Months it would take to complete, all winter.

*

'Bring Miss Gault her tea.'

Behind the bread counter in the café the wife of the baker gave the order to a child in a flowered overall. So she was safely back, the observation had been in the café when she had returned from Switzerland and Italy, the purpose of her journey known but not remarked upon.

She hung her umbrella on the back of her table's other chair. Rain had suddenly blown in that afternoon.

'That's shocking weather,' the woman behind the bread counter called out to her.

The woman's red hair was greying now and a look of relief had become established in her eyes, as if she gave silent thanks for no longer being of child-bearing age: she'd had ten girls and a boy. Never putting in an appearance in the café, her husband baked half the town's bread, and cakes and buns and doughnuts.

'Cakes, is it, miss?' the child enquired, scattering with her hand the crumbs on the stained tablecloth and wiping away the milk that a cork mat hadn't entirely absorbed. 'Will I bring them assorted?'

'Thank you.'

The child's features were pinched, the hand that was rearranging the sugar bowl and milk jug affected by chilblains. Her other hand was bandaged.

'Isn't the rain heavy for itself, miss?'

'It is. Are you Eileen? I confuse you with your sister. I'm sorry.'

'Is it my older sister?'

'I think it might be.'

'My older sister's Philomena.'

'And you're Eileen?'

'I am, all right. Wait till I'll bring you the tea now.'

Above the door that led to the back regions, a plaster figure, fingers raised, blessed the café. Lucy watched the child pass beneath it, then rooted in her purse for a threepenny piece in case she forgot later. She dropped it into her glove, knowing she would feel it there. She watched the rain through the painted letters on the glass of the wide half-curtained window. People were hurrying on the street, raincoats over their heads.

'You'll have us drowned, Mattie!' the woman behind the counter shouted at a ragged man who'd just come in, whose drenched clothes were dribbling on to the floor. He was often on the streets, playing his accordion for coppers.

'Sure, won't it wash the floor for you?' He sat down at a table near the door, his accordion on the table in front of him.

'There's only these ones left,' the girl called Eileen said, referring to the cakes she'd brought. A wedge-shaped piece had been cut out of the sponge of each, artificial cream and raspberry jam inserted and the piece replaced. Six there were on the plate. 'They're the nicest anyway, miss.'

'They're lovely, Eileen.'

A dinged metal teapot was carefully lowered on to the cork mat, a knife placed beside an undecorated white plate.

'Would I bring you a slice of the brack, miss?'

'No, no, I have plenty, Eileen.'

She poured out the strong, dark tea and weakened it with milk. She peeled the paper from the bottom of one of the sponge cakes. Other people came in from the rain, a pram pushed to the table next to the accordion player's, drops shaken from a red umbrella, one of its ribs protruding awkwardly when it was collapsed. 'It's here for the duration,' someone remarked and there was laughter.

How she would like to be addressed in the easy way the accordion player had been! How she would like to take part in the badinage! 'The Protestant woman's still waiting for her change,' one of the counter girls had said in Domville's not long ago. It was how they thought of her, how they described her when her name escaped them or if they didn't know it, what her appearance and her dress suggested, as her voice did, as their manner with her did. A Protestant woman was a relic, left over, respected for what she was, not belonging. And she among such women was more different still. After she'd left Domville's that day, the girl who hadn't known her would have been told.

She poured more tea and asked for hot water, which came with time. Blurred sunlight weakly lit the window, was lost and then flickered back again. The colour-wash of the houses across the street brightened – pink and green, slates of a roof glistening. She was as used to being different as she was to feeling alone. The same thing perhaps it was, and anyway it was ridiculous to mind.

The moment passed. Elation – exhilaration almost – had been her mood during the months she'd stitched her embroidery of poppies. She had not sought to understand, only continuing in her obedience to an intention that was entirely her own, to do what she was drawn to do. She watched the people in the café for a little longer, the accordion player finishing the cup of tea he was not asked to pay for, the baby sleeping in its pram, a couple eating fish and fried potatoes, two women intently conversing. She found the threepenny piece in her glove and left it under the rim of her saucer. She paid at the counter.

Outside, the pavement had already begun to dry in patches when she walked to where her car was. Tinker children begged; behind her somewhere the accordion music began. Blue spread in the sky.

She drove on to find a place where she might turn and then drove back again, past the Bank of Ireland and Coughlan's warehouses, on through the town and into the country.

When she came to the iron gates she drew on to the verge, as she had before. The embroidery that had taken her all winter to complete was framed in ash-wood so pale it was almost white. She reached into the back of the car for it and carried it with her to the pillar where the bell-chain hung.

Rusty on its pivot, the heavy bell swung soundlessly at first before its clanging echoed against the hill. She waited, but no one answered. No gardener or workman came. No one appeared on the short, steep avenue. She stayed a while, then drove away.

She stopped when she saw a line of men approaching a crossroads ahead of her. Ten or eleven of them there were, all darkly clad. A keeper walked in front, another brought up the rear. She waited until the men were closer and then got out of her car.

'He's not with us today,' the keeper at the head of the line said when she gave the name. 'But if you've something for him I'll pass it on.'

She gave him the framed embroidery. The other keeper said:

'Did you make it yourself, ma'am?'

They crowded round to see. 'Beautiful,' the same keeper said. 'Beautiful,' one of the men repeated, and then another said it, and another.

She asked if it would be possible, once in a while, to visit the recipient of her gift.

*

'Sure, what sense does it make?' Henry muttered when the spring and summer of that year passed and another winter had settled in.

Bridget dried a cup and placed it inside another, both on their sides, their saucers beneath them. Her fingers today were slow in what was required of them, the knuckles reluctant to unstiffen.

'No sense,' she said. 'But then.'

'Is she all right, would you think?'

Not knowing what to say, Bridget didn't answer. She carried the cups and saucers to the big green dresser, hung the cups on their hooks, settled the saucers upright, behind the ridge on the shelf. It was the damp in the air that made a bad day of it. When it was cold the knuckles weren't so affected.

'She comes back tired,' Henry said.

'Ah well, she would.'

Five years it was since the man had come to the house, thirty-four since he had come before. Bridget remembered walking down the avenue from the gate-lodge the morning after the first time and Henry saying something was wrong, how he had mentioned the dogs being poisoned a week or so ago, how he'd cleared away the gravel pebbles because they had blood on them. She remembered Lucy, dressed up, coming into the kitchen when the man came again, saying she'd carry the tea in. And afterwards Lucy not saying what she and Henry and the Captain had: that the insane maybe couldn't be held responsible for being a nuisance. You couldn't have blamed Lucy. You couldn't have blamed her for hating the man.

'There's people talking about it,' Henry said. 'Her going there.'

'There would be, all right.'

They'd talk about it because they wouldn't understand it, any more than it was understood in this kitchen. Wasn't it enough that things had settled in the end – the Captain persevering with his sympathy, the jaunts they went out on, his fondness and his companionship at last accepted? Wasn't it enough again, the memory of her friend's love all down the years, still there for all anyone would know? 'Why d'you want to go out to that old place?' – Bridget had her protest ready, had had it ready for ages now, but she kept it to herself.

'Snakes and ladders they play,' Henry said.

3

One day, not long after she first came, the keeper said to him, 'I'll instruct you how to sharpen the razors.'

The breakfast dishes were on the tables at the time, knives and forks across them, all the knives blunted with a file, the tin mugs with dregs of tea in them. His turn it was to gather up what there was, piling everything on to the tray and passing it through the hatch, waiting there until it came back, while the keeper put other things in the cupboards – the salt and pepper, any cutlery that would not have been used, the sugar dishes. Matthew Quirke the keeper was that morning. He had his coat off, bands on his shirtsleeves, his cap on the chest by the door. No one else was there.

'A privilege,' Mr Quirke said. 'The razors.'

No one was allowed near the razors only Matthew Quirke himself. It was he who shaved the men; since Eugene Costello had kept a razor by him and they found him the next morning, it was Mr Quirke who shaved the men, a rule made then.

'How's that then?' a voice called out from the other side of the hatch, hands pushing back the tray, the spills wiped from it. MacInchey's hands they were; you'd know the voice.

'You understand me?' the keeper said. 'You know what I'm saying to you?' Mr Quirke let what he said stay where it was, not pressing it. 'Ah, you do, you do,' he said, squeezing out a cloth into a basin of water. Matthew Quirke would take a glance at you and know was he understood or not. 'There's not another man I'd trust with the razors,' he said. South Tipperary he came from, set for the priesthood only something went wrong. 'Brush down that table now,' he said. 'Leave the long one to me and then we'll go out the back.'

The shed that had black-painted windows was across the big yard with the drain in the middle. There were two padlocks on it, one high, one low. Inside there was a light to put on.

The door closed behind them, a bolt shot into place. The light was a bulb hanging down over the workbench. The keeper unrolled a bundle in green baize and lifted out the razors, then oiled the sharpening stone.

'Isn't it a grand thing she comes by?' he said.

The first razor went into the vice for a speck of rust to be rubbed off with sandpaper, then the edge was passed over the stone, wiped with a rag before the strop was pulled taut on the hook it hung from.

'You'd get the way of it,' the keeper said. 'Isn't it grand, though?' he said.

You didn't have to answer. Matthew Quirke knew you wouldn't. The new keeper who came instead of Mr Sweeney didn't get it at first, not until Briscoe told him there was a man who didn't want to speak.

'Ah it is, it is,' Mr Quirke said.

Myley Keogh's bar was on the road back that day, a jug of water on the counter. 'That's a great cycle you're after getting off,' the woman said, and the only thing was you couldn't ask for a sup from the jug and the woman'd be waiting. No person would be fit to ask for water after seeing the house the way it was and people living in it. No person'd be fit to speak at all.

'It's coming up good,' the keeper said. 'Continue with the sand-paper a while yet.'

When it was shining in the light he said to stop. 'You have a friend in her all right,' he said. 'Sure, isn't it that that matters at the heel of the hunt?'

Mr Quirke handed him more sandpaper. He tightened the vice on the next razor he took from the baize. There was more rust on this one than on the last, Mr Quirke said. 'Don't be in a hurry with it.'

You wouldn't want to be in a hurry the way the days were. Any day at all, its hours would go by without haste. You'd take a line from that. No need for hurry.

'That's good, that's good,' Mr Quirke said. He was whistling, soft, under his breath. He was whistling 'Danny Boy' and then he sang. The razor had gone dark wherever it had been kept, but it could be made shiny again, Mr Quirke said, easy enough. By the time they'd finished with it, it would be better than new from the factory.

For an hour and then longer the work continued in the little shed. There was a calendar hung up, a picture of a mountainside on it, trees felled and lying down, the days laid out on it. At the beginning and in the middle of a month she always came, and when you woke up in the morning you'd know. You wouldn't know what day it was, only that it was the one when she came. It wouldn't be today.

'We've made a job of that,' the keeper said.

He folded the baize around the first of the sharpened blades and then around another one. He held them there with a rubber band around the baize.

'Would you think of a little bird-box?' he said. 'You put it on to a tree trunk and the robins would nest inside.'

He drew it out on a piece of ply-board. He showed how you'd cut the wood, two sides with a slant, the piece for the back taller than the front, a hinge marked where you'd lift open the lid and look in. The measurements were written down in red pencil on the ply-board. 9×4 the back, $6\frac{3}{4} \times 4$ the front. 5×4 and 4×4 were the lid and the bottom, $8 \times 4 \times 6\frac{3}{4}$ the sides. 'Would you think of it for her?' Mr Quirke said.

The bell went for twelve o'clock. 'We'll shut up shop,' Mr Quirke said, propping up the ply-board against the ledge of a window-sill. 'Wouldn't it be something for you to be thinking about?' he said in the yard, and again in the passageway. 'When she'd win with the dice wouldn't you give her a prize one time?'

In the hall the men had gathered for the Angelus prayer. Mr Quirke was in charge this morning and he went forward to the platform. Father Quirke he'd be now if he'd gone for the priesthood, giving out his orders on a Sunday, everything different for him.

Feet shuffled when the prayer was over; there was talking again and someone shouting out and then someone else. You'd have it wrapped up ready, made the way Mr Quirke would instruct you. She'd throw a six and go up and then she'd throw a four and she'd be home. You'd give it to her and she'd say what it was. She'd say it for you, like she always did.

SIX

The hand of her watch says twenty past five, the early-morning light gauzy and then becoming brash. She closes her eyes again. First thing once you'd lie there and hear the turkeys gobbling in the yard, Henry calling in the cows. On the wash-stand a crack runs from the lip of the jug through delicate green tracery and then is lost: always that has been there. The same green decorates the basin, is repeated on the wash-stand's single row of tiles. One of the three high windows is open a few inches at the top because she likes the air at night even when there's a storm. The outside paint has flaked away, the wood bleached by the sun.

She bundles her nightdress over her head, the floorboards creaking comfortingly when she crosses to the bent-wood chair where her clothes are still folded from the night, stockings draped, shoes tidy in shoe-trees. She pours out water and slowly washes, and slowly dresses. A seagull alights on the window-sill, its beady stare impertinent before it swoops off. Kitty Teresa said she'd like to be a seagull, but Bridget said Kitty Teresa hadn't the brains for it.

She presses in her hairpins, sets her collar as she likes to have it, looks at herself in her dressing-table glass, stands up to pull her dress straight, still guided by her reflection. She pours away the water from the wash-stand basin and carries the enamel waste-bucket across the room to the door. On the bed she makes the top and bottom sheet taut, stroking away the creases, smoothing each blanket also, shaking the pillows, tucking the quilt in.

After the first time, whenever she pulled the bell-chain on the pillar the shouting began, reaching her dimly from far away. And then the keeper appeared on the steep avenue, picking his steps because the surface was furrowed, keys jangling when he was nearer. 'Ah no, the Horahans don't come,' he said the first time, speaking of brothers and a sister who had moved away from Enniseala, who had last been back for their mother's funeral. 'A family would be ashamed,' he said, beside her in the car when he had locked the gates. He always said to wait when they reached the house. Not until the din inside quietened was the grey hall door opened.

In those days she dressed up a bit: this morning, finishing in her bedroom, she remembers that. She dressed up for them because they liked it. They said it sometimes when she passed through the hall, where some of them loitered, when they came to her until they were restrained, incoherent in their mumbling speech. They didn't mind restraint. Those who did were elsewhere, the same keeper said, a step ahead of her on the stairs. He looked over his shoulder, pointing down at the five stone steps in case she would trip. He turned the corner into the wooden stairway, turning again into the long, yellow-distempered passage in which all the doors were closed and the boards uncarpeted, the walls without pictures. The room set aside for visitor and inmate was bare, the same yellow on the walls, a light burning beneath Christ in glory, her embroidery given pride of place. 'Well now, well now, a visitor today.' That keeper had a laugh you'd remember. He'd been amused when he'd told her that on the road that day some of them had taken her to be the wife of the inmate whose name she'd known. Arguments about it there'd been, he said, and later on arguments as to whether on one visit or another the correct day had been observed. The first day of a fortnight she always came on, but several times it was spread about that she'd got it wrong, that she'd miscalculated. 'You never did, though,' that keeper said. 'In all the years.' Seventeen it was in the end.

That keeper's face comes back to her on her way across the landing to the bathroom. Some faces do, more readily than others. Was it he who said he would arrange for her to have her own key to the gates? One day in winter, when the panes of the barred windows had iced up so that you couldn't see out? A day in spring it was when the key was ready, specially cut for her and they tried it in the lock because a new key doesn't always turn. A ceremony they made of it, showing her the knack.

She pours away the water she has washed in, tipping the enamel bucket on the bath's edge. On her way downstairs she goes into all the rooms, only to see what yesterday she saw, but wanting to do that. A spider clings to a cobweb that is within her reach, that has been woven in the night. She takes the spider to the window, releasing it when she has eased up the sash, flicking away that remains of the cobweb also. This time of year, every morning there is one somewhere.

In the kitchen she turns on the plate of the stove that heats more swiftly than the others. She watches its coils redden, listening when the News begins: in the night a farmer has been murdered for the money he kept by him, a golfer somewhere has set a record. It was when Henry's sister emigrated to America that the little blue Bakelite wireless came into the kitchen, turned on on Sunday evenings for Joe Linnane's *Question Time* and for nothing else. Nineteen thirty-eight or so.

The groceries came yesterday, the bread still fresh in the tin. 'If you're not on the Internet,' a brisk voice warns, 'you're not at the races.' Making tea, she wonders what that means, remembering Baltimore Girl coming in at nine to one, her father's money on it at Lismore, hers on Black Enchanter. 'You're not going to tell me you've never been to the races!' His astonishment comes back to her and the memory trails into something else, she doesn't know why: she wonders if Ralph ever read Lady Morgan. Henry sat close to the range, chilled to his bones, he said, and she drove off to get the new lady doctor, and the priest came out with his stuff all ready in his flat black case. A year after that it would have been when Bridget didn't come down one morning.

She eats slowly, the radio turned off now. When she finishes – after she has poured what remains in the kettle over her cup and saucer and plate, and wiped the knife clean, after she has emptied the tea-leaves and turned the teapot upside down on the draining-board – she carries a chair out to the yard. She carries another, and then a third, her gait hardly affected by the limp that has become slighter with the years. She sits and waits, dozing in the sun.

The colours were what he liked: the red and the green, yellow and purple, the blue his favourite. He liked the forked tongues, the eyes as black as pitch; two boards from Ronan's they'd worn out.

'Sit by the window, shall we?' she said the day they heard the cuckoo, and they looked down at the ragwort-laden grass of the hill, no trees breaking its green monotony, no fence or rail bounding the brief avenue, the high brick wall. 'Oh, listen!' she said when the two notes of the cuckoo's song began.

He threw the dice and moved his disc; he always wanted her to win, not that he ever said so, but she knew. She heard his voice that one time, in the drawing-room, not ever again: the oblivion that possessed him was his secret. There were many secrets in the asylum, a younger keeper said; in asylums everywhere there were secrets preciously guarded because there was so little else. Oblivion often was an inmate's last, his sole, possession. That younger keeper was given to talk that was a bit on the fanciful side.

When they looked down, squirrels searched the unkempt grass, heads occasionally cocked, ears suddenly alert. Once a fox had strolled about among them, too wise to make enemies of them. She said so, and wondered if he understood.

That's there again when she slips deeper into sleep. The keeper says it's time now and on the stairways and in the passages the wild faces draw back from her. Hands reach out and then are harmless in the air.

*

'Well, there you are!' Sister Mary Bartholomew exclaims.

Clean and tidy in the habit they wear nowadays, the two nuns cross the cobbles, each bringing her something, and bringing her the news as well – of a change there is to be at the convent, new lockers outside the refectory. There is something else but she doesn't quite hear and doesn't ask because Sister Mary Bartholomew is already going on, about the two novices who have begun this week. Sister Antony brings her currant shortbread today, Sister Mary Bartholomew some kind of herbal tea.

'Enniseala?' Sister Mary Bartholomew repeats what she has been asked. 'Oh now, what's new?'

The car is giving them trouble, the radiator heating up. They'll have to come on bicycles if the car gives out. Not that it would come to that, of course; and there is laughter.

'Condon's closed,' Sister Antony said. 'Young Halpin's back from America.'

'You wouldn't call Eddie Halpin young.' Sister Mary Bartholomew softly murmurs her contradiction. 'No way.'

'I meant young when he left.'

'Oh, young then right enough.'

'Say about Father Leahy.'

'Father Leahy's maybe going out to the Equator.'

It's pleasant, listening to the nuns, usually on a Tuesday. Not once since they've begun to come have they forgotten her.

'It's good of you,' she says. Good of them to bother with someone who isn't of their faith, whose solitude they heard about. Good of them to come all this way. 'Kind,' she says.

An outing for them, they replied when she said it before, and told her that last summer at the Mount Melleray Retreat a crotchety old nun was critical when she heard they drove fourteen miles to visit a Protestant woman. 'Wouldn't her own do that for her?' the old nun grumbled and they didn't say how they'd replied. Ever since they heard all that's still talked about they have come; one morning they just drove up. It's famous in Enniseala that years ago she walked behind the funeral through the town, as famous as it is that for so long she visited the asylum. It shouldn't be, her own view is, for does it matter, really, why people visit one another or walk behind a coffin, only that they do?

'The swans?'

'They're still there always.'

She usually asks about the swans, reminding herself earlier to do so. If the swans left Enniseala it would be a loss. The last thing her father said to her was about the honey bees in the orchard.

Their faces smile at her, Sister Mary Bartholomew's elongated, a hair curling out of a mole on her chin, Sister Antony's as round as the sun. Already in the yard there is the aroma of the coffee they've made. Freshly ground in O'Hagan's, Sister Antony says, and Sister Mary Bartholomew sets up the green-baized card table she has carried out from the dog passage. Rickety it is, going on beyond its time.

'I thought we brought scones,' she says, noticing they're not on the table when Sister Antony spreads the cloth.

'They're in the tin yet,' Sister Antony says. 'They'll keep fresh in the tin.'

There are the macaroons that one of the lay sisters bakes, and slices of her fruitcake, the scones in a flowery tin.

'How lovely it is, the autumn sunshine!' Sister Mary Bartholomew remarks.

'Yes, it's beautiful.'

Her tranquillity is their astonishment. For that they come, to be amazed again that such peace is there: all they have heard, and still hear now, does not record it. Calamity shaped a life when, long ago, chance was so cruel. Calamity shapes the story that is told, and is the reason for its being: is what they know, besides, the gentle fruit of such misfortune's harvest? They like to think so: she has sensed it that they do.

Their wonderment is in their gestures and in their presents, and gazing from their eyes. They did not witness for themselves, but others did, the journey made to bring redemption; they only wonder why it was made, so faithfully and for so long. Why was the past belittled? Where did mercy come from when there should have been none left? They laud the mercy and silently applaud the figure at the funeral, but hearsay tells them nothing more.

She could manage without them, they often say, since she has made an art of being solitary. Nothing is dirty in the kitchen: she has seen them thinking that. She dresses more carefully than when she was a girl. Once in a while a hairdresser comes out from Enniseala to attend to her in her sedate old age.

'All things Italian I love,' Sister Mary Bartholomew remarks when the conversation for a moment lapses.

Italy is often talked about, the trip to the town called Montemarmoreo. They know about its narrow, cluttered streets, the walk to the marble quarries, the black sour cherries on the way. They know about the honouring of St Cecilia, a saint she introduced them to, whom they have taken to their hearts.

'Poor girl,' Sister Mary Bartholomew commiserates. 'Poor little Cecilia, I often think.'

For a few minutes they talk about all that, the acts, the punishment, the life. They pour more coffee, milk added as she likes it. She cannot explain what so astonishes them. She might say that chance was in charge again when she noticed the old-fashioned bicycle propped against the sea-wall, when she looked and saw a figure standing still. It was chance that she was passing then, as it was when her father looked down and saw what the O'Reillys' dog had tired of burying in the shingle.

But the nuns do not believe in chance. Mystery is their thing. *Take from the forest its mystery and there is standing timber. Take from the sea its mystery and there is salted water.* She found that somewhere when first she read the books in the drawing-room bookcases; long afterwards she repeated it to the nuns when it came back to her. 'Well, isn't it tidily put!' Sister Antony exclaimed in admiration, and Sister Mary Bartholomew asked if it was Charles Kickham or Father Prout who was the author. But she said no; someone foreign, she thought.

'I think what will happen,' she predicts, passing on a thought that came in the night, 'is that they'll make a hotel of the house.' She lay sleepless and the transformation lingered: a cocktail bar, a noisy dining-room, numbers on the bedroom doors. She doesn't mind. It doesn't matter. People coming from all over, travellers like never before; that is the way in Ireland now. Young fishermen from Kilauran with waiters' suits on them, and cars drawn up. In

Enniseala people walk about the streets chatting on the telephone.

'Ah no, no,' Sister Mary Bartholomew says when she mentions a hotel again, and Sister Antony shakes her head.

They don't like to think about all the changes, even though they're there already. They like the safety of what has been, what they can come to terms with. The nuns will be displaced, as the family that is still hers was, as the Morells of Clashmore were, the Gouvernets of Aglish, the Priors of Ringville, the Swifts, the Boyces. It had to be; it doesn't matter. But it would hurt her visitors to say that maybe it has to be again and she holds that back, an unimportant lie of silence.

They ask and she tells them: about Paddy Lindon and the fisherman who communicated with his fingers, the trap standing waiting on the sea-gravel, the oil lamps lit. All gone, it feels like, and yet not gone at all.

'We best be off,' Sister Antony ends the morning, the conversation down to earth again.

*

The O'Reillys' cattle graze all the fields now, big brown-speckled creatures. She looks down from the edge of the cliffs but does not descend by the easy way to the strand, for it is not easy any more. A dragonfly flutters up from the grass, then flies away into the afternoon lull.

She likes this day of the week best, even though she is lonely for a while after her friends have gone. In winter they light the drawing-room fire for her and they have the coffee there. Sister Antony came to the convent from a farm, Sister Mary Bartholomew from an institution. Sometimes they talk about that, recollecting the neighbourhoods they knew in their childhood, reminiscing about people she might have heard of.

The heat of the day has cooled. Late afternoon has a sunlit haze about it, the sea as calm as she has ever seen it, waves lapping so gently you could listen to the sound for ever. She does not hurry; there is no need to hurry. Better it should be a mystery, better in the story that still is told, even though Bridget was cross because of it, and Henry too. The gift of mercy, the nuns have said: forgiveness was the offertory of St Cecilia, while music played and her murderers were in the house. They would visit that church in Italy; one day, they said.

She smiles all that away. What happened simply did. The cow parsley was white every month of May when she drove away from the high spiked gates, the fuchsia bright in autumn at the cottage where the greyhound was always on the wall. Her visits were the joy in that inmate's life, an old keeper said years later, before they pulled the place down. A flicker in the dark, he said, even though the inmate never knew who she was.

She should have died a child; she knows that but has never said it to the nuns, has never included in the story of herself the days that felt like years when she lay among the fallen stones. It would have lowered their spirits, although it lifts her own because instead of nothing there is what there is.

She watches the tide coming in. She watches it turning before she goes back, through the fields and the orchard. The nuns have collected the fallen apples, but still some lie about. The bees are safely there, browsing through honeysuckle, the hives fallen away to nothing. The lines where clothes were once pegged out to dry are still there too, grey with moss and damp.

The stick she keeps to assist her on the steep track down to her crossing stones is where she left it weeks ago, leaning against the archway wall. She feels up to that difficult journey today, although nothing will have changed: the bark grown over the initials she once carved, the stream curving as it always has, filching no more from its banks than it did before her time. Her journey takes all afternoon, and evening comes without her noticing.

In the house she boils an egg, makes toast, and finishes her kitchen chores before she goes again from room to room. Thunderflies lie beneath the glass of her embroideries where they have crept, tiny corpses decorating rock pools and flowers. In the downstairs bathroom the bath is streaked, discoloured green and brown; the blind, half down, has a gash; the electric bulb hangs without a shade.

She walks about the drawing-room, touching the surfaces with her fingertips – the glass of a cabinet door, the edge of a table-top, the writing-desk beneath the portrait of the unknown Gault, a shepherd's head. Again there is the scent on her mother's handkerchief; again her father calls her lady.

She settles in her chair by the window, to gaze out at the dusky blue of the hydrangeas. The avenue has gone shadowy, the outline of its trees stark against the sky. The rooks come down to scrabble in the grass as every evening at this time they do, her companions while she watches the fading of the day.

If you enjoyed this special edition of
The Story of Lucy Gault then please look
out for William Trevor's new paperback:

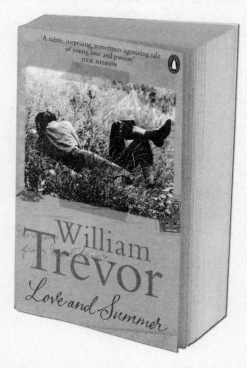

'A subtle, surprising, sometimes agonizing tale
of young love and passion'
JULIE MYERSON

William
Trevor
Love and Summer

Love and Summer is a heartbreaking story of young
and illicit love in rural Ireland told with William Trevor's
trademark compassion and understatement.

By the same author

DEATH
IN SUMMER

The sudden death of Thaddeus Davenant's wife leaves him with the problem of childcare for baby Georgina. When none of the nannies interviewed is deemed suitable, Thaddeus's mother-in-law fulfils the position herself. But in rejecting one of the applicants, they have overlooked the beginnings of a fixed and unnatural obsession . . .

'Trevor at his best . . . The subtlety with which he draws the threads of the narrative together, and the skill with which he deploys a surprisingly large cast of characters, each of whom takes on a clear reality, are quite marvellous' Allan Massie, *Scotsman*

By the same author

FELICIA'S JOURNEY

Winner of the 1994 Whitbread Book of the Year Award.

' "You're beautiful," Johnny told her and so, full of hope, seventeen-year-old Felicia crosses the Irish Sea to England to find her lover and tell him she is pregnant. Searching desperately for Johnny, she is, instead, found by Mr Hilditch, pudgy canteen catering manager, befriender of homeless young girls.

'So brilliant that it compels you to stay up all night galloping through to the end ... exquisitely crafted' Val Hennessey, *Daily Mail*

'Immensely readable ... The plot twist – a characteristic mix – is both sinister and affecting, and so skilfully done that you remember why authors had plot twists in the first place' Philip Hensher, *Guardian*

By the same author

THE CHILDREN OF DYNMOUTH

A small, pretty seaside town is harshly exposed by a young boy's curiosity. His prurient interest, oddly motivated, leaves few people unaffected – and the consequences cannot be ignored.

'A very fine novel. It is the work of a master craftsman and a deep creative talent ... stunningly subtle ... simple yet brilliant' Peter Tinniswood, *The Times*

'A sensibility reigns here which is at once inquisitive and loving ... Trevor's is among the most subtle and sophisticated fiction being written today' John Banville, *New York Review of Books*

refresh yourself at penguin.co.uk

Visit penguin.co.uk for exclusive information and interviews with
bestselling authors, fantastic give-aways and the
inside track on all our books, from the Penguin Classics
to the latest bestsellers.

BE FIRST

first chapters, first editions, first novels

EXCLUSIVES

author chats, video interviews, biographies, special
features

EVERYONE'S A WINNER

give-aways, competitions, quizzes, ecards

READERS GROUPS

exciting features to support existing groups and
create new ones

NEWS

author events, bestsellers, awards, what's new

EBOOKS

books that click – download an ePenguin today

BROWSE AND BUY

thousands of books to investigate – search, try
and buy the perfect gift online – or treat yourself!

ABOUT US

job vacancies, advice for writers and company
history

Get Closer To Penguin . . . www.penguin.co.uk